Here, killer, killer, killer...

For the first time in sixteen years, Lara Caphart has returned to her hometown of Whisker Jog, New Hampshire. She wants to reconnect with her estranged aunt Fran, who's having some difficulty looking after herself—and her eleven cats. Taking care of a clowder of kitties is easy, but keeping Fran from being harassed by local bully Theo Barnes is hard. The wealthy builder has his sights set on Fran's property, and is determined to make her an offer she doesn't dare refuse.

Then Lara spots a blue-eyed Ragdoll cat that she swears is the reincarnation of her beloved Blue, her childhood pet. Pursuing the feline to the edge of Fran's yard, she stumbles upon the body of Theo Barnes, clearly a victim of foul play. To get her and Fran off the suspect list, Lara finds herself following the cat's clues in search of a killer. Is Blue's ghost really trying to help her solve a murder, or has Lara inhaled too much catnip?

ESCAPE CLAWS

A Cat Lady Mystery

Linda Reilly

LYRICAL PRESS
Kensington Publishing Corp.
www.kensingtonbooks.com

First Electronic Edition: December 2017
eISBN-13: 978-1-5161-0416-1
eISBN-10: 1-5161-0416-1

First Print Edition: December 2017
ISBN-13: 978-1-5161-0419-2
ISBN-10: 1-5161-0419-6

Printed in the United States of America

In loving memory of my dad, Unico "Mike" Gregory

Acknowledgments

A huge thank-you goes to my agent, Jessica Faust, whose enthusiasm for the Cat Lady mysteries helped bring this series to fruition. Jessica, thank you for pushing me until I got it right!

To my editor, Martin Biro, for taking a chance on me and on the series. Your insightful suggestions were spot on! You helped make the book come together in the best way possible.

To my fabulous former coworkers, Mary Newman and Chris Newman, thank you for lending your names to the story. I had fun shaping your personalities, and hope you'll enjoy what I did with them!

To Maureen Nix and Stephan Nix, land surveyors extraordinaire, I can't imagine how I would have described the disturbance of the boundary marker without your expert advice. Any errors, whether accidental or by design, are mine alone.

To Jenny Kales, whose keen eye and passion for cozies helped me fine-tune the manuscript, I owe a million thanks.

Most of all, to all those who have made the world a happier and better place by loving cats, this is for you.

Cast of Feline Characters

Callie   A gray-and-white long-haired kitten, still wary of humans

Luna   Callie's shy sister, a gray-and-white kitten, the pink dot on her nose giving her an extra touch of adorable

Izzy   A cuddly calico with an ever-quizzical expression, she loves curling up with her sibling atop Lara's bedspread

Pickles   Izzy's calico sister, who has a penchant for chewing strands of Lara's hair

Twinkles   An orange-striped tiger cat with big gold eyes, he's fond of snoozing with his best bud Dolce

Ballou   A black, short-haired feral with a darling white mustache, his fear of people is slowly fading

Munster   A striped orange male, he's the sociable, unofficial greeter of all human visitors

Dolce   Long-haired and solid black, he's as sweet as his name, a lovable lap cat

Bootsie   Slender and gray, she's the cuddly mom to Lilybee and Cheetah

Lilybee   White with black markings, this kitten has developed a serious crush on the chief of police

Cheetah   Lilybee's gray-spotted brother, he's usually first at the food bowls in the morning

Blue   An elusive Ragdoll with a fluffy coat and azure eyes, she's been around since Lara was a girl. Or has she?

Chapter 1

Lara Caphart paused at the foot of the wide porch steps and stared up at the old Folk Victorian. She was startled, and oddly relieved, at how little the place had changed. The white wicker settee still sat on the wraparound porch, its colorful cushions now sun faded. A hanging planter, devoid of any foliage, dangled from a metal hook in front of the green-shuttered window.

She glanced over the yard she hadn't laid eyes on since she was eleven. The lawn was a bit unkempt, and the shrubs along the base of the porch needed tending. Lara easily recalled the days when Aunt Fran had kept everything trimmed and tidy—postcard pretty, in fact.

Heart thwacking against her chest, Lara slowly climbed the steps. Could it really be sixteen years since she'd seen her aunt? She tapped her knuckles on the wooden doorframe, lightly at first, then with a tad more vigor. After a wait of at least two minutes, the door creaked open. She took an involuntary step backward. "Aunt... Aunt Fran?" she asked with a slight gasp.

The woman clutching the doorframe in one hand and a gray-spotted kitten in the other tottered sideways. "Well, if it isn't the prodigal niece, returning to her roots. To what do I owe the pleasure? Did someone tell you I was dying?"

All at once, Lara felt tongue-tied. She didn't need a psychic to tell her that her aunt was in trouble. It was etched, like cut glass, in the hollows beneath her aunt's green eyes—eyes that at one time had looked at Lara as if she were the niftiest thing since peanut butter on toast.

"No. I, um..."

"I suppose Sherry called you about my knee problems," Fran Clarkson said, a bit more softly. "I can't imagine why else you'd have driven all the way up here from Boston." With a sigh and a slump of her thin shoulders, she opened the screen door. "You may as well come in."

"Thank you." Lara stepped inside the once-familiar kitchen, a room where luscious aromas like cinnamon, apple, and cloves once lingered in every corner. But today a sour smell permeated Lara's senses—an odor she'd never before associated with her aunt. According to Sherry Bowker, Lara's bestie when she was a kid, some of the folks in town had begun calling Aunt Fran the crazy cat lady.

At that moment, Lara noticed her aunt was grasping a cane in the hand that clung to the doorframe. Without a second thought, she cupped her hand firmly under her aunt's upper arm and guided her to a padded chrome chair at the head of the Formica table. "Why don't I take this little furball for a while?" Lara asked, gently removing the kitten from her aunt's hand.

"Thank you," her aunt said quietly. "That's Cheetah you're holding, if you're interested."

Lara felt herself bristling at the comment, but quelled her annoyance. "Of course I'm interested. Haven't I always loved your cats?" *All cats?* She tucked Cheetah under her chin, reveling in the softness of the darling kitten.

Aunt Fran's eyes misted with a faraway look. "That you have," she said. "You'd best set him down now. If he starts to get antsy, which he will, you'll get a sample of his razor-sharp claws."

Very gently, Lara set Cheetah on the floor. The kitten scooted away toward the jumble of food bowls lined up near the sink.

"I wasn't expecting you," her aunt said, her tone slightly accusatory. "I suppose I could make some tea—"

Lara held up a hand. "Why don't I take care of it, Aunt Fran? You sit for a while, okay?"

Aunt Fran nodded her assent. Lara stripped off her faux-suede jacket and draped it over the back of a chair.

It felt strange, rummaging through her aunt's glass-front cabinets, the way she had as a child. She found the tea bags exactly where they'd always been—in a battered tin container advertising Hershey's Cocoa.

Within minutes, two cups of steaming tea sat on the table in front of them. To Lara's delight, a thin gray cat leaped up from under the table and onto her lap. "Oh my, and who are you?" Grinning, she stroked the cat's head and was rewarded with the revving of a purr engine.

"That's Bootsie." Aunt Fran smiled wanly. "She's Cheetah's mom. Bootsie and her three-week-old babies were found by a state DPW worker on the side of Route Sixteen, tied inside a trash bag." Her face darkened at the memory.

"That's terrible!" Lara said. "How did you manage to rescue them?"

"The worker was one of my students, back in the day. He knew exactly where to bring those poor abandoned cats."

He sure did, Lara thought.

"One of the kittens didn't survive. But Cheetah and Lilybee were tough little darlings."

Another cat strolled in to check out the commotion—a long-haired black kitty who made a beeline for her aunt's lap. "And this is Dolce," Aunt Fran said, stroking the cat.

"Which is the Italian word for sweet," Lara piped in. "I live in the North End, above an Italian bakery. In fact, I work at the bakery part-time...in exchange for rent I can actually afford," she added dryly. "My landlady owns the studio apartment upstairs."

Lara knew she was babbling, but she wasn't even close to achieving a comfort level with her aunt. There was a time when they'd been as close as mother and daughter.

"I see." Aunt Fran stirred her tea thoughtfully. "I assume you're still painting?"

"I am," Lara confirmed. "Mostly watercolors." She took a sip from her teacup.

For a long moment Aunt Fran was silent. Then, "So what are your plans? Are you here for any particular reason? Or is this just a casual visit?"

Her aunt's tone stung. Lara swallowed back a lump. "I don't have any plans, per se, Aunt Fran. I... I mean, Sherry did call me. She and her mom are worried about you. Extremely worried."

Sherry Bowker and Lara had known each since childhood, from the day they entered first grade together at Whisker Jog Elementary. But the summer after Lara had completed sixth grade, her family moved away. She and Sherry were devastated—they missed each other horribly. Lara had been especially lonely, moving to an unfamiliar school in another state. The girls kept in touch by letter, and later by e-mail, until they both graduated from high school. It was during Lara's hectic art school years that they lost the thread of communication. Then one day, about five years ago, Lara plunked her old friend's name into a search engine and discovered that Sherry and her mom had opened a coffee shop in downtown Whisker Jog. She contacted her, and was thrilled to get an instant response. Every summer now, Sherry and her mom took a day off to drive to Boston for a lunch/shopping expedition with Lara.

Lara realized her mind was wandering. Her aunt obviously knew that she and Sherry had been in touch.

Aunt Fran's gaze skimmed Lara's face. Her eyes brimmed with tears. "It's been so long since I've seen you. I don't know what to think."

Lara sucked in a hard breath. She didn't want to cry. "I know, but I'm here now and I want to help with the cats. How many do you have?"

"Eleven. Two of the kittens—Callie and Luna—are afraid of people, and one adult male is feral. The kittens are young enough to socialize eventually, but Ballou won't go near a human."

Lara inhaled, then winced inwardly. She didn't know how many litter boxes her aunt had, but from the scent coating her nostrils she felt sure all of them needed to be cleaned and changed. "Aunt Fran, will you rest while I check out the litter boxes and clean things up a bit?"

With a sag of her shoulders, her aunt nodded. "That…would actually be a big help. The supplies are in the utility closet, next to the bathroom."

Lara grinned. "I know exactly where that is."

It took Lara the better part of two hours to scrub and replenish the twelve litter boxes scattered throughout the house. Fortunately, she'd found a pair of rubber gloves under the bathroom sink, along with earth-friendly cleaning supplies, trash bags, and scads of paper towel rolls.

Her heart melted at the sight of the furry faces watching her as she worked. She would have to learn all their names, if she was here long enough.

By the time she was through, the rooms smelled minimally better. In the kitchen, she collected the myriad food and water bowls, washed them, and replenished them with kibble and kitten food. She'd been relieved to find her aunt's cabinets well stocked with cat food. Lara wondered how her aunt shopped for supplies with her knees in such bad shape.

It was already two thirty, and she was starving. She headed upstairs and knocked softly at her aunt's bedroom door, which was slightly ajar. "Aunt Fran?" she called.

"Come in, Lara."

Her aunt was sitting in her padded rocking chair reading a paperback thriller. Dolce rested in her lap, looking every bit like a furry black shawl.

Lara had to swallow to keep her composure. The room was almost exactly as she remembered it, with its braided scatter rugs and white, iron bedstead, a handmade quilt folded at the foot of the bed. The white-painted dresser, its oval mirror silvered in places, sat in the same corner. From where she stood, Lara could see her own reflection.

"Come on, I'm famished," Lara said. "I'm treating you to lunch at Sherry's. She doesn't know I drove up here today, so we're going to surprise her."

Her aunt frowned and rubbed her left knee. "I don't think so, Lara. I walk very slowly, you know. It takes me forever to get in and out of a car."

"I'll help you," Lara cajoled. "I'm not going without you."

* * * *

Bowker's Coffee Stop sat in the center of Whisker Jog's downtown block, about a half-mile downhill walk from Aunt Fran's home at the end of High Cliff Road. So far Lara had only seen photos of the place, supplied by Sherry via her smartphone or on the coffee shop's Facebook page. The pictures, Lara realized, failed to capture the cozy essence of the inviting cafe.

The walls were painted in swirls of pastel, graced with vintage photos and artifacts from the 1960s. On one side of the shop was a counter lined with bright red stools. Square oak tables and padded, mismatched chairs made up the rest of the seating. Daily specials were announced on a stand-alone chalkboard framed in pale-green distressed wood.

The moment Lara and her aunt approached the counter they were rushed and assaulted.

"Oh my God, I can't believe it!" Sherry Bowker, her short black hair poking the air in gelled spikes, raced around the end of the counter and threw her arms around Lara. She squeezed and rocked back and forth until Lara laughingly begged for mercy.

"Sherry, this place looks wonderful," Lara said.

"Thank you." Sherry hugged Lara again and then looped her arm through Aunt Fran's. "And Fran, you haven't been here in like, forever," she said in a mock-stern voice. "I'm so happy to see you."

Aunt Fran smiled and allowed Sherry a quick hug. "I'm glad to see you, too, and my pal Daisy over there." She waggled a hand at her old friend Daisy Bowker, who was busy serving a table of four. Daisy's face morphed into one of sheer joy when she spotted Lara and Aunt Fran.

After more hugs were doled out, Lara and her aunt settled onto stools at the counter, which, Aunt Fran explained, was easier on her knees. Sherry instantly produced two steaming mugs of coffee, along with two of the oversized sugar cookies Daisy was known for. With Halloween only a few weeks away, today's cookies were shaped and frosted like mummies. Lara couldn't help giggling as she bit off a chunk of the mummy's frosted arm.

"Eating dessert before you've even ordered lunch?" Aunt Fran asked wryly. "I guess some things never change."

Lara smiled, feeling her nerves loosen. For the first time since she'd arrived in Whisker Jog, she thought her aunt looked almost happy.

They both ordered tuna salad sandwiches and sipped at their coffee. Between serving customers, Sherry and Daisy took turns plying them with bits of local gossip.

Aunt Fran waved at a table of four opposite the counter. Its occupants—two women, an older man, and a teenage girl—returned the greeting. The girl, who looked about thirteen and sported aqua-tinted hair, smiled curiously at Lara. Lara smiled back and took a napkin from the dispenser on the counter. The girl's face intrigued her—oversized brown eyes, roundish cheeks, slightly large ears lined with silver studs. And that hair... She removed a pencil from the depths of her flowered purse and began to sketch.

Sherry sidled up to the counter and leaned over to sneak a peek at Lara's handiwork. "Hey, that's Brooke you're drawing, isn't it?"

"Brooke?" Lara said.

Sherry laughed. "Sorry. You haven't been introduced yet. Brooke Weston is the girl sitting at that table over there." She tilted her chin at the table of four. "They all belong to a book club that reads the classics. Brooke comes here directly after school every Wednesday so she won't miss any of the discussion. The coffee shop closes at four, but sometimes I stay a bit longer so they can finish up without feeling rushed."

"That's nice of you," Lara said. "But why don't they just have the club at the library?"

Sherry smiled. "They like it better here. Can you blame them?"

Daisy came up beside her daughter. "So, Fran," she said, "I've been thinking about you, sweetie. Have you been able to plant your tulip bulbs yet?"

"I don't think I'm going to get to it this year, Daisy. The bulbs were shipped to me last week, but they're still sitting in burlap bags out by the shed."

Tulips! That's right—Lara remembered now. Back when she was a kid, Aunt Fran was known for the gorgeous tulip varieties that skirted her house from front to back along the brick walkway. Apparently she'd kept up the tradition.

In fact, Lara remembered one year when she "helped" her aunt plant a row of the bulbs, only to learn that she'd stuck them all in the ground upside down. Instead of getting annoyed, Aunt Fran had only laughed, ruffled Lara's curls, and said, "Oh well, next year you'll get it right."

But there never had been a next year. Lara's folks had moved out of state, and she'd never seen Aunt Fran again.

Until now.

Lara didn't want to embarrass her aunt by bringing up her current physical limitations. Instead, she made a mental note to try to plant the tulip bulbs before she returned to Boston.

Daisy went off to clear one of the tables. Lara was putting the finishing touches on her napkin sketch when the door to the coffee shop swung open. A broad-shouldered man wearing a red-and-black-checkered jacket strode in. His bushy eyebrows matched his thick white hair, and he wore the look of someone quite enamored with himself. "I'll take a black coffee to go," he said to Sherry in a rather rude tone.

A muscle in Sherry's face twitched, but she gave him a sharp nod. With a quick tilt of her head in his direction, she shot Lara a meaningful look.

Who's that? Lara mouthed to her aunt, after he strode off.

Aunt Fran leaned closer to Lara. "Theo Barnes," she whispered. "I'll tell you later."

The man's hard-looking blue eyes scanned the room, and then he sauntered over to the book club table. "So how are all my buds today?" he said in a voice like a sonic boom. He touched the younger woman's cheek, eliciting a smile from her. The older woman beamed up at him, and with a theatrical motion he took her left hand and kissed it. Then he clamped a meaty hand onto the shoulder of the club's sole male member, a sixtysomething with a pasty complexion who cringed visibly at Barnes's touch. Barnes leaned over and growled something in the man's ear. The man nodded, slunk out of his chair, and stalked out of the cafe.

Barnes came up to the counter to collect his takeout coffee, stopping between the stools where Lara and Aunt Fran were seated. Lara stifled a shudder. Barnes was standing far too close for her liking. She looked at her aunt, whose face had gone pale. Lara was about to tell Barnes to take a hike when he announced, "I need to talk to you, Fran."

"I don't think so," Aunt Fran hissed at him. "You've talked quite enough."

Barnes's piercing eyes shifted and rested on Lara. "My proposal stands, my lovely, but I think I can make it even sweeter for you. We *will* chat later. I promise you that."

Aunt Fran squeezed her eyes shut and said nothing.

With a smug look, Barnes reached across the counter and took the lidded paper coffee cup Sherry was holding out. Then, without so much as a thank-you, he left.

"What an oaf," Lara said after the door closed. "I mean, could he have been any louder?"

"Theo Barnes is the town bully," her aunt murmured. "I'll tell you about him when we get back to the house."

"But he didn't even pay for his coffee!"

Sherry slid two plates in front of Lara and her aunt. "Don't worry about it, Lara. He never does. He thinks he owns the place."

"He does own the place." Daisy came up behind her daughter. She reached under the counter for a bottle of spray cleaner. "Unfortunately, he's our landlord. For now, anyway. But that's not for you to worry about. You two go ahead and enjoy your lunch."

Lara looked down at her tuna salad on wheat. A pile of rippled chips and two pickle rounds sat beside it—exactly the way she liked it. She set aside her pencil sketch and dived into her lunch. The tuna salad was perfect—lightly seasoned, and with just the right amount of celery and onion to give it crunch. Aunt Fran nibbled at hers, but with far less gusto.

Lara was attacking the last bite of her sandwich when her aunt, who'd barely eaten half her lunch, suddenly pushed aside her plate. "Why are you here, Lara?" she asked quietly. "I mean, why are you *really* here?"

Lara felt a hard lump form inside her stomach. The cats weren't the only reason she'd driven to New Hampshire. Sherry had confided that a local businessman had been harassing her aunt, making her life a living nightmare. She hadn't given details, but Lara now suspected she knew who it was.

Theo Barnes.

In a voice that came out shakier than she intended, Lara said, "I came because I want to help you. Because I care about you."

"You care about me," Aunt Fran said flatly. "Isn't it strange, then, that I haven't seen or heard from you in sixteen years."

Her aunt's sudden vitriol surprised Lara. Feeling tears push at her eyelids, Lara snatched up her crumpled napkin and blotted her eyes. "I don't know what else I can say, Aunt Fran. I care and I want to help. Can we talk about this back at the house?"

Aunt Fran looked suddenly flustered. "Of course we can. I shouldn't have brought it up here." She reached into her purse for her wallet, but Lara quickly covered her hand.

"No, Aunt Fran. It's my treat, remember?"

"Actually, it's our treat," Sherry said, coming up to the counter. "When you walked in together, I was just…so glad to see you both."

"Thank you, Sherry," Lara said.

Since Aunt Fran hadn't eaten her mummy cookie, Sherry slipped it into a paper bag and handed it to her. "You'll both come back tomorrow, right?"

"You bet," Lara said.

Aunt Fran only smiled. "I'll try."

Lara helped her aunt off the stool. Just then, Brooke, the teenager, excused herself from the book club and dashed over to them.

"Hey, are you Lara?" she asked, beaming as if she'd spotted a rock star.

"I am, and I understand you're Brooke."

"Yup. Guilty as charged. Your hair is like, so gorgeous. Is that the natural color?"

Lara laughed and fingered a coppery strand. "It is," she said, charmed by the girl's bluntness. "I'm glad you like it, but I wouldn't mind doing with fewer curls. By the way, I have something for you." Lara handed her the napkin sketch.

Brooke pushed a strand of aqua hair behind one ear. "You drew this?" she asked, gawking at the napkin. "It looks just like me!"

"Lara is an artist," Aunt Fran put in. Lara detected a hint of pride in her aunt's voice.

"Can...I mean, *may* I keep it?"

"You sure can." Lara smiled at her. "It was a pleasure meeting you, Brooke."

"This is so cool!" She gave it back to Lara. "Would you bring it back to the house for me? If I put it in my backpack it'll get wrinkled."

"Um, yeah, sure," Lara said, perplexed.

"Thanks!" And then to Aunt Fran, "See you in a few, Ms. C."

Chapter 2

Back at the house, her aunt had insisted on tidying up the kitchen counter, and Lara didn't argue. She knew Aunt Fran needed something to make herself feel useful, in spite of the strain it put on her knees. Lara took that opportunity to explore her favorite room—the room where she'd spent so many hours as a kid.

The smaller of the two parlors resembled a playroom more than a parlor. Thick brocade curtains, somewhat faded now, hung from black, wrought iron rods. The room's papered walls were lined with shelves crammed with children's books. One entire corner, Lara remembered, had once been devoted to books that taught children how to draw. Curious, she went over to that spot, the special place where those treasured how-to books once sat. But they weren't there. They'd all been removed. She knew it was silly, but a tiny bit of her heart felt empty.

Through one of the windows, Lara spied a short, yellow school bus rumbling up High Cliff Road. It chugged along slowly, its engine idling for a minute or so before turning around at the end of the road and motoring back down the hill.

In front of one of the windows, a low table painted cherry red was strewn with books. Lara smiled when she saw *The Jungle Book*, a childhood favorite of hers. She started to pick it up when she heard the kitchen door open and then close again. The low murmur of a child's—no, two children's voices—drifted into earshot. She returned to the kitchen, and was surprised to see Brooke Weston and a little boy of about eight or nine. Ah, so that was why Brooke asked her to hold on to the napkin sketch. She'd planned to pay a visit later.

"Hey, Brooke." Lara retrieved the napkin from atop the fridge and gave it to her. "Here it is, safe and sound. I put it in a clear plastic bag for you." Brooke lowered her turquoise backpack to the floor. "Hi, Lara. Thanks for this. It really does look like me!"

Aunt Fran slid an arm around the boy's shoulder. His chocolate-brown eyes were only a shade lighter than his straight, dark hair. "Lara, this is Darryl Weston, Brooke's younger brother. He and I practice reading aloud every day. Darryl, this is my niece, Lara. Lara is an artist from Boston."

Lara grinned at the boy and stuck out her hand. "Pleased to meet you, Darryl."

Darryl took her hand shyly, then quickly withdrew it. His face lit up. "You're a real artist?"

Brooke waved her sketch in his face. Her brother slapped it away.

"As real as it gets," Lara said with a laugh.

"Lara, if you don't mind," her aunt interrupted, "Darryl is going to spend some quiet time reading in the small parlor while Brooke does her homework. He's asked if he can practice without me today, so I won't be joining him."

"But I will," Brooke sniped, "so you'd better not try to slack off, dork face."

Darryl stuck out his tongue at his sister. "You're not the boss of me. I'm—"

"Brooke. Darryl." Aunt Fran spoke with a sternness Lara suspected was only half-serious. "Please go into the parlor and do your schoolwork. I'll bring you both a snack in a few minutes."

The siblings argued and picked at each other as they made their way into the parlor. Lara followed them to be sure they got settled without killing each other. She watched as Brooke dumped the contents of her voluminous backpack onto the floor. The girl then dropped down next to it all and plucked an algebra textbook from the jumble in the pile.

Lara noticed that the edges of the books were damp, and stained with something purple. "Oh wow, what happened to your books?" she asked Brooke.

"After you left the coffee shop I spilled my grape soda. The whole bottle went, like, right into my backpack. What a mess it made. I had to dump out all my books on the table so Dora and Mary could help me wipe them up. I'm such a klutzo sometimes."

"Nah. Everybody spills things."

Brooke dug a pair of earbuds from her pocket, stuck them into her ears, and started fiddling with her smartphone. She threw a dark look at her brother. "Do *not* bother me while I'm studying, Darryl, or you'll be sorry."

The boy stuck out his tongue behind his sister's back and then snatched up *The Jungle Book*. Chuckling softly at their antics, Lara closed the door nearly all the way and went back into the kitchen.

"I'll make the kids a snack, if you'd like," she told her aunt.

Aunt Fran looked pale. Lara knew she needed to sit for a while. "Thank you. I would appreciate that. That way I can take a few minutes and skim through the paper."

Her aunt sat at the kitchen table, the newspaper spread out before her. Lara took a box of salty crackers from the cupboard and hunted around for the peanut butter.

"In case you're wondering," Aunt Fran explained, "Darryl struggles with reading. I've been helping him after school. It also helps his mom, who has a day job. I guess I'm sort of a tutor-slash-babysitter. As for Brooke, for some reason she likes doing her homework here. On Wednesdays, when she has book club, the school bus driver lets her hop on Darryl's bus in front of the coffee shop. It gives their mother peace of mind, knowing where her kids are every day."

Because you're a natural at nurturing, Lara wanted to say, but kept the thought to herself. There were so many other things she wanted to say, so many questions she wanted to ask. But right at the moment she was chicken, so she stuck to a safe subject. "They seem like great kids. Is Darryl dyslexic?"

"No," her aunt said. "But in school he's extremely shy, nearly phobic about reading aloud in class. He knows the words, but when he has to pronounce them he gets all tongue-tied. He's making progress, but it's slow going."

Having located the peanut butter, Lara made the kids a bunch of cracker "sandwiches." She set them on plates, poured two glasses of milk, and plopped everything on a tray. It was the same treat, she remembered, that her aunt used to give her every day after school.

A sudden wave of nostalgia washed over her—a longing for things to be the way they used to be. In her mind's eye she saw Aunt Fran, young and healthy with her knees in perfect condition. The kitchen scrubbed clean, the linoleum gleaming. Lush pots of spider plants hanging in the windows. A pan of butterscotch brownies cooling on the stove. And on the kitchen table, a large pad of sketch paper and a package of colored pencils waiting for her when she got home from school.

Home from school, but not really home. Lara had never actually lived with Aunt Fran. But since her folks had regular day jobs and Aunt Fran taught middle school, she went to her aunt's each afternoon and stayed until her dad picked her up.

Shaking herself of her memories, Lara carried the tray into the small parlor and abruptly stopped short. On the floor sat Darryl, *The Jungle Book* open before him on the red table. He was reading aloud without hesitation, pronouncing each word perfectly. But that wasn't the most shocking part. Next to Darryl was a beautiful Ragdoll cat with shining azure eyes. Peering over Darryl's arm as he read, the cat glanced up at Lara in mild recognition and swished her tail. Lara took in a sharp breath.

"Blue?" The name escaped her lips in a ragged whisper. Her heart pounded. Adrenaline gushed through her like a busted water pipe. *But it can't be Blue.* How could it be? After all these years, Blue would be long passed. This cat looked young and vibrant, her eyes bright and inquisitive.

The cat looked up at Lara, swished her tail again, then returned her gaze to the book. It was almost as if she were reading along with Darryl.

Lara's knees felt wobbly. She wanted desperately to dash over and stroke the cat, to see if it was really her Blue. But Darryl was obviously on a roll, reading every word aloud with amazing ease, so she didn't want to interrupt. She couldn't help wondering, though, if her aunt had exaggerated the boy's reading problem.

With a quick wave at Brooke to let her know the snacks had arrived, Lara set the tray on the floor. She backed quietly out of the room, pulling the door almost closed.

"Aunt Fran?" she asked, back in the kitchen. "Didn't you say Darryl had trouble reading out loud?"

Her aunt looked up from the newspaper. "He does, yes. Why?"

"Well"—Lara scrubbed at her eyes with her fists—"he's in there reading aloud at the level of a...a...high school senior! And there's a Ragdoll cat sitting next to him. She looks exactly like my Blue. Remember Blue?"

An odd expression came over her aunt's face. Slowly, she rose from her seat and grasped her cane. "Lara, I don't have a Ragdoll cat," she said quietly. "As for Darryl, he can barely read a simple sentence without stumbling over the words. Are you sure?"

Lara aimed a hand at the parlor. "See for yourself."

For a long moment, Aunt Fran studied her niece's face. Then she grabbed her cane and moved toward the parlor, taking every step with care.

Lara rubbed her eyes again. Maybe they'd played a trick on her. Could her stress over her aunt have pushed her senses into some crazy mode where she imagined things the way she wished them to be, not the way they were?

She was tired, that was for sure. The day already seemed twenty hours long, and it was only a little after four.

Thirsty, she went to the fridge and scanned the top shelf. She was pulling out a carton of OJ when Brooke paraded into the kitchen. The girl pulled out her earbuds, plunked her smartphone on the Formica table, and dropped into a chair. "Ugh, I hate algebra. If I have to look at it for one more second, I'll... I'll scream."

Lara held up the juice carton, but Brooke shook her head. She poured herself a small glass and went over and joined Brooke. "So how did you get to be part of the classics book club? It seems like an eclectic group."

"Eclectic." Brooke grinned, displaying even white teeth. "I like that word. Someone, I think it was Mary—she's the pretty one—posted a note in the library. I only joined because I'm going to have to read a lot of the classics once I'm in high school. I figured the others could help me if I got stuck on something." She snorted. "Of course Glen is useless. He's only there 'cuz he's crushing on Mary. He's, like, this weirdo who can never keep a job. Dora, she's the older lady, is really nice, though. I just wish we could ditch Glen."

"Well," Lara said, not sure how to respond. It wasn't her place to comment on a man she didn't know. "So, what classic are you reading now? The book looked pretty thick."

Brooke rolled her eyes at the ceiling. "*The Pickwick Papers*. The most utterly boring book ever written."

"I've never read *Pickwick*," Lara said. "What's the premise?"

A striped, orange cat hopped onto Brooke's lap. Brooke plopped a soft kiss onto its furry head.

"That's Munster, I think," Lara said, recalling her aunt's earlier introduction to the resident felines.

"It is," Brooke confirmed. "Anyway, it's about a band of lame old dudes who roam all over England having these so-called *adventures*"—she made air quotes around the word—"and then when they get back, some ditzy landlady sues dumpy old Pickwick for not marrying her!"

Lara couldn't help laughing at Brooke's description of the classic Dickens novel. She'd never read it, so she couldn't honestly critique it. "One of these days I'll check it out," Lara said. "Lately—in my rare spare time—I've been reading biographies of some of my favorite artists. Van Gogh, O'Keeffe—"

A light tap at the kitchen door interrupted her. Munster slipped off Brooke's lap and padded out of the kitchen.

Before Lara could react, the door opened. A thirtysomething woman with short brunette hair and a bright smile peeked through the opening.

"Hey, Mom, you're early," Brooke said, without much enthusiasm.

The woman stepped into the kitchen and closed the door. "I am, a little, but—oh, hello there," she said when she saw Lara.

Lara rose from her chair. "Hi. I'm Lara Caphart, Fran's niece. You're Brooke's mom?"

The woman smiled, her resemblance to Darryl startling. "Yes, I'm Heather Weston. Pleased to meet you, Lara." She extended her hand and Lara shook it briefly.

"Can I get you something?" Lara asked. "Water? Juice?"

"Thanks, but we have to be going. It's food shopping day, remember?" Heather asked her daughter.

Brooke groaned. "Don't remind me."

"The kids hate helping me lug all the heavy stuff inside the house," Heather explained. She focused her gaze on Brooke. "But we all have to pitch in these days, don't we?"

With a glum expression, Brooke nodded. "I'll get Darryl." She scooted off her chair and went to fetch her brother. Moments later, Darryl trailed his sister into the kitchen.

"Mom, you should see how good I read today!"

"Really?" Heather asked. "Can you show me after we get home?"

Darryl nodded eagerly.

Heather gave a tiny wave to Lara. "Tell Fran I said hi. Hope I see you again."

"I'm sure you will," Lara said.

After Heather and the kids left, Lara stuck her juice glass in the sink. Aunt Fran came from the direction of the bathroom into the kitchen.

"Oh, there you are," Lara said. "The kids' mom just picked them up."

Aunt Fran nodded distractedly. "I watched Darryl read for a few minutes. It's...inexplicable. You were right—he was reading that book aloud without a single hesitation." She sat in one of the kitchen chairs, flinching as she bent her knees.

Lara dropped onto a chair adjacent to her. "Did you happen to see the cat with him?"

Aunt Fran looked at Lara as if she'd asked if she'd spotted the kangaroo in the room. "There was no cat in there, Lara."

From her aunt's tone, Lara decided not to press it. "Hey, I like the Weston kids."

Aunt Fran smiled. "They're sweet children, but right now they're struggling. Their dad bailed on them several months ago. It's been tough on the family. Heather does her best, but I think she's getting worn out from being the sole supporter."

"Oh, I'm sorry to hear that."

"The man was somewhat of a ne'er-do-well, but he always loved his kids. Unfortunately," she said with an edge to her tone, "the words 'child support' were not in his personal dictionary. I don't think Heather even knows where he is right now."

"That's a shame," Lara said. "Where does Heather work?"

"Knowles Transitional Care, in Wolfeboro," her aunt said. "She's an LNA, a licensed nursing assistant. The place is so understaffed that she often has to work extra hours. Although, as she often points out, it's better than working for Theo Barnes."

"Barnes? That rude man we saw in the coffee shop?"

"The very same. Up until a few years ago, Heather worked in his office. He was such a miserable employer that it prompted her to go to school for her LNA. She did, and she's never looked back."

Theo Barnes again, Lara thought. "You make Barnes sound like the devil in disguise, Aunt Fran."

Her aunt pointed a finger at her, her green eyes blazing. "Yes, Lara, you nailed it. He *is* the devil in disguise. The problem is, his disguise has slipped away and now he's just the devil."

Chapter 3

"Thank you for making dinner, Lara. That omelet was scrumptious."
Settled in the wing chair in front of the unlit fireplace, Aunt Fran folded a crocheted throw over her legs and patted her knees. Dolce accepted the invitation and sprang onto her lap, green eyes gazing up at her adoringly.

"Anytime," Lara said, genuinely pleased. She was sitting on the floor next to her aunt, Munster curled in a half-moon atop her folded legs. "My landlady—her name's Gabriela—calls them *frittate*, the plural of frittata. She's the one I told you about—the one who owns the bakery."

"And she's teaching you some Italian, I see." Aunt Fran smiled.

Lara waggled her hand back and forth. "A little, but I'm kind of a crappy student."

"Lately," Aunt Fran went on, "I've been making do with frozen dinners and canned soup. Not exactly my style, but it's easier on my knees. I don't do well standing at the stove or at the sink for long periods." She rested her hands over Dolce and softly stroked the cat. "And thank you again for helping today. The house already looks much better."

And smells better, Lara thought, though in reality she'd only skimmed the surface of what needed to be done. Tomorrow she hoped to give the place a good vacuuming and maybe some dusting.

Aunt Fran's smile wilted. "I still don't know why you're here, Lara. Do you want to enlighten me?"

Okay, the moment of truth.

"Aunt Fran, I'm going to be honest. I've been here less than half a day and already I'm very worried about you. I remember this house before…before—"

"Before your mother and Roy moved away?" The bitterness in her aunt's tone surprised Lara.

"Y-yes, before that." Lara stroked Munster's soft head for courage. "But what I meant was, um...before you got so overwhelmed with cats. And I don't mean to pry, honestly I don't, but...have you seen a specialist about your knees?"

"I'm not a fool, Lara. Of course I have." She sighed. "My doctor calls my condition *rapidly destructive osteoarthritis*. It means the deterioration in the cartilage happened quickly, not over a long period. He's urging me to have replacements done in both knees."

Oh, boy. That sounded bad. No wonder Aunt Fran had so much difficulty walking.

Lara tickled Munster under the chin, triggering a loud purr. "So what are you waiting for? Why don't you just have the surgery?"

"You sound like everyone else," her aunt said, a touch of snark in her tone. "You don't see it, do you?"

"See what? I—"

"How can I have knee surgery with no one to care for the cats? It requires several days in the hospital, and even more in a rehab facility, like the one where Heather works. And after that, a long period of recovery at home, with therapists making home visits. And that's only for one knee."

"Okay, I get it. But isn't there anyone you can ask for help? Maybe pay someone to house-sit/catsit for a few weeks?"

Aunt Fran shook her head. "I tried finding someone, but no one was willing to work for the pay I could offer. Besides, a few weeks wouldn't be enough."

"Your knees," Lara said. "That's why you quit teaching this year, isn't it?"

"It is, and before you ask, I do get a monthly disability check. The problem is, it's barely enough to keep this house up and running. Once winter sets in, the heating bills will skyrocket."

Munster began chewing on the sleeve of Lara's paisley pullover. She smiled and bent down to kiss his whiskers. "What about Brooke?" she suggested. "She obviously likes your cats. Could she give you some help with the litter boxes?"

"She could and she offered to do so, but I refused. And since I can already see a question mark forming in that inquisitive head of yours, I'll tell you why. You probably don't remember your grandmother—my mother—do you?"

Lara shook her head. "Not really." A vague memory of a scowling woman with a caustic tongue came to mind. Lara had been quite young at the time. She wasn't sure if that had been her grandmother or a neighbor.

"Well, when I was a young girl," Aunt Fran explained, her voice tight, "my mother suddenly declared one day that she was a semi-invalid. No doctor had ever told her that, or diagnosed her with anything in particular. But the label worked well for her so she stuck with it." Her hands shook a little. "I was forced to perform all sorts of chores that a child should never be charged with. Including personal hygiene tasks that were mortifying to me."

Dolce stared up at Aunt Fran, as if he felt her sudden angst.

"Oh, I..." Lara swallowed. "I'm so sorry. That sounds truly awful. Look, I get what you're saying. But if Brooke really wants to help. Wouldn't it be a good after-school job for her?"

Aunt Fran's expression softened. "It might be, but I know Brooke quite well. When she does something she enjoys, especially if it means helping someone, she puts her whole heart into it. I'm worried that if she started helping with the cats, she'd get so involved that her schoolwork would suffer. Plus, she'll be entering high school next year, and will have even more homework than she does now."

That is so Aunt Fran, Lara thought. *You can take the teacher out of the school...*

Finally, Lara relented. She didn't want to badger her aunt anymore. She'd have to figure out another way to get her some help. "So you've been doing some private tutoring?"

"Not really. So far I've only helped Darryl with reading, but I'd like to do more if I can. Actually," she said, "I don't get paid for working with Darryl. His mom barely makes ends meet as it is. And speaking of Darryl..."

"Yes, speaking of Darryl," Lara repeated. "Why do you think he suddenly started reading practically at high school level?"

Slowly, her aunt shook her head. "I can't explain it, Lara. I saw it with my own eyes and I still don't believe it. Just yesterday he couldn't pronounce the word *quarry*. But this afternoon..." Her words drifted sideways, and she seemed to lose the thread. She leaned her head back in the chair and closed her eyes. She remained that way for so long that Lara wondered if she'd nodded off.

Taking advantage of the awkward silence, Lara glanced around, drinking in all the treasures that had fascinated her as a girl. When she was young she'd called this room the "fancy" room. She could still picture herself stretched out on the floor with her sketch pad and colored pencils, trying to copy the swirly patterns in the Oriental carpet. What had delighted her most was her aunt's collection of Victorian flue covers. Lara was happy to see they were still displayed on the mantel, each one depicting a colorful cat or kitten.

There was, of course, a cat tree in the front window. Covered in sturdy beige carpeting, it had ledges and cubbyholes and a perch at the top. Two gray-and-white kittens were nestled inside the lower cubby. Lara cooed to them in a soft, singsong voice, hoping to entice them closer. Instead they huddled into a tighter ball, as if protecting one another.

Lara's gaze drifted to the doorway that led to a back hallway. Beyond that was another porch—one that was screened in. When Lara had been hunting down litter boxes to clean, she'd found three of them out there. For some reason, she didn't recall her aunt ever having spent much time on that porch, even with its short set of stairs that led out to the side yard. Aunt Fran evidently preferred the openness of the wraparound porch in front, and the padded wicker chair in which she could rock to her heart's content.

Aunt Fran's eyes opened abruptly. "Tomorrow, *if* you're still here," she said, "maybe you could sit with Darryl for a while. What happened today might have been a complete fluke. I'd welcome your opinion, Lara." She rested a hand on Dolce, who snuggled farther into her lap.

"I'll be happy to do that," Lara said. She was miffed at her aunt's implication that she was going to hightail it back to Boston the next day and leave her without any help. "And unless you toss me out, I have no intention of bailing on you."

Lara knew she sounded cranky, but she was tired and beyond frustrated with her aunt's situation. How could Aunt Fran have let things get this dire? Why hadn't she tried to find homes for some of the cats? Wasn't there a local humane society that could give her some assistance?

"Why would I toss you out, as you put it?" her aunt asked testily.

Lara blew out a breath. "Listen, Aunt Fran," she said evenly, "from the time I got here this afternoon, I've sensed that you're angry with me." Her aunt started to interrupt but Lara held up a hand. "Granted, I haven't tried to contact you for a very long time. I honestly can't explain why. When Dad first got that new job and we moved to Sudbury, I was utterly miserable. I missed you so much. Plus, I was dying without Sherry. But I remember sending you a bunch of cards and you never wrote me back."

Aunt Fran looked genuinely puzzled. "I only received one card," she insisted. "It was about a week after you'd moved. I wrote several letters to you, but never heard from you again. One day I tried to call, but the number had been changed to a private one."

Lara was stunned. She'd never received those letters. As for the phone number, she remembered her dad saying that because of his job they needed to get an unlisted number. She assumed he'd given the number to Aunt Fran, his only sister.

Her aunt's eyes misted. "I'm sorry if I sounded cross," she said. "My emotions are all over the place right now."

Yeah, tell me about it, Lara wanted to say. "I know. Mine, too." She placed a hand over her aunt's thin fingers and was rewarded with a squeeze. "So maybe we can start fresh, okay?"

Aunt Fran smiled, and her eyes brightened. "That sounds like a plan. You can start by telling me what I've missed all these years. Your career, boyfriends..." She let the words dangle.

Lara skimmed over the details of her art career, which, so far, had been less than impressive. She'd sold a few watercolors, but her earnings hadn't been spectacular. Her online art projects supplemented her income, but the work was sporadic—nothing she could depend on. Her part-time job at the bakery kept her in food and rent, but with little left over. Not having a car helped. Taking the T to get around Boston, while annoying, gave her plenty of opportunities to find interesting faces to sketch. She occasionally did it surreptitiously between the seemingly endless T stops.

"Is there...anyone special in your life?" Aunt Fran asked.

The question surprised Lara. The dismal truth was that she'd never had anyone truly special in her life. Oh sure, she'd had boyfriends. But none had ever risen to the level of a "significant other."

"No, no one. Aunt Fran, you were going to tell me all about that awful Theo Barnes. Why is he bothering you?"

Her aunt's face clouded. "He's been trying to coerce me into selling part of my land. You know the vacant stretch below the crest of the hill, behind the town's parcel?"

Lara nodded slowly. She realized she was smiling to herself. She'd spent much of her early childhood exploring that empty field. It stretched from the back of the town's tiny park to the bank of the narrow stream that formed her aunt's rear boundary line. The meadow was a haven for a wealth of small animal species. Her favorites had been the red salamanders that darted along the water's edge.

Aunt Fran continued. "Theo desperately wants that land so he can build luxury condo units. According to him, he already has interested buyers."

"First of all," Lara said, "he can't force you to do anything with your own property that you don't want to do. And second, think of all the animals that would be disrupted! And besides," she added, picturing the location in her mind, "isn't it landlocked?"

Her aunt nodded. "Right on all counts. Unfortunately, Theo owns the parcel adjacent to mine—it's part of the town block where Bowker's Coffee Stop is. If he consolidates my land with his, then the problem of street access will disappear. But that's not all. His latest ploy is to claim he owns a big chunk of my land. Supposedly he had a survey done. My vacant parcel, he insists, doesn't stretch as far as I think it does."

Lara rolled her eyes. "What a royal toad. No offense to frogs."

"He's not a nice man," her aunt said tartly. "And that's as much as I can say without using a few choice descriptors that are *not* in the dictionary. Not in my dictionary, anyway." Her green eyes twinkled a bit.

Munster rose, stretched, and lumbered off Lara's lap. Lara took advantage of the sudden freedom and stretched out her legs. "Aunt Fran, have you talked to a lawyer about this?"

"Not yet. But I did try to find a survey of my property at the town hall. The only thing they had was the assessor's map. The town clerk told me I'd have to go to the Registry of Deeds in Ossipee to get the recorded survey."

"If you need it, Aunt Fran, I'll drive up there and get it for you."

Aunt Fran's smile was warm, if a bit awkward. "Thank you. That means a lot to me."

There were so many other questions Lara wanted to ask. She was beginning to realize how much she'd missed during all the years she'd been away. But when she looked over at her aunt, she saw that her eyelids were drooping. She needed a solid night's rest. They both did.

"It's after ten," Aunt Fran said, as if reading her mind. She lifted Dolce gently and set him down on the faded Oriental rug. With the help of the cane she'd hooked over the arm of her chair, she pushed to her feet. "Why don't we call it a night? We can chat more in the morning." Her voice sounded hoarse with fatigue.

"Should I…sleep in my old room?" Lara asked.

"Of course. There are fresh sheets in the linen closet upstairs. If you don't mind, I'll let you put them on yourself."

Lara smiled. "Not a problem."

After ensuring that her aunt had made it safely to her room, Lara fetched her suitcase from her rental car.

Right after they'd eaten dinner Lara had scooped the litter boxes, so they should be all set for the night. After checking to be sure all the lights were off, except for a night light turned on in every room, she made certain the cats had food and fresh water and that the doors were securely locked.

Tomorrow she would assess what else needed to be done, and try to come up with a game plan.

"If you leave your bedroom door open," Aunt Fran said, "you'll no doubt have some furry friends join you in the night."

Lara grinned. "If they're feline friends, they're more than welcome." It'd been years since she'd slept with a cat snuggled beside her. Her mother never let her have a cat, and her landlady refused to allow an animal in the studio apartment Lara leased from her. Gabriela, immaculate to a fault, imagined cat hairs floating magically through the air vents and into the bakery, landing on all of her baked goods.

"Maybe Blue will reappear, if that *was* Blue," Lara said pensively. "More likely it was one of her descendants."

Aunt Fran's brow furrowed. "Lara, I don't have a Ragdoll cat. Are you sure that wasn't Bootsie? She's mostly gray fluff, but has blackish ears."

Lara was already shaking her head. She didn't want to argue, but she was sure. Well, almost sure.

"You could be right, Aunt Fran. Don't worry about it." She leaned over and placed a kiss on her aunt's cheek. "I'm glad I came up here today. Thanks for letting me stay."

The room she used to sleep in had barely changed at all. The wallpaper, emblazoned with clusters of lilacs, was in good shape except for a few tiny spots where it had peeled. Lara wondered if she could repair those sections with small dots of glue. The fuzzy rug next to the single bed looked as thick and cozy as ever. The maple bed, which had a bookshelf-style headboard, was covered in the same ivory chenille spread she remembered.

In the morning, she'd throw open the windows and give the room a good airing out. For tonight, she'd settle for a hot shower, after which she planned to slip under the covers and sleep like the dead.

She located a set of sheets in the linen closet and quickly made up her bed. Then she pulled off her funky parrot earrings and dropped them onto the maple dresser. After shedding her jeans and paisley knit pullover, she took the world's fastest shower, then wrapped herself in a terry cloth bath towel and scooted back to her room. She giggled when she saw Izzy and Pickles, the two calico sibs, curled around each other atop the bedspread. Izzy glanced up at her as if to say, "What took you so long?" She unzipped her suitcase and dug out her favorite sleep tee, the one imprinted with a repro of Van Gogh's *Starry Night over the Rhone*.

The cats stirred when she slipped under the covers. They rearranged themselves, one against her leg and one pressed to her shoulder, and revved up their engines. Their purring sound was soothing, like the calm whisper of a surf. Almost immediately Lara drifted off.

It seemed that only minutes later Lara jerked upright. Something outside had awakened her—a searing cry, followed by the sound of raised voices. Careful not to dislodge a cat, she swiveled her legs off the bed and padded to the window. She lifted one of the blinds and peeked into the yard. The old shed was still there, hunkered at the rear of the property. In the vacant field below the hill, she thought she spied the quick flash of a light. But after an instant it disappeared, and then, only darkness.

"I'm definitely going crazy," Lara mumbled to the cats. They graciously allowed her back into the bed, and after that she slept.

A short time later, a second noise awakened her. A muffled cry that seemed to come from the far edge of the meadow.

Lara leaped out from under the covers and dashed to the window. A lone figure was standing near the shed, her outline unmistakable.

Aunt Fran.

Lara gulped back a lump of surprise. Should she run out and see if something was wrong? Or would that make it look as if she'd been spying?

She hesitated, then watched her aunt move slowly along the rear walkway, aided by her four-pronged cane. Aunt Fran didn't appear to be in any distress. She was making her way back toward the house without any difficulty, as if it were a ritual she performed every night.

With a sigh of relief, Lara slid back under the covers. After a few minutes, more sounds floated into earshot. This time they were faint thumping noises, coming from her aunt's room. Almost as if Aunt Fran were shifting things around.

Those were the last sounds Lara heard. She didn't awaken until the first trickle of daylight was squeezing through the blinds.

* * * *

A paw batting at her nose awakened Lara. She squinted at the clock—only six fifteen. Half-asleep, she grinned at the perpetrator—Izzy. The calico cat balanced on her chest while Pickles chewed on a strand of her tangled hair.

Although she was tempted to sleep half the morning, Lara hauled herself out of bed. The room felt chilly. She gave her arms a brisk rub. After a quick trip to the bathroom, she threw on her jeans, topping them with the multicolored cowl-neck sweater she'd scored for a fiver on eBay.

Lara headed downstairs and immediately turned up the thermostat. She felt sure her aunt wouldn't mind, especially since the cats needed to stay warm.

In the kitchen, furry felines danced around her legs in a parade of tails that made her grin. Twinkles, the orange-striped tiger, reached up with one adorable paw as if to say, "Feed me first!"

"I know, I know, you're all starving." Lara gently peeled Izzy off her thigh, then pulled cat food cans and kibble out of the cupboard. "Don't worry, there's plenty for everyone."

She made quick work of popping open cans and pouring dry food. Callie and Luna approached the bowls with hesitation, but eventually hunger won out. They began scarfing down wet kitten food as if they hadn't eaten in a week. Only Ballou, the feral cat who hadn't yet made an appearance, was missing. Lara hoped he might join the others if she made herself scarce.

After scooping the litter boxes and wrapping up the trash, Lara headed outside through the kitchen door. The sun sat slightly above the horizon, blinking with the promise of a bright day. The air was crisp with the intoxicating scent of autumn—wet leaves, smoke, and apples. She sucked in deep, cleansing breaths, expelling the lingering smells from the house.

Lara ambled around the backyard, her feet kicking up scads of leaves from her aunt's shedding maple. She'd missed this place. Until now, she hadn't realized how much.

The old shed, once white with green trim like the house, was in sore need of a paint job. Propped against the front of the shed were two bulging burlap sacks. Were those the tulip bulbs Aunt Fran had mentioned? On the side facing the vacant lot, a steel tool rack had been bolted to the shed wall. A row of garden tools hung from its hooks.

She grinned when her gaze landed on her favorite spot. At the edge of the yard, about ten feet from the crest of the hill, sat a huge stone. About six feet tall, it was roughly shaped like a curved hand. Lara used to nestle inside that curve with her pad and pencils and sketch to her heart's content.

Feeling like a kid, she dropped down to the grass and pressed her back against the rock. It cupped her with its hard edges, not quite fitting the way it used to. The ground felt cold and uneven. Almost immediately, she hopped to her feet and laughed. *I guess I'm getting old*, she thought, smirking to herself. She brushed her posterior with her hands to get rid of any stray dirt.

Hugging herself against the morning chill, Lara strolled toward the top of the hill and looked out over the landscape. A light wind lifted the ends of her hair. In the meadow below, behind the town park, the field grasses tilted in the breeze. How many winters had she sledded on this hill, gliding down the snowy slope on her aunt's ancient Flexible Flyer?

This was the parcel of land, she realized, that Theo Barnes had been pressuring her aunt to sell.

From where she stood, the block that housed Sherry's coffee shop was visible. Across the street from that was the town library, a one-story red brick affair that looked as if it hadn't changed in decades. Another old building squatted next to the library. With its dreary gray shingles and shallow front steps, it had all the trappings of an ugly apartment house.

A sudden flurry of movement in the meadow caught Lara's attention. It was an animal on the prowl, sleek and stealthy, and—

Lara took in a quick breath.

It was Blue, stalking through the field toward the base of the hill, her aquamarine eyes seemingly fixed on Lara.

"Blue," she called softly to the cat. "Come here, sweet kitty."

The cat continued moving but then shot off through the tall grass, heading in the direction of the brook.

Lara scuttled down the hill as quickly as she could, determined to catch up with the elusive feline. The cat was trotting through the grassy field as if on a mission. Lara was so focused on keeping Blue in her line of vision that she didn't notice the jutting rock embedded in the ground. It caught the toe of her boot. In the next instant she pitched forward, her arms flailing in a clumsy attempt to break her fall. She tumbled to the ground, skidding on her stomach, almost to the bottom of the hill.

For a moment Lara lay there, her breath coming in sharp gasps. She rolled over and sat up, groaning as she tested her limbs. Everything worked, although the palm of her right hand was scraped and sore.

After tossing a few colorful curses at the rock that had betrayed her, she hauled herself to her feet and began brushing dirt and grass from her hands and sweater. She slapped at her jeans to dislodge the clinging bits of dirt and grass. She hoped Aunt Fran's washing machine was in good working condition. At the rate she was going, she'd be running a load through very soon.

One last time, Lara glanced around for any sign of Blue, but the cat was MIA. By now Aunt Fran was probably awake and wondering where she'd disappeared to. She felt her stomach rumble. It was time she made breakfast for the two of them.

Lara turned to start back up the hill when something caught her eye—a swatch of red, maybe thirty feet away, that she hadn't noticed before. Whatever it was, it was lying behind the granite bench at the rear of the town's property. Had someone left an old blanket there? Could it be something that belonged to Aunt Fran?

She moved gingerly toward the red lump. A weird chill crept up her spine. Nothing in the meadow had ever frightened her before, but now she felt oddly afraid.

Lara halted abruptly in her tracks.

It wasn't a blanket, as she'd first thought. It was a jacket—a red-and-black-checkered jacket.

A jacket still worn by its very dead owner, Theo Barnes.

Chapter 4

Lara sipped from a steaming mug of mint tea, her brain still trying to delete the vision of Theo Barnes's bloodied head.

"I need you to focus, Ms. Caphart." Chief Jerry Whitley's gruff tone made her jump a little. He sat at her aunt's kitchen table, adjacent to where Lara was hunkered in one of the padded chrome chairs. "You still haven't explained why you touched the deceased's body if you already knew he was dead."

Stay calm. Don't get rattled, Lara told herself. "I'm sorry, Chief Whitley, but you're wrong. I did explain it, at least three times." She couldn't help getting touchy, even if it did cast a shadow of suspicion on her. Why did he keep asking the same question? Was he trying to get her to change her story? Entrap her into confessing?

"I could tell he was dead," she said evenly, "because his head was facing sideways. I saw his eyes. They were—" She swallowed hard. *They were dead eyes*, she wanted to say. "They were open and staring. It didn't look, you know, natural. And yet—in case I was wrong, I wanted to see if there was any sign of life."

A hand the size of a catcher's mitt flipped to a new page in a tattered blue notebook. "So you went over to the victim and pressed a finger…?" The chief pulled off his cheaters and imitated the gesture, placing one thick finger at his own throat. "A *finger* to the victim's carotid artery? Why not two fingers?"

Lara felt like snatching up his blue notebook and drop-kicking it into the next room. First of all, she didn't want to admit that she had a phobia about dead bodies. The one time she'd had to attend a wake, she'd stayed in the back of the room, as far from the casket as she could manage. "Listen,

Chief Whitley, maybe they use two fingers on TV, but I'm not a medical professional. I didn't want to touch him any more than I had to. What difference does it make how many fingers I used?"

The chief regarded her for a long moment, and then, "And you're sure you didn't move the murder weapon? Maybe set it aside to get a closer look at the victim?"

Okay, now he was trying to trick her. "As I've said several times, I did not see a murder weapon. I do not know what the murder weapon was, nor do I know how the poor man died. I'm afraid I'll have to leave that to you professionals to determine." She looked him straight in the eye, but he only stared right back with a granite gaze.

"This is ridiculous, Jerry," Aunt Fran interjected. "Lara didn't even know Theo. I'll thank you to stop badgering my niece right now." Her tone was more bluster than bite, but it seemed to work its magic.

Whitley closed his notebook with an audible snap. "That's all I need for now, Ms. Caphart. You'll no doubt be hearing from us again. And while I don't have any right to detain you, I'd appreciate it if you didn't leave town. Not without contacting us first." He scraped back his chair and rose, shifting his attention to Aunt Fran. "The state crime scene techs will be sectioning off a big chunk of your property, Fran. No one is to cross those lines. Not for any reason."

Aunt Fran nodded. "We understand."

The sound of a vehicle turning around at the end of High Cliff Road caught Lara's attention. Through the kitchen window, she spied the Carroll County medical examiner's white van. It cruised slowly past the house, heading toward the main drag.

Aunt Fran sagged in her chair after the chief left. "Oh, Lara, how did this happen? Who could have done such an awful thing?"

Lara couldn't help shooting a glance at her aunt's cane, which was propped against the table between them. One of the prongs was coated in dirt—dirt that had apparently dried overnight. Why had Aunt Fran gone outside last night? Was it before or after Barnes had been killed?

"I don't know, Aunt Fran. The police will have to figure that out. Do you think you can swallow a little breakfast? I thought I'd make us some oatmeal."

"That sounds good," she said. "There's a package of English muffins in the freezer. You can thaw a few, if you'd like."

Lara went through the motions of preparing breakfast, but her appetite had taken a direct hit. Her discovery of Barnes's body was giving her stomach a bad case of the jitters.

Aunt Fran sat quietly, a distant look in her eyes. The worry lines etched on her face seemed even deeper this morning.

After splitting an English muffin with her aunt and gulping back a few spoonfuls of oatmeal, Lara went to work scooping and freshening the litter boxes. She persuaded Aunt Fran to rest in her room while she vacuumed through the downstairs. Blue had yet to reappear, but Izzy and Pickles—the only cats who hadn't fled at the sound of the vacuum—had a grand old time wrestling with the hose as it wound around the edges of the furniture. Their antics lifted Lara's spirits a bit. When she was through, she gave them each a sound kiss on their respective snouts. She then hunted down a new vacuum-cleaner bag. She felt sure that the current one was now packed with forty or fifty pounds of cat hair.

Lara was pulling a vacuum-cleaner bag out of the walk-in supply closet when she spied a new feline face watching her from the doorway. His coat was shiny and black, and his perfectly symmetrical white mustache gave him a slightly comical look. The tip of his right ear was missing.

Lara grinned. "I know who you are," she said in a soft, singsong voice. "You're Ballou, aren't you."

The cat's eyes widened. For a moment Lara thought he would bolt. When he stayed put, she very slowly reached out a hand to him. Ballou dipped his head toward her outstretched fingers, but his paws stayed rooted in place.

A sudden noise above Lara's head startled them both. Ballou turned and fled with the speed of a jet.

Lara dropped everything and raced upstairs, terrified that her aunt might have fallen. She dashed toward her aunt's room, the door to which was open. Lara rushed in and found Aunt Fran sitting on the edge of her bed, her head in her hands.

"What's wrong, Aunt Fran? Are you hurt?" Lara slipped an arm around her aunt's thin shoulders.

"No, I… I'm fine," her aunt said, her face suddenly flushed. "I was trying to reach a box in the back of my closet, but my arm wasn't quite long enough and the silly thing tipped over."

Lara glanced over at her aunt's closet. The door was wide open. A gold-speckled box had toppled to the closet floor, spilling part of its contents. Lara went over and started to scoop up the envelopes that had fallen from the box.

"Wait! I'll get those," Aunt Fran said, waving her hands urgently. "Leave them right where they are, Lara."

Lara stopped short at her aunt's sharp tone, her hand inches from an envelope she was sure she'd seen her own name on. Had she detected a hint of panic in her aunt's voice? Slowly, she got to her feet. "Um, sorry, Aunt Fran. I was only trying to help."

Her aunt looked pained. "I know you were, Lara. But there are some things I need to do myself." She smiled, her green eyes glistening. "Listen, you've had a rough morning. Why don't you take a break and go to the coffee shop to visit with Sherry? I know she'd love to see you."

"Will you come with?" Lara asked her.

"No, you go without me today. I need to sit and think about some things." Her expression darkened. "Theo's body was found at the edge of my property, Lara. That troubles me deeply. I want to give some thought to who could have done such a horrible thing."

"It is bizarre," Lara agreed. "On the other hand, I can't help thinking that Barnes must have made more than an enemy or two in his day." She gave her aunt a flat smile. "The man didn't exactly impress me as a good-will ambassador."

Her aunt's gaze grew distant. "I can think of only one person Theo truly loved—his niece, Mary. She was the young woman sitting at the book-club table yesterday."

An image of the attractive brunette flitted through Lara's mind. She recalled Theo touching the woman's cheek with affection, right before he kissed the other woman's hand and then barked something into the older man's ear. "Oh, that's sad, then. I didn't realize they were related."

"Mary's adoptive mother, Elena, was Theo's sister," her aunt explained. "Elena died several years ago from uterine cancer." Aunt Fran patted Lara's knee. "You go ahead. Don't worry about me. Why don't you leave your cell number on the kitchen table in case I need to call you?"

"Sounds like a plan." Lara kissed her aunt's cheek and trotted downstairs. She located a piece of paper, jotted down her cell number, and left it on the kitchen table. There was no sign of Ballou, but Munster sidled over and rubbed against her leg. Lara reached down, scooped up the kitty, and kissed his furry head with a noisy smack. "I'll be back soon, I promise," she told him.

After plunking another kiss on Munster's soft white whiskers, she set him on the floor, grabbed her flowered tote, and tucked her phone in one of the pockets. Outside, a state police car sat parked in her aunt's driveway, directly behind Lara's rental car. She couldn't help wondering if they'd blocked her car on purpose. *Too bad for them if they did*, she thought. The coffee shop was only a six- or seven-minute walk from her aunt's.

The door to the state vehicle swung open without warning. A sturdy, middle-aged woman who looked about forty hopped out and stepped in front of Lara. "Ma'am?" she said, one carefully plucked eyebrow rising to her crisp hairline. Her uniform was dark green, pressed to perfection, and her steady gaze was somewhat intimidating. "I believe you were asked not to leave the premises?"

Lara gave the woman a smile that she hoped looked benevolent. "Actually, Officer, it was suggested—and it was only a suggestion—that I not leave town. Besides, I'm only heading down the street to the coffee shop. My friend and her mom own it. Have a nice day." She stepped around the officer and marched toward the road, half expecting the woman to run after her and whip her around by the arm. When neither happened, Lara turned and waved at her. The trooper, stone-faced, only stared back.

On her way to the coffee shop, a twinge of guilt poked at Lara. The state trooper was only doing her job—a tough job, at that—and Lara *had* been a tad sarcastic. But honestly, the woman could've cracked a smile, couldn't she? Even a half smile would have sufficed.

In spite of the October breeze that chilled Lara's cheeks, the sun was casting pale, golden rays from an azure sky. Sugar maples lined the main drag, their leaves dry and faded. They rustled overhead with soft, soothing sounds.

She passed some of Whisker Jog's oldest homes, including Hendricks House, a once-elegant restaurant. A large sign on the lawn announced that it was now a holistic massage practice.

Although Lara loved her hectic neighborhood on Boston's popular Hanover Street, with its bakeries and restaurants and ever-present pigeons, it felt good to be back in Whisker Jog. She wished desperately she hadn't been the one to find Barnes's body. If only she hadn't gone searching for Blue, she'd never have spotted that red-and-black-checkered jacket.

Lara tucked her tiger-striped scarf more tightly around her neck. It was the favorite of all her scarves, and she was glad she'd remembered to pack it. She was almost at the coffee shop when she realized she was walking past the local beauty salon. Kurl-me-Klassy, the lettering on the glass front window announced. She sneaked a peek through the glass. A young stylist with crimson hair was snipping away at the curly gray head of a woman who looked at least eighty. Both spotted Lara looking in. They waved at her and smiled.

Lara returned the greeting and moved on. Even before she pulled open the glass door to the coffee shop, she could see that the place was bustling. She recognized some of the official-looking types from the crime scene. She also spied Daisy, moving at warp speed as she delivered steaming plates to a table of diners.

From behind the counter, Sherry spotted her instantly. "Lara!" she called over the din of chattering customers.

Lara stepped toward the counter, the ambient warmth in the coffee shop wrapping around her. She went over to the only unoccupied stool, on which rested a velvety-brown homburg. Next to that sat an elderly gent whose bald head sprouted long white tufts. "Is this seat taken?" she asked, indicating the hat. She gave him a pleasant smile.

He did not smile back. "That's Herbie's seat," he answered gruffly. "He's been sitting there every day for thirty-seven years."

Sherry looked wide-eyed at Lara, giving a rapid little shake of her head. Lara got the message: *don't ask questions.* Sherry held up a finger, the tip of which was painted glowing orange, then scurried around the edge of the counter. She marched over to Lara. "It's like a mob scene here today," she said, darting her gaze all around. She clamped her neon-tipped fingers onto Lara's arm. "Lara, what happened this morning? Everyone's saying Theo Barnes was murdered, and that you found the body!"

"He was," Lara said quietly. "And I did find the…body. But I have no idea what happened to him, or who did it. Sherry, listen, I can come back later. I can tell you guys are really slammed today."

"No! You have to stay." Sherry shot her gaze all around the coffee shop. Still clutching Lara's arm in a grip worthy of a wrestler, she tugged her friend over to a table at which a young woman and a fortysomething man were hunched over cream-colored mugs. The woman was crying into a crumpled tissue. Lara recognized her as one of the book club members from the day before.

"Mary Newman, Chris Newman." Sherry jabbed a finger at each one as she recited their names. "This is my best friend in the whole world, Lara Caphart. She's going to sit with you today, okay?" Using two hands, she shoved Lara down into one of the vacant chairs. "I'll bring you coffee in a jiffykins, Lara. Hang tight." She turned and bolted with all the grace of a roadrunner. Lara would've sworn she saw a tail feather float to the floor.

Lara turned to her tablemates, both of whom were staring at her as if she'd just been lowered from a spacecraft. She looped her flowered tote over the back of her chair. "Hello, it's nice to meet you. I hope you don't mind me joining you. Sherry kind of foisted me on you, didn't she?" She gave out a laugh that she knew sounded nervous.

For a moment no one spoke. Then the woman, Mary, who wore a beige sweatshirt embroidered with a pumpkin patch design, said, "No, of course not." She squashed a tissue against one watery brown eye. With her freckles, turned-up nose, and dark hair curled into a flip, she didn't look much older than a college student. "Except...I hope you don't mind my crying. I just can't seem to stop." With that, she let loose a fresh waterfall of tears.

"Theo Barnes was her uncle," her husband explained. He stuck out a hand to Lara. "Chris Newman, in case you missed the introduction."

Lara shook his hand. It was smooth, but the nails looked chewed to the quick. "Glad to meet you, Chris. I'm so sorry for your loss." Technically it was Mary's loss, but her husband, no doubt, shared her grief. With his wire-rimmed glasses and gentle brown eyes, Chris Newman put Lara in mind of a kindly pastor.

"We were all shocked at the news," Chris quietly told Lara. "I write feature stories for the town's weekly rag—*The Whisker Gazette*. I guess I'll really have something to write about this week," he added grimly. "Mary wants me to write her uncle's obituary."

"Because I know you'll write it with sensitivity," Mary said, pouting a little. She sucked in a stuttering sob. "Not everyone loved Uncle Theo the way I did."

Lara remembered what Aunt Fran had said about Mary—that she was the one person Theo truly loved.

Chris stared down at the table, frowning. "Theo was not an easy man to deal with. He—"

"Here you go!" Sherry swooped in from behind and placed a steaming mug of coffee in front of Lara. With her other hand, she plonked down an oversized basket crammed with warm muffins, butter, and blueberry preserves, along with plastic knives individually wrapped in carrot-colored napkins. "These are left over from breakfast so they're on the house, everyone. If you'd rather have lunch, let me know, okay? Enjoy!"

"Thanks, Sherry," Lara said to her friend's retreating form.

Chris shot a guilty look at his wife and then leaned toward Lara. "Do you know if the police have any suspects?" he asked in a low voice, reaching for an apple-cinnamon muffin.

Ah, so the reporter wanted the skinny on the murder. Lara mulled it over for a moment and then said carefully, "Not as far as I know. They didn't tell us very much."

"Hmm. Did they...say how he was killed?" Chris asked.

"Chris!" Mary slapped her hands over her ears. "I don't want to hear any of that. Please stop!"

Chris's cheeks flushed a hearty pink. "I'm sorry, honey. I didn't mean to upset you." He reached over and hugged his wife, pulling her close. Mary sobbed into the shoulder of his blue crewneck sweater.

"To be honest," Lara said, "even if I knew anything, which I don't, I'm pretty sure I'm not supposed to talk about it." The police already had her penciled in on their suspect list. She didn't need to antagonize them by blabbing about what she had witnessed at the crime scene.

Lara started to reach for a blueberry muffin but then snatched her hand back. The herd of gremlins that had settled in her stomach would probably stage a revolt if she tried to eat anything right now. The miniscule blob of oatmeal she'd swallowed back at her aunt's already felt like a leaden lump weighing down her insides. Maybe she should finish her coffee and get the heck out of there.

Chris Newman patted his wife's back, and she lifted her head from his shoulder. With a loud sniffle she snagged one of the orange napkins, unfurled it, and pressed it to her leaky eyes.

Chris pushed aside his mug and removed his wallet from his back pocket. He withdrew a business card and slid it over to Lara. "If you think of anything you *can* tell me, Lara, would you give me a call or a text?"

Lara stared at the card, amazed at the man's boldness in the face of his wife's angst. It read CHRISTOPHER NEWMAN, CPA, and beneath that, Certified Public Accountant, along with his contact info.

"I thought you were a reporter?" Lara said, slipping the card into her tote.

"Accountant by day, journalist by night," he said, without much enthusiasm. "That is, if you call reporting on things like the town's upcoming pumpkin festival journalism." He shot his wife a furtive look, but Mary didn't seem to notice.

Over the low clamor sifting through the coffee shop, a feminine voice suddenly rang out from the doorway. "Cheer up, everyone—don't look so glum. Theo Barnes is dead!"

Chapter 5

The coffee shop chatter ceased abruptly, as if a magician had waved a wand over the room and flash-frozen everyone's tongues. All eyes, including Lara's, followed the curvaceous brunette who weaved across the dining room, her stiletto heels clicking, her faux-leopard jacket perfectly complemented by a black velvet beret.

Lara couldn't help gawking, especially since the woman seemed to be moving in their direction. With the woman's approach came a swirl of floral perfume, a scent that hovered over their table and settled there in a potent cloud.

Mary leaped out of her chair. "Aunt Josette, you're here!" She stumbled toward the newcomer, nearly falling over the leg of Chris's chair, and threw her arms around her. Another cascade of tears began flowing from Mary's eyes.

"Mary, darling," the woman cooed, returning the hug. She patted Mary on the back as if she were a fussy toddler. "There, there, darling. It'll all be okay. I promise. Everything will work out just fine."

Mary cried for at least a minute, then sucked in one last sniffle. She stepped back and swiped the heels of her hands over her runaway tears. "But Uncle Theo is dead, Aunt Josette, and someone killed him. You're...you're not really glad about that, are you?" She said that with all the innocence of a newborn, as if she couldn't conceive of anyone disliking her uncle.

Looking somewhat embarrassed, the woman pushed a stray lock of dark hair away from Mary's forehead. "No, of course not. I'm sorry I came off sounding so harsh about Theo. I keep forgetting he was your mom's only brother."

"That's okay. Aunt Josette, this is Lara," Mary said. "She's Fran Clarkson's niece. You remember Fran, right?"

Josette's mascaraed eyes widened. "Oh my, of course I do. Lara, I am so very pleased to meet you." She held out a smooth hand tipped with gorgeously manicured nails.

Lara pumped it briefly with her own unadorned hand, blinking at the baseball-sized diamond glittering from Josette's right middle finger.

"Same here," she said.

"How *is* Fran these days?" Josette inquired, her voice laced with pity. "Does she still have all those, you know—"

"Cats?" Lara finished for her. "She has several, and they're all doing fine. Everything is under control, in fact." She had no intention of fueling any gossip about her aunt's overflowing feline community. Besides, things were already better. Lara intended to see that they stayed that way.

"Well, that's good," Josette said, sounding unconvinced. She turned to Chris, greeting him with an airy kiss that didn't quite make contact, then pressed a hand to Lara's shoulder. "By the way, I can't imagine what you must be thinking of me, Lara. I didn't really mean that I was glad Theo was dead. Naturally, I'd never wish murder on anyone, but...well, you see, Theo and I didn't exactly have an amicable divorce."

And probably not an amicable marriage, Lara thought. She wondered how long Josette had been married to Barnes. Long enough to make her do a mental happy dance over his demise, that much was obvious.

"I understand your feelings," Lara said, though she thought the woman was a bit crass for broadcasting them to everyone.

"Now dry your tears and come with me, Mary," Josette said crisply. "I insist on taking you shopping. You'll want something chic to wear to your uncle's funeral, won't you?"

Mary stared at her aunt through red-rimmed eyes. "I haven't really thought about it, Aunt Josette. I don't think I need to look chic, do I? I mean, I'm sure I have a navy dress—"

"Mary, I insist," Josette said, taking her niece's hand in her own. "If nothing else, it will take your mind off Theo."

"Honey, maybe it would help if you went out shopping with Josette for a while," Chris said. "Clear your head a little."

"But I have to be at work by two!"

"Can't you get time off?" Josette crinkled her tiny nose over a sharply drawn frown. "You certainly have good reason."

"I know, but we're super short-staffed this week. I'd hate to let my boss down. She's been so good to me. Besides, I'll need time off for the funeral, so I should really go to work today."

Josette hesitated, then released a sigh. "All right. Then we'll just go window-shopping for a bit, okay?" She chucked her niece under the chin, a gesture that made Lara cringe. Did she always treat Mary like a child? With a nod, Mary relented. "Okay, but only for a little while."

The pair made their farewells and headed for the exit. Josette led the way, high heels reverberating off the linoleum, while Mary shuffled dolefully behind her. Lara took that as her cue to make a hasty departure.

"I'm afraid I need to go as well," Lara said, gathering up her tote. "I want to pick up a few groceries for my aunt. My rental car is back at the house." *Still blocked by a state police car?* she wondered.

Chris looked relieved. He pulled a twenty from his wallet, dropped it on the table, and rose from his chair. "That's for all of us, okay?" His laugh sounded nervous. "I'd appreciate it if you'd call me when you find out anything new, Lara."

Lara nodded, doubtful she'd be able to supply him with the kind of juicy tidbits he was angling for. "Thanks, Chris. I don't think the police will share with me, but I'll definitely keep you in mind."

The clot of people who'd filled the coffee shop earlier had loosened. Daisy was taking orders and delivering meals, but she didn't look quite as frazzled as she had when Lara first came in.

Lara went over to the counter to let Sherry know she was leaving. She found her friend expertly stacking bacon, lettuce, turkey, and tomato slices into a hearty club. Lara leaned over the counter and gave her Chris's twenty, explaining that he'd offered to pay.

"Not necessary, but I'll take it," Sherry said. "I'll make sure his next meal here is on the house. Hey, you have to come back later, okay? We never got a chance to dish!"

"I know, and I'll try. I want to get as much done for Aunt Fran as I can. This little matter with...*you-know-who* hasn't helped things any."

Sherry gave a nod of acknowledgment. "I hear you, girl. When do you have to go back to Boston?" she asked glumly.

Lara didn't know how to answer that. "I guess that remains to be seen. The police kind of hinted that they don't want me to leave town—"

"Seriously?" Sherry's eyes widened. "I read somewhere that, technically, the cops can't do that."

Lara shrugged. "I guess I'm a person of interest, as they say on TV. But, like I said, it was only a suggestion." She said it with far more nonchalance than she felt. In reality, it was terrifying to be a suspect in a murder. If that's what she was.

"Ridiculous," Sherry sputtered. "Never mind. Come back when you get a chance, okay? Even if it's only for a few minutes."

Lara promised she'd do her best.

Chapter 6

Outside, the temperature had dropped by at least ten degrees. Lara glanced at her watch. Two minutes till noon. Almost five hours from when she'd first stumbled upon Barnes's body.

She'd just started the short trek back to her aunt's when she noticed a woman coming toward her on the sidewalk. Fiftysomething, with blond hair melding into gray, the woman moved slowly, taking each step with care. Recognition clicked in Lara's brain. This had to be Dora, the other woman in Brooke's book club. Lara recalled her sitting at Brooke's table the day before in the coffee shop.

The woman stopped and stared unabashedly—through a pair of stylish lilac-tinted spectacles—at Lara. "You don't remember me, do you?" she said.

Lara smiled. "I think I do, from yesterday. You're in the book club with Brooke, aren't you?"

"I don't mean that," the woman said sharply. "I mean, you don't remember me from before, from when you were a girl. I'm Dora Pingaree, an old friend of Fran's."

Lara gave her what she hoped was a contrite look. "No, I'm sorry. I don't remember that far back. Until yesterday, in fact, I hadn't seen my aunt in a number of years." The admission made her feel like the worst niece on the planet. "But it's lovely to meet you, Dora."

Dora nodded. "I remember you from when you were a girl. Such a darling thing you were—all those plush red curls. How Fran adored you."

Adored—past tense. *Is that intentional?* Lara wondered. Either way, she decided she liked Dora. Something about the woman seemed genuine, even if she was a bit blunt.

"Well, thank you," Lara said.

In the next instant, Dora's face drooped. "I'm awfully sad about Theo Barnes. I suppose you heard all about what happened."

More than you know, Lara was tempted to say. She wondered if Dora was testing her, trying to entice her into admitting she'd been the one to find Theo's body.

"Yes, it was a terrible thing, wasn't it," Lara said quietly.

"The police will have their work cut out. Theo had enemies, you know. Lots of them." She stared over Lara's shoulder, as if she were seeing the enemies lined up and waiting for interrogation.

"I'm sure they'll find the killer soon," Lara offered. "Well, listen, it was nice chatting with you, Dora. I really need to get back to my aunt's to see if she needs any help. She'll probably have a grocery list a mile long ready and waiting for me. Before I leave town, I want to be sure she's stocked up on supplies."

Dora snapped her attention back to Lara. "One of those fancy new supermarkets opened up just outside of Whisker Jog, but you can get the same things right here in town at the Shop-Along. Prices aren't bad, either. Fran usually does her shopping there." She gave Lara directions.

Lara thanked her, eager, now, to get away. She had the feeling that, if given the chance, Dora would chat for another hour.

Dora grimaced, and with one fist she rubbed her lower back.

"Are you okay?" Lara asked her.

"I wear a back brace," Dora explained. "It's very restricting. But if I don't wear it, the pain gets unbearable."

Poor woman, Lara thought. "I'm sorry to hear that. If there's anything I can do—"

Dora waved a hand at her. "Oh no, I'll be fine, dear. I'm used to it. We all have our crosses to bear, don't we?"

Lara smiled at the cliché, but she had to admire Dora's pluckiness. "I guess we do."

After saying a final good-bye to Dora, Lara walked briskly back to her aunt's, the fresh chill in the air biting her cheeks. Even from the road, she could see the yellow crime scene tape. Two police cars remained in the driveway, but they'd pulled off to the side to avoid blocking Lara's car.

And whoever the killer was, he—or she—was still out there.

* * * *

Lara was surprised to find her aunt at the kitchen sink, her hands buried in a pan of sudsy water. Dolce lay curled at her feet, his nose resting on the shoelaces of her blue sneakers.

"What'cha doing?" Lara asked, skimming her gaze over the freshly washed cat bowls in the dish drainer. Dolce blinked up at her, and Lara bent and gathered the cat into her arms. "You have to be careful around people's feet," she told the cat, and then plunked a kiss on his head. "You don't want to get accidentally smooshed."

Aunt Fran rinsed her hands, then turned and smiled at Lara. "Don't worry, I'm always aware of him. I was just cleaning up some of the bowls. You did such a good job yesterday that I wanted to keep up the tradition." She pulled a clean dish towel out of a nearby drawer.

"Can I take over for you?" Lara asked her.

"I can finish later," Aunt Fran said, drying her hands. "There are only a few left. Let's sit for a moment, shall we?"

Lara didn't press the point. She sensed her aunt was trying to show that she wasn't totally helpless, that she didn't always need rescuing.

In truth, the hint of pink in Aunt Fran's prominent cheekbones was a huge improvement over the pallor of earlier that morning. Her green eyes had a touch of their old sparkle. Even her smile seemed more natural.

All of which was strange, considering the circumstances. Was Theo's death the reason for the sudden improvement in Aunt Fran's appearance? Or had Lara's unannounced arrival the day before made the difference in her demeanor? Lara hoped it was the latter.

Aunt Fran retrieved her cane from the corner of the counter where she'd propped it. Lara couldn't help shooting a glance at the prongs. All four looked clean, without a trace of dirt.

At the kitchen table, Aunt Fran eased herself into a chair. Lara sat facing her, Dolce parked on her lap.

"The police are leaving us alone, for the time being," Aunt Fran said. "The crime scene van left, but they'll be back. They've cordoned off the vacant field and the town park. I told the chief I'd call the station if we spotted any nosy-posies hanging around in the area."

Lara nodded. People could be so ghoulish. "Aunt Fran, do you think the killer could've met up with Theo near the bench at the back of the park?"

"That's my guess. The police haven't exactly shared their theories with me. But if someone wanted to have a late night secret meeting, that would be the perfect place."

"Yeah," Lara said. She thought about the voices she'd heard after she'd gotten into bed the night before. "It's not as if Theo would have been wandering around the park at midnight just to see the sights. He must have been meeting someone there."

Aunt Fran frowned and looked away. She reached out toward Dolce, who was more than happy to abandon Lara's lap and climb into hers.

She needs Dolce for moral support, Lara thought. *Is she hiding something? Why had she gone outside so late?*

"Chief Whitley asked me if I touched the murder weapon. Aunt Fran, I never even saw a murder weapon! For all I know, someone hit Theo with a rock and then tossed it into the field to get rid of it."

"I only hope they find the killer soon." Aunt Fran looked at the wall clock above the sink. "How about a bite of lunch, Lara? I have some cold cuts in the fridge. Did you eat much at the café?"

"Not really." Lara filled her in on her encounter with the Newmans—topping it with the appearance of Theo's ex, Josette, and her elation at the news of his untimely demise. She also told her about running into Dora.

"Don't take Josette too seriously," Aunt Fran said. "She has a penchant for drama, but she's actually a kind soul. I think years of living with that buffoon, Lord rest his soul, did a number on her."

A rumble of hunger roiled through Lara's stomach. Until now, food had been a turnoff, the image of Theo's bloodied head still encroaching into her thoughts. But several hours had passed since she'd found the body, and her own body was reminding her that she needed to eat.

Lara threw together two ham-and-cheese sandwiches and made two cups of tea. She wolfed down her own lunch, while Aunt Fran ate hers slowly and deliberately.

"Aunt Fran," Lara said, after stuffing in the last bite, "I was thinking that you might need some supplies—food, cat stuff, things like that. Can I make a trip to the market for you? Dora told me you buy your groceries at the Shop-Along."

An amused smile formed on Aunt Fran's lips. "Leave it to Dora. She notices things most people wouldn't. But actually, that would be wonderful. The last time I had delivery from them, I'd told the clerk I wanted a package of Dove bars. Instead of the chocolate bars I'd been craving, I got two bars of heavenly smelling Dove soap."

Lara laughed. "Easy mistake, I guess. But I promise to get exactly what you want."

The two prepared a list, and Lara hopped into her rental car. The state police vehicles were still in the driveway, but no one even glanced in her direction as she eased her rental sedan out onto High Cliff Road.

The Shop-Along was only a two-mile drive from her aunt's. Snugged between a fenced-in day care center and a newish-looking dental practice, the parking lot in front of the squat yellow building was packed. Lara was happy to find a space near one of the carriage corrals.

Next to the market's wide glass entrance was a large wooden crate packed with pumpkins. Lara couldn't resist—she lifted a medium-sized one from the pile. Inside the store she grabbed a shopping cart and plopped in the pumpkin. It would set her back four dollars, but she thought about how cute it would look sitting on her aunt's front steps. If she had time, she might even draw or carve a cat on it.

Aunt Fran's list consisted mostly of staples—sugar, milk, tea bags—along with a substantial amount of kitten and cat food. No surprise there. The aisles were neat and well organized, and within ten minutes she'd loaded everything she needed into her grocery cart.

"Oh, wow, you must, like, really have a lot of cats!" said the checkout clerk, a young woman with roundish cheeks and a bright smile. "Do you run some kind of, like, shelter or something?"

Lara smiled. "Not exactly. I'm just stocking up on supplies."

"Oh. Then you should be all set for the winter!"

Not hardly, Lara thought. She thanked the friendly clerk and wheeled her cart out to her car. After loading her last bag into the backseat, she swung the cart into the nearest corral. She was climbing into her car when she spotted a white SUV parked nearby, its engine running. Mary Newman sat in the driver's seat crying into a tissue. Even from where Lara was standing, she could see Mary's shoulders heaving.

Poor woman. Lara locked her car and went over to Mary's. She tapped her knuckles against the driver's-side window. Mary jumped, and after a slight hesitation, she powered down her window. "Hi," she said, her face flushing.

"Mary, are you okay? I thought you were going window-shopping with your aunt."

Mary shook her head and sniffled. "I feel awful about it, but I blew her off. I told her I was getting a bad headache. Actually, that much was true. The thing is, Aunt Josette loves to shop and I...I—" She let out a strangled sob and wept into her tissue.

Lara waited for a moment and then said, "Mary, let's talk, okay? Do you mind if I hop into your front seat?"

Mary nodded, which Lara took as assent. She scurried around to the other side of the SUV and opened the door, stopping short when she saw a pile of magazines stacked on the passenger seat.

Mary gave a sudden start. "Oh, God. Wait a second. Let me get all this junk out of your way." She grabbed the magazines with both hands and tossed them onto the backseat. They landed with such force that a few of them slid to the floor. Lara managed to snare a glimpse of one, and had to stifle a gasp at the title—*Confessions in Lace*. The glossy cover depicted a young woman smiling coquettishly over one bare shoulder, her dress a silky affair that barely covered the essentials.

Lara couldn't help feeling embarrassed for Mary, who was having trouble making eye contact. She gave her what she hoped was an empathetic smile. "Mary, is there anything I can do to help? Your uncle's death must have been a terrible blow."

Tears leaked from beneath Mary's lids. "It was. What makes me sad is that so many people disliked him. I'll be amazed if anyone even goes to his funeral. I know some people thought he was ruthless in his business dealings, and I guess he could be, but…but to me he was always wonderful."

"You were his niece, Mary," Lara said gently. "I'm sure he loved you very much."

"He did. It's just—" She looked off to her left, as if remembering something painful. "I'm afraid the police will be looking at the wrong people, you know?" she said in a shaky voice.

The wrong people? Like maybe his ex-wife, Josette?

"Are you thinking of your aunt?" Lara asked, as tactfully as she could. She didn't want to accuse anyone, but Josette hadn't exactly disguised her delight over her ex's earthly departure.

Mary looked at her in horror. "Aunt Josette? Heavens, no! She wouldn't swat a mosquito. Besides, she was in Connecticut last night with a new beau. Someone she met online. She only drove back to New Hampshire this morning."

Taken aback by Mary's defensive tone, Lara was quiet for a moment. She sensed Mary knew more than she was saying. She might even know something that could point to her uncle's killer. If only Lara could persuade Mary to open up to her.

"I'm sorry," Mary said, her cheeks flaming. She gave Lara a wobbly smile. "I didn't mean to sound so witchy."

"You didn't," Lara assured her. "I understand how bummed you are over all this. It's a lot to absorb."

Squirming in her seat, Mary glanced at her car's digital clock. "It's twenty to two. I have to go now. My shift at the crafts store starts at two."

That was another strange thing. Why hadn't Mary asked for time off? Surely she had good reason. Lara couldn't imagine any employer faulting her for taking off a few days after a close family member was murdered. She decided not to press it. Mary obviously had her reasons. Lara opened her door. "I won't keep you any longer, Mary. But if you ever want to talk—about anything—I'm a pretty good listener."

Mary swallowed hard. "It's just that Chris—" She shook her head. "Never mind. I can't talk about it now. Thank you for being so kind, Lara."

On impulse, Lara leaned over and gave Mary a hug. Then she got out of the SUV and closed the door, her gaze skittering to the stack of mags on Mary's backseat. *Confessions in Lace.* Lara made a mental note to Google it later.

Lara waved as Mary pulled out of her parking space, but Mary didn't seem to notice. The SUV zipped off quickly toward the exit, then zoomed away down the main drag. Lara started to head back to her car when she spotted a slip of paper on the ground, almost under the tip of her boot. Had it been there when she'd climbed into the SUV? She didn't think so.

She stooped to inspect it. The paper was somewhat flimsy, as if it had been torn from a napkin. On it, the words MIDNIGHT MARY had been printed in pencil in bold letters. Before a breeze could whisk it away, Lara picked it up and slipped it into her jacket pocket.

Lara got into her car and started the engine. Right before Mary left she'd started to say something about Chris. If only they could have talked longer, Mary might have confided in her.

Chapter 7

Bowker's Coffee Stop was quiet by the time Lara returned. The moment she opened the glass door, her senses were treated to the scrumptious aroma of warm vanilla and spices. Smiling, Lara inhaled deeply. Daisy must have prepared a fresh batch of sugar cookies. Lara couldn't wait to see what today's design would be.

The hullabaloo of earlier in the day had settled into a pleasant hum. Customers chatted over coffee and dessert, some thumbing away at their smartphones. Sliding onto a stool at the counter, Lara was grateful she didn't recognize any of the customers. She wanted a chance to dish privately with Sherry.

A head graced with gelled black spikes popped up from behind the counter. "Hey, you made it back!" Sherry plunked a package of napkins on the counter and immediately poured Lara a steaming cup of coffee.

"Ahh…thanks. That's exactly what I need." Lara emptied a packet of half-and-half into her mug and took a long swig. "It's been a day, let me tell you."

Sherry gave her a worried frown. "Oh, Lara, I can't believe this is all happening. I mean, why now, you know? You haven't seen your aunt in, what, like, fifteen or sixteen years? And the day you show up, the town tyrant is murdered?" She shook her head, her raven-tinted spikes remaining firmly in place.

"Uh, yeah, that didn't sound too good," Lara said wryly.

"Lara, no one would seriously consider you a suspect. I mean, what would your motive even be?"

Oh, how about Barnes's ongoing clash with Aunt Fran over the land he was trying to force her to sell?

"Although—" Sherry started to say when Daisy came through the swinging metal door holding a small tray of frosted black bats.

"I had some dough left over from this morning," Daisy announced. "I hated to see it go to waste, so I whipped these up." She glanced at the wall clock. "I'm hoping I can unload them before closing time."

Lara's gaze skimmed the cookies. "Seriously, those are too adorable to eat."

"Want one?" Daisy grinned.

Lara snagged one off the tray. "Twisted my arm." She bit into a bat's wing and groaned. "Okay, this is ridiculous," she mumbled over a mouthful of cookie. "How do you make cookies that taste like this?"

Daisy winked at her. "My secret will die with me. I mean—" She flushed. "Sorry. I shouldn't have used that word."

Sherry squeezed her mom's shoulder. They exchanged a look.

Lara felt her stomach flip. "What's wrong? What is it?"

"Lara," Daisy said in a low voice. "There's something I think I ought to mention to you about Fran. About her dealings with Theo. She might have already told you, but—"

"About her land? About Barnes trying to coerce her to sell it?"

Daisy nodded. With a pained look, she set the tray of cookies on the counter. "Did she tell you about the screaming match she had with him at the town hall?"

With a sense of dread, Lara slowly shook her head.

"A number of weeks ago," Daisy went on, "Fran had—well, kind of a fight with Theo in the town clerk's office. Evidently, Fran wanted a copy of the plan that showed her property. Theo must've seen her go into the town hall. He trotted right in there after her and started harassing her."

Lara squeezed her hand into a fist. "He *was* a tyrant, wasn't he? So, what happened?"

Daisy sighed. "I guess the shouting got out of hand. At one point Fran raised her cane at Theo. She came close to clipping him in the eye. He got furious and said he was going to have her arrested for assault."

Lara covered her face with her hands. "Oh, Lordy. Then what?"

"The town clerk, Bernice Markell, intervened." Daisy flashed a droll smile. "She's the sweetest, nicest woman. But if her feathers get ruffled, she can come on like a battleship. From what I heard, Bernice marched around the counter and grabbed each of them by the arm. She told Theo to get his, um, *posterior* out of there before she kicked it out."

"I'd like to have seen that," Lara said with a chuckle. Then she frowned. "What about Aunt Fran?"

"Bernice took Fran into her office in the back and gave her some tea to calm her down." Daisy sighed. "Unfortunately, three other people were in the town clerk's office that day. They witnessed everything. I heard two of our customers gossiping about it later that day. By the next day, everyone in town knew about it."

Lara's heart sank. Would the police chief use it against Aunt Fran? Would he try to say she had a motive for killing Theo? That she'd displayed violent tendencies toward him in the past?

"This is crazy," Lara said. She recalled what Mary had told her—that no one liked Theo. "Theo must have had dozens of enemies. Josette certainly didn't show any love lost for him."

Sherry rolled her mascaraed eyes. "No kidding. Josette's been doing the dance of joy ever since she heard Theo was dead."

"You noticed." Lara bit off the bat's head.

"Who didn't?" Sherry hunched over the counter, closer to Lara. "But get this. Mom and I found out it wasn't only because she hated him. Turns out Josette stands to get the remainder of her yearly alimony allotments in one lump sum from Theo's estate—to the tune of fifty grand."

"Whoa," Lara said.

"Yup." Sherry fetched the coffeepot and topped off Lara's mug.

With a miniature spatula, Daisy began sliding her few remaining cookies into the Plexiglas case on the counter. She glanced around to be sure no one was within earshot. "Apparently, she was awarded five thousand a year for each year of their twelve-year marriage. So far she's only collected ten thousand. Once her ex-hubby's estate is probated, she'll get the rest. In one big fat lovely chunk."

Fifty thousand dollars. Lara turned this over in her mind. It wasn't a fortune, but it wasn't chicken feed, either. Josette, she decided, was looking better and better as a suspect. "That's a pretty strong motive," Lara said. "How'd you find out about the alimony?"

Daisy winked slyly at her. "This morning, before you got here, I was bringing coffee over to Mary and Chris's table. I heard them whispering about it. It was right after we'd all found out about Theo's murder. 'Course it helped that I pretended to drop some sugar packets on the floor right behind their chairs. I picked up that sugar *verrrry* slowly, if you get my meaning."

Lara laughed and swallowed the rest of her cookie, which consisted of approximately one-half of a bat wing. "You were always a good detective, Daisy. Isn't that how you figured out Sherry had been wearing your eyeliner to school every day? When she was nine?"

"Oh, for the love of Humpty Dumpty," Sherry sputtered. "Did you have to remind her?"

"I'd forgotten about that." Daisy narrowed her eyes at her daughter. "I kept finding tissues in the bathroom wastebasket with traces of coal-black eyeliner and gooey makeup remover on them. It didn't take a rocket scientist to figure out what was going down."

Lara giggled. "I remember this one day, Sher, when you put it on so heavy you looked like Cleopatra."

Daisy twisted her lips into a smirk, but Sherry's attention had already shifted. She was staring at the lone diner sitting at the corner table near the restroom.

Sherry touched Lara's arm. "Poor Glen," she murmured. "He's been there all day, nursing cups of coffee and staring at the table."

Lara tilted her head sideways so she could see the man more clearly. Ah yes, Glen—the sole male member of Brooke's book club. The one Brooke claimed was "crushing" on Mary.

"Why does he look so glum?" Lara asked.

Daisy closed the Plexiglas case. "He'd been renting a studio apartment from Theo in the building across the street, the one next to the library." She tilted her head toward the door, indicating the drab apartment building across the street. "Anyway, yesterday Theo tossed him out. Glen usually pays by the week, but I guess he was several weeks behind in his rent."

"Poor old dude slept in his car last night," Sherry added. "For now, the library is letting him park it in their lot overnight, since the lot empties out once the library closes. Actually, it's the circulation manager who said he could park there. She has, well, *had* a thing for Theo—God only knows why. A few weeks ago, I caught them canoodling in the front seat of Theo's car." She stuck her finger into her mouth to mimic a gag.

Lara's heart went out to Glen. "Does he work?"

Sherry shook her head. "He's worked sporadically in the past, but he's such a know-it-all that no one keeps him on for long. Frankly, people around here are sick of him. No one even feels bad for him anymore. He's one of those people who's his own worst enemy, you know? Oddly enough, he's quite intelligent. Problem is, he's never put his brainpower to good use. Plus, he has zero personality. I don't know where he'll go from here."

Lara glanced over at Glen. A strand of gray hair dangling over his left ear, he was idly twirling circles on the table with his forefinger. He did look like a dreary soul. Of course, having Theo Barnes for a landlord couldn't have helped his attitude any. And now he was pretty much homeless.

"Dora insisted on buying him breakfast this morning," Daisy said with a sigh, "but he barely touched it. I heard her reminding him to take his heart medication, but he seemed to be ignoring her. I really don't know what's going to become of him."

Lara suddenly remembered what Daisy had said yesterday about Barnes owning the place. "Daisy, Barnes was your landlord, too, wasn't he? Aunt Fran told me he owns—excuse me, *owned*—this entire block."

"He does—did," Sherry said before her mom could answer. "He sent us a letter about a month ago. It said we're going to have to move the coffee shop out of here by the end of the year."

"What?" Lara yelped. "That's only a few months away!"

Daisy pressed her lips into a furious line. "Nice of him to give reasonable notice, right?"

"But what about your lease?" Lara said. It horrified her to think that he could act in such a cavalier way toward his tenants.

"Technically," Sherry explained, "we're now tenants at will, on a month-to-month basis. Theo insisted on making that change to the lease when we renewed it this past winter."

"We should have known something was up," Daisy said quietly. "Turned out he had plans to raze this entire block. Our coffee shop, Quint's Hardware, and Kurl-me-Klassy were all going to have to move. Relocating would have been almost impossible, especially for us. We need restaurant facilities to operate. Quint's has already found a bigger and better space across town, so they don't really care. It's us and Kellie at the beauty salon who are getting the shaft."

Sherry craned her neck around the dining room. Aside from Glen, the few remaining customers were gawking at their phones. She gently elbowed Daisy. "Show her, Mom."

Nodding, Daisy stooped for something beneath the counter. She rose and placed a folded sheet of paper in front of Lara. "I got this from a friend at the town hall," she said in a low tone. "This is the proposal Theo had for the downtown." She unfolded the paper. "It hasn't been made public yet. It was scheduled to go before the planning board next month."

Lara scanned the colored sketch. Prepared by an architect, it depicted a modern, brick-front strip mall facing the main drag. A curving, paved road led to the ritzy condo complex behind it. The stretch of meadow where she'd frolicked as a kid was swallowed up by landscaped parking. She had to admit, it was fancy looking. It would appeal to anyone who thought newer was better. She folded the sketch and gave it back to Daisy.

Lara drained her coffee mug and set it down. She understood, now, why Barnes was so desperate to get his mitts on Aunt Fran's land. The downtown block wouldn't have provided access alone. He'd intended to build a whole new plaza. One that would bring him a nice influx of cash. But he couldn't have done it without first buying Aunt Fran's vacant parcel. She was the fly in his ointment, so to speak.

"So, what's going to happen now?" Lara said. "With Theo gone..."

Sherry shrugged. "I guess for now we've gotten a reprieve. At least until we find out who's taking over Theo's business interests." She squinted at the wall clock and let out a gusty sigh. "We're closing in ten. I'll sure be glad to see this day end."

The last customer finally trickled out, but not before buying five bat cookies. Daisy stuck the last two bats in a paper bag, then walked over and gave them to Glen. She leaned and spoke softly to him. He nodded, and finally he left.

"I gotta run, too," Lara said. She hugged Sherry, then started to dash out the door. "We'll talk more tomorrow, okay?"

Sherry's eyes welled up. "Okay," she said raggedly. "I'm so glad you're here, Lara."

"Me, too." Lara turned toward the exit, her own eyes feeling misty. She was tugging open the door when a twentysomething woman with a crazed look in her eyes rushed inside the coffee shop.

Chapter 8

"I'm so glad I caught you before you closed!" The young woman sounded breathless as she plopped a sheaf of fliers on the counter. Her thick black curls were fastened into a messy ponytail. She looked positively frantic. "I was afraid I wouldn't catch you in time."

The woman's apparent desperation tore at Lara. She turned back inside the coffee shop to see if she could help.

"Um, actually..." Sherry began, looking at the clock.

"Please," the woman begged. "I only need a few seconds of your time. My new cat is lost and I'm terrified something happened to her. Can I put some fliers in your window?"

"Of course!" Sherry said instantly. "Come on. Sit down for a minute."

Breathing hard, the woman sank onto a stool. Sherry filled a glass with water and set it down in front of her.

Lara looked at the flier on top of the stack. A not-too-clear photo of a striped gray cat stared back at her.

The young woman gulped down a mouthful of water. "Thank you." She jabbed a finger at the pic. "I've only had her three days. Her name's Goldy. The old woman who used to own her died about a month ago, and she ended up in the shelter. That's how I got her." She sniffled. "Anyway, when I opened the door to bring in the mail yesterday, she escaped outside and disappeared. I'm scared to death she's been hurt...or worse!" She swallowed hard, tears resting on her lashes. "I hardly slept all night."

Lara hated thinking of all the things that could happen to a lost cat. Whisker Jog was rural. Nocturnal enemies abounded. Fishers and coyotes in particular had been known to prey on small pets. It was one reason Aunt

Fran had always kept her cats inside—at least to the extent she could. Lara prayed that Goldy, wherever she was, had found a safe place to hunker down.

"What's your name?" Lara asked, sliding onto the stool next to the woman.

"Sorry. I'm Wendy." She handed Lara and Sherry each a flier. "Take this home with you, okay? If you see my Goldy, call me, please—no matter what time it is. I won't be able to sleep till I know she's safe." She looked at Sherry with pleading eyes. "Is it okay if I tape two of these in your front windows? I brought my own masking tape. I promise to remove them once Goldy is found."

"You sure can," Sherry said.

While Wendy taped the fliers to the storefront windows, Lara studied the cat's photo. It was far from top quality. Wendy had probably taken it with her smartphone, but the angle was bad. It was also partly in shadow.

One thing in particular, though, caught Lara's eye. With dark stripes that curved into a graceful V on her chest, Goldy's markings were somewhat distinctive. She also had huge gold eyes. Someone would have to study the pic close up, however, to see the real Goldy.

Lara slid her purse off her shoulder and dug out her mini-pack of colored sketch pencils. She flipped over the flier Wendy had given her. Using quick strokes, she sketched Goldy's likeness. She held it up. "Does Goldy look something like this?"

Wendy's eyes widened. "Oh my gosh, that's her. That's my Goldy! How did you do that?"

"Practice," Lara said. She turned to her friend. "Sherry, if I put this on my Facebook page, will you share it? A lot of your friends are probably local. They can keep an eye out for Goldy."

"You bet I will!" Sherry reached over and clasped Wendy's wrist. "We'll do everything we can to help, okay?"

Wendy swallowed. "Thank you."

Lara pulled out her cell and took several photos of the sketch. She handed the original to Wendy.

"Thank you both," Wendy said, swiping at a tear. "At least you've given me hope. I feel sure I'm going to find her now."

After Wendy left, Lara bade Sherry good-bye again and hustled out the door. Guilt was starting to gnaw at her.

She'd left her aunt alone long enough.

Chapter 9

The police cars had finally vacated Aunt Fran's driveway. The few that stuck around had chosen to commandeer the town's prime parking spaces in front of the small park area. Lara wondered if the crime scene techs had finished collecting evidence, since their van was also gone.

She was relieved to find Aunt Fran sitting at the kitchen table, her nose buried in the paper. Dolce, curled in her lap, blinked up at Lara as if to say, "Please don't disturb us, we're nice and comfy."

"Oodles of groceries, coming up." Lara grinned, holding aloft four overstuffed bags. "I'll lug in the kitty-litter bags after I unpack all these."

Aunt Fran beamed at her niece. "Well, that's quite a haul. I'd offer to help you put things away, but I know you'll do it much more quickly."

"I'll have it done in a jiffykins, as Sherry would say."

Aunt Fran folded the paper. "Before you do that, Lara, would you please take a peek into the small parlor?" Her green eyes twinkled cryptically.

"Uh...sure thing."

Intrigued, Lara set down her bags on the counter. The door to the small parlor was partway open. She pushed it open a tiny bit more and poked her head in. A low gasp escaped her.

Darryl was sitting in the same spot at the red table at which he'd been reading the day before. Propped in his hands was a large book boasting giraffes on its glossy cover. He was reading out loud in his sweet, childlike voice—smoothly and without hesitation. Blue sat at his elbow, staring straight at the book. Her bright turquoise eyes seemed to be following the text as Darryl read aloud.

As improbable as Lara knew it to be, this cat had to be Blue. She was identical in every way to the elusive feline who'd warmed her heart as a child. Who'd been there all those times when she felt sad or lonely.

"Blue," Lara said in a hoarse whisper.

The Ragdoll cat lifted her gaze and met Lara's. Her tail twitched. Her blue eyes closed and opened again in a slow blink.

It is you. It is!

Darryl suddenly realized Lara was looking in at him. A cheery smile broadened his cheeks. "I have a new book. It's about giraffes!"

"I see that." Lara smiled at him. "And I can tell you love reading it. Um, would you like a snack?"

The boy shook his head. "No thanks. I already had one." He went back to reading his book.

What nice manners he has, Lara thought. And while she didn't want to appear to be spying, she stood there for at least another minute. She watched as Blue moved closer to Darryl and rested her chin on his arm. If Darryl noticed, it wasn't obvious. He was completely engrossed in his giraffe adventure.

Surely he must be aware that the cat was there?

As silently as she could, Lara pulled the door nearly all the way closed. She tiptoed back to the kitchen.

"He's reading a giraffe book," Lara told her aunt. "It's...amazing."

Aunt Fran nodded. "I know, isn't it? It wasn't until yesterday that he started reading so...well, effortlessly. It's wonderful, of course. But it's also baffling."

"And the cat—she looks so serious." Lara smiled. "She's listening to him read as if she's reading along with him."

Aunt Fran looked sharply at her. "Which cat? I hope it's not Twinkles. He got stuck in there one day with the door closed. He ended up tearing one of the books to shreds."

"Definitely not Twinkles," Lara said. She hesitated. Maybe she shouldn't have mentioned Blue again. Her aunt had been quite adamant that she didn't have a Ragdoll cat.

Still, Lara saw no reason to lie about what she'd seen. "No, it's the cat I told you about yesterday. The one who looks like Blue." *The one who is Blue.*

Aunt Fran's face paled. "Lara," she said in a soft but firm tone. "Even if you had Blue as a child, it's impossible that she would be—" She stopped abruptly. "I just heard voices. Outside, in the backyard. Are the crime scene people back?"

Lara held up a finger, signaling that she would check it out. She went outside onto the porch. A car she'd never seen before was in the driveway—an older model navy sedan. When had that gotten there? She peered into the yard. When she saw who was there and what they were up to, she couldn't help grinning.

Next to a sack of tulip bulbs, Brooke was kneeling on the ground, while Dora, outfitted in hot-pink sweats, clutched Aunt Fran's hoe for dear life. She waved at Lara from where they'd parked themselves at the starting point of the brick walkway.

Lara popped back into the kitchen to let her aunt know who was there. Then she scrambled down the porch steps toward the pair. "Hey, what are you two doing?"

Brooke sat back on her heels, her aqua-tinted strands moving slightly in the breeze. "It was Dora's idea, but I'm glad she recruited me. We felt so bad that Ms. C. couldn't plant her tulips this year. We really want to help." Trowel in hand, she reached into the burlap sack for a bulb. "We're gonna do as much as we can today. But we'll keep coming back every day until we're finished. Right, Dora?"

"You betcha." Dora beamed down at Brooke. Her back slightly bent, she leaned on the hoe, almost as if she needed it for support.

Two oddly matched BFFs, Lara thought—two wonderful, thoughtful helpers. Aunt Fran was lucky to have such caring people in her life.

Lara swallowed over the knot of guilt that was twisting her insides. She'd hoped to get the planting job done herself before she returned to Boston. Now these two kindly elves were doing the task for her.

Rubbing her arms for warmth, Lara stared out past the shed. A strand of yellow crime scene tape stretched across the top of the hill—an ugly reminder of the vicious crime that had played out less than a day ago. She was surprised—and grateful—that the crime scene ribbon hadn't been extended to include Aunt Fran's yard.

No doubt the police had surmised that whoever killed Barnes had probably met him near the bench at the rear of the park. Maybe they had argued and things had escalated. Angered, the killer attacked. Were those the sounds Lara heard after she'd first climbed into bed last night?

She didn't want to think about it anymore. She'd told the police about the voices she'd heard close to midnight. It was their job to find the killer, not hers. Right now, she had to help Aunt Fran—it was she who mattered most.

Although, she remembered with a twinge of unease, *I didn't exactly tell the police everything.* Aunt Fran had gone out in the yard very late the night before. When Lara gave her statement to the police, she'd conveniently omitted that little nugget. But whatever her aunt's reason had been for her late night excursion, it had nothing to do with Barnes's murder.

Lara would stake her life on that.

She looked down at Brooke, who was carefully inserting a tulip bulb into the hole she'd just dug. With her hand, Brooke scooped the loosened dirt over the bulb, then moved along to dig the next hole. Dora used the flat of the hoe she was gripping to tamp down the earth over the newly planted bulb.

Lara cringed when she saw Dora biting her lip in pain. From the way the older woman was bent over, Lara suspected that her back brace was digging into her.

"Dora, why don't I take over for you?" Lara said, reaching for the hoe. "You can go inside and visit with Aunt Fran for a while."

"Oh, I can't let you do that," she said, pulling the hoe out of Lara's reach. "My doctor says doing things like this can only help my back. He's always scolding me for being too sedentary."

Lara hesitated. "Are you sure? Because—"

Brooke's sudden shriek made them both jump. "Dora, what's that?" Brooke pointed at the business end of the hoe. "It looks like…like…"

Following the direction in which Brooke was aiming her finger, Lara dropped to her knees. She bent her head low and peered at the hoe.

"Don't touch it!" Brooke said.

"I won't." Lara's heartbeat spiked. She was already fairly sure of what she was looking at.

Blood.

"Dora, set the hoe down," Lara said quietly. "I think we might've landed on the murder weapon."

Chapter 10

Dora dropped the hoe as if it had suddenly gone red hot. She stumbled backward, her face turning ghostly pale. Lara grabbed her arm to keep her from toppling.

"We can't tell anyone about this," Brooke said, her voice shaky. "The hoe belongs to Ms. C. If we report it to the cops they'll think she…she…"

Lara steadied Dora and then stooped next to Brooke. She lightly touched her shoulder. "Brooke, this might be the murder weapon and it might not be. But we do have to report it."

"But—"

"Brooke."

The voice was Aunt Fran's. No one had noticed her struggling down the walkway. She stood near the edge of the brick path and leaned on her cane, her face unreadable. "If that's Theo's blood, it means the killer used my hoe to"—she cleared her throat—"to harm him. I'm going to call Chief Whitley. Come on. We all need to go inside. If we stay out here we might end up destroying evidence."

One by one, they filed into the house. No one spoke as Aunt Fran made a brief call from her kitchen phone.

"They'll be right along," she said, hanging up.

Dora, looking shell-shocked, lowered herself onto a kitchen chair. "If I'd only known," she said, her eyes unfocused. "I never would've touched that thing."

"It's not your fault, Dora," Lara said. "In a way, you did a good thing. This might help the police find Barnes's killer."

Munster strolled out from the large parlor. He stretched and yawned. Gold eyes beaming at Brooke, he sauntered over and rubbed his sleek form against her leg.

"There's my Munster," Brooke said, lifting him and pressing her face to his. Her eyes grew watery.

Poor girl, Lara thought. Seeing the blood on the end of that hoe, knowing who it probably belonged to, had upset her terribly. She was trying to be stoic, but Lara could see it in her expression. She hoped Brooke wouldn't have nightmares over it.

A few minutes later, they heard a car roar into the driveway. Lara went outside onto the porch. Chief Whitley was already exiting his unmarked Ford. A patrol car swung in and parked beside him. Two uniformed officers hopped out of the cruiser and moved swiftly into Aunt Fran's backyard.

His face stern, Whitley stepped into the kitchen, pulling the door closed behind him. "I appreciate your calling us," he told Aunt Fran. "I'm afraid we're going to need to interview each of you."

Brooke let out a tiny whimper. She buried her face in Munster's fur.

To Lara's relief, Whitley took pity on her. "Not you, young lady," he said gently. "You don't need to stay. You've done good work today. We're very grateful."

"Thank you," she choked out. "Can I go sit in the parlor with Darryl? I…I have some homework I can do."

"But your backpack is in my car!" Dora said. She sounded flustered.

Brooke groaned, but Whitley held up a large hand. "Not to worry. One of my officers will bring it in. Is it the blue Corolla?"

Dora nodded. "It's not locked. Her backpack is in the backseat."

Whitley went out onto the porch and barked an order in the general direction of the shed. Barely a minute later, backpack in hand, he opened the screen door and came back into the kitchen. "Here you go, young lady."

Brooke took her bag from him, thanked him, and let Munster slide to the floor. Looking vastly relieved to be escaping interrogation, she hurried off toward the small parlor. Lara noticed that Munster padded away in a different direction.

"Jerry, her mom needs to know about this," Aunt Fran told Whitley. Her voice shook slightly. "Brooke is only thirteen."

"Once again, not to worry. I'll get in touch with her," Whitley assured her. "Do you have a number?"

Aunt Fran supplied him with the number, then sat down again. Dora asked to be interviewed first so that she could go home and take her pain pills.

"I have some Tylenol," Lara offered. "Would that help?" She hated to see Dora suffer.

"No thanks, Lara, but I appreciate the offer. The stuff I have at home is much stronger."

Whitley looked uncomfortable. "Fran, is it okay if Dora and I go into your other room there for a few minutes?" He dipped his chin in the general direction of the large parlor. "I'd like to take her statement so we can let her go home."

"Of course."

Good, Lara thought. At least Whitley was showing compassion for the woman. He'd probably known her for decades, though she figured that didn't matter when the subject was as serious as murder.

The two went off, leaving Lara and Aunt Fran to sit and stare glumly at one another. "Aunt Fran, I'm so sorry this is happening to you. I feel as if I brought a curse with me when I showed up yesterday!"

With a forlorn smile, Aunt Fran covered Lara's hand with her own. "Don't be silly. You didn't bring me a curse, Lara, you brought me hope. Just when I thought I'd run out of options, you reached into my pit of despair and pulled me out."

Lara smiled and swatted at a burgeoning tear. "Now you're being melodramatic. It reminds me of all those stories you used to tell me when I was a kid. You told me they were true, but I swear you made half of them up."

"Of course I did." Aunt Fran smiled, and her eyes shone. "You had a lively imagination. I knew I'd have to be creative if I was going to succeed at entertaining you."

A sudden flood of memories washed over Lara. Ragged bits and pieces of the past, stitched together by an aunt who'd never been anything but kind. How could Lara have shoved all that aside? How could she have pushed her aunt so thoroughly from her thoughts, as if she'd never even existed?

"I don't know why it took me so long to come up to see you," Lara said with a sniffle. "I guess I'd fallen into a routine, between my artwork and my bakery job and—" She swallowed. "And it had just been such a long time. I wasn't sure I'd even be welcome, and because of that I was afraid to call you. Plus, I don't have a car, and—"

"Lara, stop. Enough said, okay? You and I, we're good." She winked at her niece, something Lara had never seen her do.

Lara forced a weak smile. "Aunt Fran, I… I'm not sure how long I'll be able to stay, at least for this visit. Gabriela is probably having fits at the bakery without me. In fact, I should probably text her."

Aunt Fran looked away, but then, with a lift of her chin, she turned her gaze back to Lara. "That's an excellent idea, Lara. After all, she is your employer. It wouldn't be fair not to let her know what's happened."

Lara pulled her phone from her jeans pocket. She blew out a breath and typed out a quick text to Gabriela:

Gab, I got delayed in NH. Things got complicated. Not sure when I'll be back. Everything OK there?

Before she could rethink it, Lara sent the text. Barely a minute later her phone pinged with a return message.

U OK?! Luca helping but not like U. Overnite ltr came for U. Family most important! Take all time U need!

Lara groaned inwardly. Gabriela's grandson, Luca, was about as much help in the bakery as a litter of kittens would be. Immature for his twenty-four years, he hadn't yet found his calling in life, except to fantasize about becoming an international singing sensation. If his grandmother had her way, he'd have already hooked up with Lara and produced a grandbaby or two for her to dote on.

Wait a minute. An overnight letter? Lara hurriedly sent another text.

I'm OK. Don't worry. Who sent the letter?

Gabriela's response was cryptic:

Don't know. Boston address, Louisburg Sq.

Lara felt her jaw drop. Louisburg Square was one of the poshest neighborhoods in Boston. No way did she know anyone who could afford to live there.

Maybe she should ask Gabriela to open the envelope and check out the contents. No doubt it was something silly—some sort of upscale, direct mail marketing bulletin designed to entice a poor starving artist. Or maybe an invitation to an exclusive gallery showing?

Lara sent a quick text back to Gabriela. She thanked her profusely for understanding her situation, and asked her to hold on to the envelope for safekeeping.

She set her phone down on the table.

"Trouble?" Aunt Fran gave her a worried look.

Lara slowly blew out a breath. "No, Gabriela's being very understanding." She told her aunt about the mysterious overnight envelope.

"I think you're wise not to ask anyone to open it," Aunt Fran agreed. Her eyes clouded. "Lara, if you need to drive back to Boston, I would certainly understand. You've already helped me more than you know. I… I don't know where I'd be right now if you hadn't been here."

Lara didn't hesitate. "I'd rather be here, Aunt Fran, with you and the cats." *And Blue*. "Besides, Gabriela sounds like she's hanging in there okay without me. I'll just chalk it up to vacation time."

Yeah, like she ever took a vacation. Her discretionary income, which amounted to exactly zero, didn't allow for any luxurious getaways.

As for the bakery, Lara felt sure Gabriela could get by for a while without her. Lara was mostly a glorified dishwasher, anyway, even if Gabriela did admire the way she set up the bakery cases.

Lara looked up to see her aunt studying her.

"Lara, are you all right?" Aunt Fran asked. "Are things okay at...at home?"

"Things are fine, Aunt Fran." Lara gave her a reassuring smile. "I decided that the bakery will survive without me a few more days. Besides, Gabby reminded me that family comes first. She's totally okay with me staying here for a while."

At that moment, a poker-faced Chief Whitley strode out from the large parlor. One hand curled around his notebook, he looked pointedly at Aunt Fran. Dora trailed along behind the chief, looking a bit worse for wear. Her glasses were slightly askew, and the fine lines around her mouth seemed to have deepened.

"Dora, would you like some water?" Lara was quick to ask.

The woman shook her head. "No, thank you. I just want to go home. This has all been too stressful for me. It makes the pain worse." She leaned over Aunt Fran and gave her an awkward hug. "I'm sorry we didn't get your bulbs planted, Fran."

"That's the least of our worries, Dora," Aunt Fran said. "It's enough that you wanted to help."

Whitley held out his hand, as if granting Dora permission to leave. Dora moved toward the door, looking a bit off-kilter. On impulse, Lara went over and took the woman's hand in her own. "Let us know if you need anything, okay?"

Dora smiled, and Lara saw a spark of animation in her eyes. "Thank you. You're so lovely, Lara. I'm glad you're here to help Fran." She waved at them both and left, but a moment later came back inside. "Chief, your car is behind mine."

"Oh. Yes. Right." Looking annoyed, Whitley stepped onto the porch. He growled out a short command to one of the officers and tossed his keys over the railing.

"Thanks," Dora said timidly. She shuffled off without another word.

Whitley came back into the kitchen. He stood there for a long moment, his back to the door, as if debating his options. Then he moved a step closer to the kitchen table. "Fran," he said with a crusty edge to his tone, "I'd like you to come down to the station. The state police investigator is still there. I think he'd like to be in on it when I...interview you."

Lara rose and faced the man. "You mean interrogate, don't you, Chief Whitley?"

Whitley stared hard at Lara. "Use whatever phraseology you like, Ms. Caphart. It's well known around town that Barnes and your aunt had a major beef going on. I think we need to *chat*"—he made air quotes around the word—"someplace that's a little more neutral than a cat-infested parlor. I mean, for God's sake, I had a cat in my lap and another one rubbing my leg the whole time I was in there with Dora. It was a miracle I didn't have one on my head. I kept trying to shoo the orange one over in Dora's direction, but for some reason it preferred me." He made a point of reaching down and brushing cat hair—if there was any—off his trouser leg. "Not to mention that two little ones kept eyeing me from that cat tree the whole time."

Wisely, Lara stifled the giggle she felt bubbling in her throat. She couldn't help speculating as to whether Aunt Fran had ever had a "thing" with the chief. She didn't think she was imagining that Whitley seemed to tiptoe around her. And the man was rather attractive, in a faded-glory sort of way.

"And I hope you two weren't talking about the case in here," Whitley added brusquely. "I should have made you stay in separate rooms while I interviewed Dora."

Aunt Fran's green eyes blazed with indignation. "First of all, Jerry, I do not appreciate you talking about me as if I weren't sitting right here. And second, your question is patently ridiculous. What did you think Lara and I were doing—conspiring on how to beat the rap?" Her last word rose on a wave of fury.

Once again, Lara had to suppress a smile. Watching these two parry with words was like trying to keep up with a spirited ping-pong match.

"Chief, if I can interject," Lara put in. "Dora isn't the only one who's had a stressful day. This entire, well, mess with Theo Barnes has been an absolute nightmare for Aunt Fran." She tried to adopt a humble expression. "Isn't there any way—"

"Ms. Caphart, before you go any further." Whitley held up his large palms. "Despite what you think, I'm not unsympathetic to the situation. That said, however, I'm afraid we're going to need both Fran and you to come down to the station." A slight flush tinged his cheeks. "We'd like to fingerprint you both, but only for purposes of elimination, you understand."

Lara felt an invisible clamp pinch her insides. Purposes of elimination? That was cop-speak if she'd ever heard it.

Her thoughts raced. Had *she* touched the hoe? Were her prints anywhere on it?

She rolled her mind backward, to when Brooke had first noticed the blood on the hoe. Brooke had cried out, prompting Lara to kneel for a closer look. She was sure she hadn't touched anything. She'd have known better. On instinct alone, she'd have wanted to protect the murder weapon—if that's what it turned out to be—from further contamination.

As for Aunt Fran, her prints were probably all over the hoe—at least the handle portion. What would that prove? That she was fond of planting flowers in her yard?

Lara sat down again and rested her elbows on the kitchen table, covering her eyes with her hands. She'd barely been in Whisker Jog for a day, and already it seemed everything was spiraling out of control.

She was also beginning to realize that Aunt Fran might be in trouble.

Theo Barnes had been a prominent citizen of Whisker Jog. A bully, for sure, but to some he might have been a hero. Despite Dora's claim that he'd had lots of enemies, who knew what other people had thought of him? Or what friends he might have had in high places? Surely someone other than his niece, Mary, was mourning his death. Lara hadn't been in Whisker Jog long enough to get a sense of the social scene.

Another thought gripped her. Was there something, other than the hoe, that had traces of the murderer's fingerprints? Had the police found a critical piece of evidence tucked in one of Barnes's pockets? Maybe a letter or an incriminating photo? Was that the reason they were insisting on fingerprinting both women?

Last of all, and most important in Lara's opinion, was one burning question: Why had Aunt Fran gone outside very late last night? Was it before or after Barnes had been killed?

She jumped when she felt someone shaking her arm. "Lara, you're daydreaming," Aunt Fran said.

"Sorry. I was just thinking about everything." She looked up to see Brooke and Darryl huddled together in the kitchen. Darryl had questions written all over his face, while Brooke, clutching her backpack, looked pale and scared.

"Their mom's on her way over to pick them up," Whitley said by way of explanation. "After that I'm driving us all to the station. Fran, you might want to grab a coat. It's getting chillier out there by the minute."

Lara rose slowly. A sick feeling was wending its way into the pit of her stomach.

"I'll get your coat, Aunt Fran," Lara offered. Determined not to let Whitley sense her fear, she started toward the large parlor, where the coat closet was located opposite the front door.

"Lara, wait." Aunt Fran grasped her forearm. "Before we go to the police station, there's something I need to tell you." She exchanged a look with Whitley. Whitley looked away, a red stain creeping up his neck.

"A long time ago," her aunt said in a small voice, "right after you left Whisker Jog with your mom and dad, I…started seeing Theo. Within three months of our first date, we—well, we got engaged. Theo and I were going to be married."

Chapter 11

The ride to the police station had been somber, if not excruciating. Lara couldn't stop her aunt's words from ringing in her head: *Theo and I were going to be married.*

After they'd entered the station—a squat brick affair with a surprisingly cheerful front entrance—each of them had been fingerprinted. The procedure was simple enough, yet it had made Lara feel like a criminal.

After that, Aunt Fran was led into one room and Lara into another. Whitley chose to conduct Lara's interview himself. A captain from the state police sequestered himself in a different room with Aunt Fran.

Lara shuddered when she recalled the closeness of the room she'd been stuck in. If she'd been even a tad claustrophobic, she'd have probably tried to climb those dreary walls. And if someone had asked her to paint a picture of the room, the colors on her palette would have stayed largely untouched. The room had been mostly gray with a touch of bile green.

All of it paled next to the bombshell Aunt Fran had dropped. Engaged to Theo? Betrothed to the town bully? Lara needed time to process that one.

No, she needed more. She needed an explanation.

After ensuring that both women were safely back in the house, the young officer who'd driven them home took off like a shot.

"I'll hang our coats," Lara said. "And then I'll make us a quick supper." She tried to sound upbeat, but Aunt Fran wasn't buying it.

"Lara, I'm so sorry you got dragged in to all this."

I'm sorry, too, Lara was tempted to say.

Even so, she'd have hated the idea of seeing her aunt go through that alone. Aunt Fran needed her family—and right now Lara was it.

She went over and slipped an arm around her aunt's shoulder. "I didn't get dragged in, Aunt Fran. In fact, when you think about it, if I hadn't been poking around outside this morning, I wouldn't have found the, you know, the body. Someone else would've discovered it, and we wouldn't have to be so...involved."

Aunt Fran gave her a wry smile. "I suppose." Her expression grew pensive. "But things happen for a reason, Lara. Maybe this is the way it was meant to be."

Lara suddenly remembered what had drawn her attention to Theo's prone form in the first place.

Blue.

She'd spotted the cat padding across the meadow, heading toward the river. When she'd tried to follow her, she'd tripped and tumbled down the hill.

And found Barnes.

Lara stuck their coats in the closet, put on the teakettle, and insisted that her aunt sit down and let her whip up a fast dinner.

The frittata she'd made the evening before had turned out quite delicious. But tonight they needed something different. Something Lara's limited cooking skills would be able to handle. Fortunately, she'd bought groceries earlier that day.

Thirty minutes later, they were enjoying a tangy version of American goulash with multigrain rolls and a spinach salad.

"You've turned out to be quite the cook," Aunt Fran said after swallowing a mouthful of salad. "I'm impressed."

"Uh...Aunt Fran, I'm lucky I can boil water without scorching it," Lara mumbled over a mouthful of goulash. She swallowed. "Sorry. Didn't mean to talk with my mouth full. The little bit I know about cooking, I picked up from Gabriela."

Aunt Fran nodded. "Your mother, as I recall, was somewhat of a hit-or-miss cook."

"Mostly miss," Lara said, and instantly felt guilty. Her mom had her faults, plenty of them, but at least she'd tried. For the most part, anyway. "I shouldn't talk about her that way. You must think I'm awful." Lara buttered her last piece of roll and popped it into her mouth.

"Not at all," Aunt Fran said. Her voice grew soft. "But right now we need to talk about the elephant in the room. Theo."

More like a Tyrannosaurus rex, Lara thought.

"Theo Barnes," Lara said. "Your former fiancé. Or is it ex-fiancé?" She gulped back a mouthful of her tea.

"Either one works," Aunt Fran said.

"How—how long ago were you engaged to him?"

With a quiet sigh, Aunt Fran dabbed her lips and folded her napkin. "I'm going to start from the beginning. It's easier to understand that way. That summer, after you and Roy and your mom moved to Massachusetts, was the start of a very difficult time for me. I lost all three of you at once—but it was you who'd practically lived in this house with me. It seemed you were here more than you were at your own home."

Lara felt her throat closing. *Because this felt like my home.*

"So then you wrote letters," Lara prompted. She was starting to feel impatient.

"Yes," Aunt Fran said. "Letters that, for some reason, were never delivered to you."

If Lara had to guess, she'd say her mother had been the cause of that. The letters themselves—Lara was sure now that they'd been inside the fallen box her aunt had tried desperately to hide that morning. Brenda "Breezy" Caphart had never been fond of Aunt Fran. They'd tolerated one another, but Lara had always sensed that when it came to Aunt Fran, her mom felt like a runner-up in a pageant she could never win.

As for her dad, just thinking of Roy Caphart made Lara smile. He'd been a gentle man—not a mean bone in his lanky form. He'd doted on Brenda, but he'd adored Lara. Colon cancer had claimed him six years earlier. He'd insisted he wanted no services, no calling hours. Brenda hadn't even notified Aunt Fran until long after his ashes were buried.

But I could have told her, Lara thought. *I could have called to tell her that her only brother was gone. Why didn't I?*

"You're dream-weaving again."

Lara rubbed her cheeks. "I know. Sorry. My mind keeps drifting. Please go ahead, Aunt Fran—tell me about Theo."

Aunt Fran pushed her plate aside. She'd finished everything save for a few stray macaroni shells. "I had a lot of friends back then. A few very dear friends. But it wasn't the same without you in the house. It felt... empty. Even the cats—I had three back then—felt your absence." She paused for a long moment. "And then a few months after you moved out of New Hampshire, Theo started to call me."

Interesting timing, Lara thought.

She thought back to the younger version of her aunt that she remembered so well. Aunt Fran had been pretty, for lack of a better word, but in a non-traditional way. Lara could easily see how Theo, or any man, would have been drawn to those expressive green eyes, taut cheekbones, and soft laugh.

"I have to say, I welcomed his calls. It helped take away the loneliness. Soon we started seeing each other. And before you gape at me in horror, I should tell you that he behaved like a different man back then. He didn't show any signs of the bully he later became." She laughed softly. "For a short time, Lara, he was a gentleman. One day he even helped me rescue a kitten that had gotten stuck in a tree in the park. Tore his trousers, but he got the little monkey. He came down from that tree with the kitten wrapped in his sweater." She swallowed, her eyes watering. "It was one of the sweetest things I'd ever seen. I think that's when I started to fall in love with him."

That was a Theo Barnes Lara couldn't begin to imagine. "I can't picture that," Lara said. "Not from what I saw of Barnes at the coffee shop."

Her aunt went on. "We began spending all our free time together. And then one day out of the blue, he popped the question. We'd only been seeing each other for a few months, but nonetheless I said yes." Her gaze drifted sideways, and the lines around her eyes deepened.

Lara gave her a few moments and then said, "Obviously, it didn't work out."

"No. It didn't." Aunt Fran's hand shook a little as she reached for her teacup. She took a small sip but the liquid had cooled, and she made a slight face.

"Almost as soon as we'd gotten engaged," Aunt Fran said, "Theo began to change. He wasn't content to spend his free time with me anymore. Dining out, something we'd both enjoyed, got much less frequent. One weekend Theo decided to hop on a flight to Vegas. I didn't find out about it till he'd already returned. He came by my house, unannounced, late that Sunday night. His face fairly popped with anger. When I asked what was wrong, he told me he'd lost a crapload of money in Vegas. I explained that I'd been frantic with worry, that the least he could've done was to call and let me know he was okay."

"What did he say?" Lara asked her.

"He said—" She took in a calming breath. "He said it was none of my business, and I'd better learn that if we were going to make our relationship work. Our *relationship*, mind you. He didn't even call it a marriage."

Lara sat back, her hands resting in her lap. She shook her head. "Aunt Fran, I don't know what to say. I'm so sorry—about everything. I'm appalled at the way Theo treated you. Thank heaven you didn't marry him."

Aunt Fran gave out a sad little laugh. "Thank heaven indeed. Less than a week later I ended it with him. I finally woke up to how little we had in common."

"How did he take it?"

"Oh, he was livid. You should have seen him! No one had ever rejected him before. It was a whole new experience for him."

"A well-deserved one," Lara snapped. "When did he meet Josette?"

Aunt Fran thought a moment. "As I recall, it wasn't long after we'd split up. A year, maybe two at the most. Josette had been working at the lumber company where Theo bought a lot of his supplies. One day he asked her out, and the two started flouncing around town together, acting as if they were local royalty."

Having met the flashy Josette, Lara could easily picture that. "But, unlike you, Josette was foolish enough to marry Theo."

"That's right," Aunt Fran said. "In a way, I felt sorry for her. She truly didn't see what she was in for. She found out soon enough, though. Theo cheated on her constantly. She made up for it by spending as much of his money as she could."

Lara told her aunt what Sherry had revealed about the lump-sum alimony payment Josette was entitled to collect from Barnes's estate.

"Well, that's news to me," Aunt Fran said. "Not surprising, though. Josette had a sharp lawyer. You might remember him. Gideon Halley?"

Lara felt her eyes spring wide open. "Gideon? Halley?" She laughed. "Now that's a blast from the past."

She tried to form a picture of Gideon in her mind, but she hadn't seen him in over fifteen years. What she remembered was a shy boy with straight black hair and bony arms, his nose always buried in an adventure book. His eyes were a distinctive chocolate brown, she recalled. They shone whenever he read aloud from a book report he'd written for English class.

She wondered what he looked like these days.

"He was a nice boy," Aunt Fran said. "He still is, though of course he's a man now. Quite a striking one, too. He practices mostly family law, right here in town."

Lara felt her cheeks grow warm. Once upon a time she'd had a crush on Gideon. He'd been one of the few boys who hadn't teased her about her hair color.

"I'm glad you told me about your history with Theo, Aunt Fran. The thing is—how can I put this? I can't help wondering if Theo's battle over your land was really about you rejecting him all those years ago."

"I've often wondered the same," Aunt Fran said. "And who knows, maybe that's why he harassed me with such intensity. But it's water over the dam, now. The reason doesn't really matter, does it?"

Lara shook her head. "No. I guess not."

Unless the police tried to use it as a motive for Aunt Fran to have killed Barnes. What if they thought Aunt Fran had never gotten over Theo, even though she'd been the one who'd ended things between them? It was obvious from Chief Whitley's expression earlier that he'd known about the ill-fated engagement.

A sudden ripple of melancholy washed over Lara. In the course of only a day, her life had been abruptly split in two. She felt like she was in a tug-of-war, with half the rope pulling her toward Boston, and the other half tugging harder into Whisker Jog.

She so badly wanted to ask Aunt Fran why she'd gone into the yard the night before. Yes, it would put her aunt on the spot. But she couldn't go on any longer without knowing. The truth would set them both free.

She hoped.

"Aunt Fran—" Lara began, when a dull thud somewhere in the small parlor nabbed her attention. She gave a start. "What was that? One of the cats?"

"In that room?" Aunt Fran had a strange expression on her face. "I don't think so."

Lara slid off her chair and scooted away to investigate. The door to the small parlor was open. Not a hint of a feline was in sight. She glanced around the room, seeing nothing out of place except—

And then she laughed, relieved to see that it was only a book that had fallen to the floor in front of the red table. She went over to peek at the volume, and knew instantly whom it belonged to. The book was *The Pickwick Papers*, which meant it was Brooke's.

Poor Brooke. She'd obviously left it on the table by accident after she'd come in to study with her brother. She'd probably been so rattled by finding the bloody hoe that she'd forgotten to stick it back into her backpack.

Lara picked up the volume, and then set it down flat on a nearby shelf with the title facing out. She'd have to remember to tell Brooke so she wouldn't think she'd lost the dreaded classic.

She glanced around the room again. Hadn't Aunt Fran told her that the cats didn't like this room?

If that was the case, then who'd knocked over the book?

Chapter 12

By the time Lara returned to the kitchen, Aunt Fran was already setting their dishes in the sink.

"Aunt Fran, I'll take care of that," Lara said. "There's only a few, anyway." Her aunt looked relieved. "Thank you. My knees are starting to get wobbly. It's been a long day." She unhooked her cane from its resting place on the counter and started toward the kitchen table.

Lara secretly hoped Aunt Fran would turn in early. That way she could spend some quality time alone with the cats, getting to know them better. A few of them looked in desperate need of a good brushing.

"Oh! Aunt Fran, I almost forgot to tell you," Lara said. "This morning when I was looking for a vacuum-cleaner bag, Ballou came along and watched me from the doorway of the supply closet."

Aunt Fran pressed her cane into the floor and turned slowly toward Lara. "Ballou? Are you sure it wasn't Dolce?"

Lara slowly shook her head. "No, it had to be Ballou. He was the only one of your cats I hadn't met yet. Besides, Dolce doesn't have a white mustache, right? So get this—he actually sat and watched me for about nine or ten seconds. I couldn't believe it! I took a chance and *very slowly* held out my fingers to him. He didn't come closer, but he did lean his head forward. I think he was about to sniff my fingers when that box of letters fell from your closet upstairs. It startled both of us, and he darted off. I haven't seen him since."

Aunt Fran lowered herself onto a kitchen chair. "He manages to keep out of sight during the day. He tucks himself away wherever he thinks he can't be seen. In fact, I think he hides under your bed, Lara. At night, though, I know he prowls the house. I'm sure that's also when he eats."

"Poor little cat—he probably feels trapped inside the house, even though it's the safest place he could be," Lara mused.

"But Lara, he got close to you. That's nothing short of a miracle." Aunt Fran's eyes brightened. "Maybe there is hope for him after all."

* * * *

A little after eight, Aunt Fran announced that she was heading upstairs. "I'm going to watch a British mystery on PBS and then read myself to sleep."

Lara asked her if she needed any help, but Aunt Fran refused, as Lara knew she would. Still, it'd been a trying day for them both, and fatigue had a way of creeping into your bones. She'd never forgive herself if Aunt Fran fell on the stairs.

"I'm coming up right behind you," Lara said. "I want to change out of this shirt and grab a pair of warmer socks. Do you mind if I use your washer and dryer?"

"Be my guest," Aunt Fran said. "You know where the laundry room is."

Lara smiled. One of many things she'd always loved about her aunt's house was that she'd rarely had to go into the cellar—a place where spiders lurked with abandon. The cellar was used mostly for storing old furniture and for housing the oil burner. The laundry facilities were in a closeted space adjacent to the downstairs bathroom.

After ensuring that Aunt Fran was settled in her room, Lara kissed her lightly on the cheek. On the pretext of wanting to wash her hands, she ducked into the small bathroom that was accessed directly from her aunt's bedroom. She ran the water, then peeked behind the shower curtain. She blew out a breath, relieved to see a sturdy-looking safety seat inside the tub. Aunt Fran could apparently shower without having to stand.

Dolce had decided to stay with Aunt Fran—no surprise—and Twinkles had followed suit. The pair would most likely remain with her for the rest of the night.

Lara left her aunt's door open a foot or so, as she knew Aunt Fran always did, then went into her own room. She turned on her bedside light—a hurricane lamp with delicate violets imprinted on its porcelain base. It gave off a glow that bathed the room in a soft, golden light.

After rummaging through her suitcase, she changed into a fresh sweatshirt and a pair of thick socks. Her long hair was beginning to look scraggly, so she twisted it into a ponytail, securing it with one of the colorful hair bands she'd stuck in the side pocket of her suitcase.

She realized now how shortsighted she'd been when she packed for the trip. She'd intended her visit to Whisker Jog to be short and productive—surely no longer than two or three days. Already she was running out of clean clothes. And though she always traveled with a small sketch pad and a sleeve of colored pencils, she hadn't packed any of her watercolor supplies. *Bad planning*, she scolded herself.

Lara gathered up her dirty clothes and started toward the stairs. Then she remembered she'd left her tablet charging on the shelf behind her bed. She unplugged it and plunked it atop the pile.

After dumping the clothes into the downstairs washer and turning it on, she went in search of cat supplies. She found them in the supply closet, in a plastic basket brimming with assorted feline accessories. She spied a few chewed-up catnip toys, along with several brushes. Lara plucked a red rubber brush out of the box. She liked that it didn't have steel prongs, as some brushes did.

In the large parlor, she settled comfortably into her favorite chair. With its oversized plump cushions and solid oak base, it had always felt like a fortress to her—safe and warm and secure. As a kid, she would plop into it with her head and back resting on the seat and her legs propped over the back. It was fun to read that way, even if she did have to hold the book in the air. And though the plush cushions had gone somewhat lumpy, it still felt as inviting as a treasured old friend.

Munster immediately jumped into her lap, his purring soft and even. He rubbed his face against hers. "I'll bet you miss Brooke," Lara said, nuzzling his whiskers. She felt herself smiling as she ran the rubber brush from the top of his head to the tip of his tail. His purring revved up a few decibels. By the time she was through, she'd liberated a handful of golden fur from his sleek form. She made a small pile on a page from the newspaper, sure there would be more to come.

Predictably, Pickles leaped into her lap as if to demand, "I'm next!" By the time she finished brushing her, Izzy, and Bootsie, she had a multicolored mound of cat hair large enough to make a whole new cat.

"Well," she declared, "you guys certainly needed that. I'll have to do the rest of you tomorrow." *Except for Ballou*, she thought. Would he make another appearance? Was there hope she'd ever see him again before she returned to Boston?

And what about Blue—the gorgeous, elusive Ragdoll who'd befriended her as a child? Why did Aunt Fran insist she'd never had a Ragdoll cat?

Lara wrapped up the cat hair in the newspaper and delivered it to the waste can in the kitchen.

Something nagged at her. Something she was supposed to do— "Oh, glory," she muttered to herself. "That poor missing kitty."

In all the confusion after the blood was found on the hoe and they'd been forced to go to the police station, she'd neglected her promise to Wendy. Lara returned to her favorite chair and pulled her cell out of her jeans pocket. The pics she'd taken of her sketch of the missing cat were still in her photo cache. She chose the clearest one and sent it to her Facebook page, giving contact info if anyone spotted Goldy. It was a fairly good depiction of Goldy, she thought, even if she'd never met the cat in person. She tagged Sherry, reminding her to share it. Lastly, she sent up a silent prayer for the missing kitty.

Something else poked at her brain. There was something she'd wanted to Google, something she—

She snapped her fingers when it came to her.

Confessions in Lace.

The magazine she'd seen in Mary's car!

Lara switched from her smartphone to her tablet. *All the better to see you with, my dear*, she thought dryly.

The search was a breeze—the site for the magazine came up right away. The background on the home page was a patterned charcoal gray, with small white lettering in the center. The message, clearly meant to entice, was written in fancy script surrounded by swirls of purple lace. Lara wrinkled her nose in distaste when she read it.

A periodical for the discerning gentleman ~ All adult true accounts of love lost and found.

Lara rolled her eyes and clicked the link over the words "Subscribe here." Her jaw dropped open when she saw the price. For $149.99 a year, a discerning gentleman would have the pleasure of receiving fifteen issues packed with stories and photos. Discreet packaging was promised.

"Oh, ugh," Lara muttered. "Double ugh."

Surprisingly, the site had no photos, save for a thumbprint pic directly below the subscription link—a sultry blonde wrapped in yards of white lace. Lara was tempted to search a bit further, but she honestly didn't want to see much more.

She had only one question. Why had a stack of these mags been sitting on Mary Newman's front seat?

Lara was mulling this over when a furry form sprang suddenly onto the arm of the adjacent sofa.

Sparkling blue eyes, alight with curiosity, regarded Lara from the arm of the tufted sofa.

Blue sat very straight, her dark tail curled around her fluffy form. Her coloring was stunning—like a cream-colored cookie whose edges had been dipped in a dark, exotic chocolate.

No sound came from the cat. She seemed content to have Lara watch her—not skittish in the least.

Lara held her breath and remained still. In the past, Blue had been a mystery cat—there one moment, gone the next. This time, Lara was determined not to let her out of her sight.

Where do you go? Who feeds you? Do you live outdoors? How do you get inside?

She thought back to all the times Blue had been with her as a child. Chasing butterflies in the field. Romping at the edge of the stream.

One summer day when Lara was six or seven, she remembered, she'd caught a red salamander near the edge of the brook. She'd filled her plastic pail with water and put the salamander inside. It was so cute she wanted to keep it. If she could persuade her dad to buy her an aquarium, she could create a nice little home for it.

It all came back now. That was the first day Blue had appeared in her life. The cat had crept up behind her, surprising her. She'd reached a hand out to touch her, but the cat had eluded her grasp, scampering instead toward the pail. With both paws, the cat had tipped it over. The salamander had skittered away to the safety of the stream.

Lara swallowed. *You saved that little creature, didn't you? You knew it wouldn't thrive in captivity, however well meaning I might have been.*

Blue stared calmly at Lara, then lifted her gaze toward the wall of the adjacent room. Lara turned to see what she was looking at. Nothing looked out of place—nothing she could see, anyway.

Lara perked her ears toward the staircase, listening for any sound that her aunt might have stirred. But the house was silent.

When she turned around, Blue was gone.

* * * *

In the next instant, a dull *thump* sounded from the small parlor.

It had to be Blue. But how had she gotten in there so quickly? And without Lara seeing her?

Or it could be an intruder, Lara thought, her heartbeat kicking up a notch. But the house was locked up snug and tight—she'd seen to it herself.

Lara hopped off her chair and padded over to the doorway of the small parlor. She was glad she'd dug out her thick socks. Aunt Fran had turned down the heat, and the house was starting to feel chilly.

The door to the small parlor was partway open. Lara pushed on the door with two fingers. It swung open soundlessly, as if the hinges had recently been oiled.

She reached over to her right and flicked on the switch. An overhead light came on, casting long shadows over the room. Lara glanced all around. She smiled when saw Darryl's giraffe book resting on the red table. From the look on the child's face when he was reading from it, it was obvious he'd been enthralled with it.

But then she felt her smile morph into a frown.

On the table, next to the giraffe book, was Brooke's volume of *The Pickwick Papers.*

Lara remembered leaving the book on one of the shelves, at least eight feet away. Even if the book had fallen, it couldn't have jumped onto the table by itself.

She let out a slow breath. She was letting her imagination get the best of her. Aunt Fran must have moved the book, thinking it would be more secure on the table. Except…

Except she didn't remember her aunt going in there during the evening.

But she must have, Lara told herself. *Otherwise I'm going crazy.*

Chapter 13

To Lara's dismay, the crime scene techs returned early the next morning. Not that it was unexpected—the discovery of the bloody hoe had changed the focus of the investigation.

Awakened by voices drifting in from outside, Lara had peeked out her bedroom window to see two figures outfitted in white marking off areas near her aunt's shed. The ugly yellow tape now surrounded the shed, and much of the backyard.

Great.

She put it out of her mind and started her daily ritual. Though this was only the second morning she'd been at her aunt's, she'd already fallen into a routine of sorts. Feed cats. Scoop litter. Start breakfast.

Aunt Fran rose a little after seven. Her hair looked freshly washed, and she wore a periwinkle-blue cable-knit sweater over black sweatpants. She looked pleased to see the casserole dish of scrambled eggs warming in the oven. "You remembered my favorite breakfast," she said. "Thank you, Lara."

"I made the eggs earlier," Lara told her, then kissed her on the cheek. "All I have left to do is pour the juice, turn on the coffeemaker, and pop some bread into the toaster. Would you like half a grapefruit?"

"That would be wonderful. Thank you. Actually, do you mind if I have tea instead?"

Lara slapped her forehead. "Sorry, I made coffee out of habit. I know you prefer tea. I'll put on the kettle."

Within five minutes, they were enjoying a hearty breakfast. Munster sidled up next to Lara and reached up with one golden paw.

"Beggar," she teased, tickling his nose. "I suppose you want some eggs." She plucked a sliver of scrambled egg off her plate and held it out to him. He took it gently from her fingers and then licked his lips.

"You're spoiling him, you know, feeding him from the table," Aunt Fran said. She tried to look stern, but a smile danced on her lips.

Lara grinned and slipped a few more tidbits of egg to the cat. She was stalling, trying to delay the inevitable.

"Aunt Fran," Lara finally said. She hated to spoil the mood, but she needed to get the weight off her chest. "The night Theo was, you know… murdered, I heard voices outside. I told the police about it. They concluded that I probably heard Theo arguing with the killer. The thing was, I couldn't hear enough to make out the words. Plus, it only lasted for a few seconds. But after that—"

"You saw me go outside," Aunt Fran quietly interjected. Her cheeks went pink, and she reached over and squeezed Lara's wrist. "I know you've been wanting to ask me about it."

Lara blew out a gust of sheer relief. "God, yes, I have. Actually, I never saw you go out, but I saw you heading back inside. I know there's no way on planet Earth that you did anything to hurt Theo. But when I saw the dirt on your cane yesterday morning, I got scared. Scared that the cops might find evidence that you went outside that night and try to pin the rap on you."

Her aunt nodded distractedly. "I didn't hear the voices you heard that night, but I was sure I heard something else. It was a loud wail, like a cat crying in pain. I might have dreamed it, but I don't think so."

"Why didn't you come and get me?" Lara said. "I'd have gone outside to check for you!"

Aunt Fran withdrew her hand and went back to her tea. "After the long day you'd had, you needed your rest," she fretted. "I just couldn't—"

"For pity's sake, Aunt Fran. I'm twenty-seven. I can lose a little sleep without anything dire happening."

Her aunt shrank slightly into her chair. "I'm sorry. I should have told you right away and not let you wonder."

Lara instantly felt terrible for yelling at her aunt. "No, I'm the one who should be sorry. I didn't mean to snap at you. I've been so worried, that's all. And just so you know, I did not say anything to the police about it. I knew there was a reasonable explanation."

She thought about the wailing noise her aunt had heard the night Theo was killed. Could it have been Goldy, Wendy's missing cat?

Lara gave Aunt Fran a brief rundown of her encounter with Wendy at the coffee shop the day before. She pulled her cell from her pocket and showed her the sketch of the missing Goldy.

"Pretty markings," Aunt Fran noted. "Poor little darling. She might find her way home, but she might also be confused about where she lives. I'll definitely keep my eyes and ears peeled for her."

They finished breakfast and Lara cleared the table. She'd been toying with the idea of stopping into the local beauty parlor and having her hair cut. That morning when she'd run a comb through it, it had felt like one big tangle.

"What do you think, Aunt Fran?" She held up a strand of her curly hair. "Time for a trim?"

Her aunt gave her a sly smile. "I'm not saying a word. But if you decide to get it cut, Kellie down at Kurl-me-Klassy does a great job for a reasonable price."

* * * *

"You can call me Kellie," the crimson-haired stylist said. "Or you can call me Byrd. I answer to both." Her lips were a shade darker than her hair, and her smile beamed like freshly fallen snow. She flipped a pink plastic cape around Lara and tied it behind her neck.

Lara laughed. She'd taken an instant liking to the bubbly Kellie Byrd. The fact that the stylist took walk-ins added another checkmark to the salon's "plus" column.

"I like Byrd," Lara said. "But I'd feel silly calling you that. If you don't mind, I think I'll stick with Kellie."

The stylist shrugged. "Whatever bobs your boat," she said and sifted her fingers through Lara's hair. "Man, what I wouldn't do for locks like these. The color is to *die* for—and it's natural, that's what slays me. Problem is, you're getting to what I call the Raggedy Ann stage. All hair. No flair. You need some styling, girl. *Bad*."

"Then style away," Lara consented, then gulped. "But…not too short, okay?"

With a cryptic smile, Kellie twirled the chair around and lifted the hatch to the built-in sink. She released the latch on the salon chair and instructed Lara to rest her head back.

The warm water sluicing over Lara's head felt luxurious. Kellie massaged her scalp with a coconut-scented shampoo, then rinsed and repeated. By the time she was through, Lara could feel the chill of the past few days leaving her bones.

While Kellie collected her haircutting supplies, Lara scoped out the salon through the mirror. Gold-toned wallpaper with vertical pink stripes gave the salon an open, elegant ambiance. Instead of harsh overhead fluorescents, Kellie had placed gold wall sconces between the ornately framed mirrors to provide the salon's lighting. Above each of the mirrors, a thick band of gold, wire-edged ribbon was twisted loosely and draped between two pink porcelain birds.

Kellie rolled a tall tray over next to Lara and began toweling the excess water from her hair. Lara glanced over at the empty salon chair next to where she was sitting.

The stylist followed her gaze, and her glossy lips pursed. "That's…I mean that *was* Yoko's chair."

"Yoko?"

"She was my other stylist, until last week," Kellie said sourly. "She left to take a job at one of those *mall* salons." She dragged out the word "mall" like it was a cuss word.

"Oh, that's too bad," Lara said. She wasn't quite sure why it was bad, but Kellie was clearly distressed by her former employee's move.

"I mean, those places are okay if you're still learning," Kellie went on. "But Yoko has real talent, ya know? She's too good to work in a *chain* salon."

Lara nodded in sympathy, but she wasn't sure she agreed. She knew an artist who got her hair cut regularly at a so-called chain salon, and the woman always looked gorgeous.

"Not that I can really blame her," Kellie said. "See, here's the thing. Our patoots are supposed to be tossed out of here by the end of the year. Theo Barnes—you know, the dead guy—AKA my nasty landlord? He had plans to tear down this whole block and build a shopping complex." Kellie pulled a wide-toothed comb from her drawer.

"I think I heard something like that," Lara said vaguely. "So, what's going to happen now?"

Kellie lifted her shoulders in a shrug. "Who knows? I probably still have to relocate. Thing is, I'm having trouble finding a place in town that has the facilities I need. A lot of my customers said they'd come to my house. But I can't run a business that way, ya know?"

Lara's heart went out to the woman. She knew how grueling it was to keep a small business running. Gabriela did it every day.

"I'm sorry to hear that, Kellie. I can tell you have a lot on your plate right now."

It occurred to Lara that Theo's sudden demise had left his tenants with a big question: Who was going to succeed to his business interests? And how would it affect them?

The police, no doubt, were wondering the same thing. Had they interviewed all the tenants whose leases were being terminated? She was about to ask Kellie if the police had talked to her when a familiar voice warbled from the doorway.

"Yoo-hoo!"

Kellie whirled around, and a cheery smile filled her face. "Dora! Where've you been, girlfriend?" Switching the comb to her left hand, she scooted over to Dora and looped her right arm around her in a hug.

Dora set a foil-covered plate on the Lucite reception counter. "Oh, well I'm doing." She sniffled and reached behind her back to massage her lower spine. "The pain gets worse when I'm stressed," she said. "It's so horrible about Theo, isn't it? Have you heard any more news?"

Kellie shook her head. "No. Nothing. You?"

"Nary a thing," Dora said. "By the way, I brought you some—" A sudden little gasp escaped her as her gaze wandered to the mirror. She adjusted her lilac-tinted specs. "Oh, Lara, I didn't see you there. You look so...different with your hair wet."

Lara smiled at Dora in the mirror. "Hi, Dora. I thought I'd see about getting a trim this morning. Luckily, Kellie was able to fit me in."

"Well, you came to the right gal," Dora said, winking at the stylist. "She's the best there is, bar none. Kellie, honey, I won't keep you. I just wanted to pick up some of that shampoo and conditioner you recommended last month. It did wonders for my hair!"

"Of course." Kellie set down her comb. "Lara, would you excuse me? This'll only take a minute."

"Take your time," Lara said.

Kellie went over to a set of shelves behind the reception desk. She pulled two large bottles from the top shelf and dropped them into a pink gift bag. Then, as if reconsidering, she tapped a manicured finger to her lips and then reached up for another, smaller bottle. She added it to the bag.

"Thank you, dear," Dora said softly. She opened her voluminous purse and began pulling out a wallet.

Kellie instantly clamped her hands over Dora's. "Put that away, Dora. There's no charge for the supplies, remember? And I added a special treat—some new body cream I'm testing out. It smells heavenly—like almonds and vanilla."

Even through the mirror, Lara saw Dora's eyes well up. "You're so generous, Kellie. And such a good friend. Thank you, honey. I don't know what I'd do without kind people like you."

"No worries. I'm happy to do it." Kellie hugged her, then peeked under the foil covering the plate Dora had given her. "You brought me more of those delicious cookies—that's thanks enough. But you shouldn't have gone to the trouble."

"Least I can do," Dora said, and then sidled over closer to Lara. "Please give Fran my love, would you Lara? I wanted to stay longer yesterday and chat, but...well, things kind of devolved, didn't they?"

"They did, but I'll tell my aunt you were asking for her." Lara freed one hand from beneath the cape and squeezed Dora's arm.

Dora smiled, and with a tilt of her head she said, "You know, Lara, your aunt is the only person I know who still sends hand-written cards to people. It's such a treat to get a note from her in that lovely penmanship of hers."

A sudden pang struck Lara in the chest. She thought of all the hand-written cards Aunt Fran had given her during her childhood years—for every imaginable occasion. A perfect report card. A winning entry in her elementary school's art contest. Almost every accomplishment, however small, earned Lara a handwritten note from Aunt Fran. Each one had been unique. Her aunt always bought note cards from a museum gift shop—cards with exquisite art prints on the front.

Lara frowned to herself. Where were those cards? She was sure she'd saved them. She'd stuck them all in a special box. Where did that box end up? Had it gotten lost when they moved to Massachusetts?

She felt Dora touch her shoulder and realized her mind had drifted again. "Thanks, Dora. I'll be sure to tell her you said that."

After Dora bade them both good-bye and left, Kellie shook her head. "Poor woman," she murmured, pulling the wide-toothed comb through Lara's damp hair. "She hasn't been the same since the accident."

"Accident?"

Kellie set her comb on the tray and picked up a pair of scissors. "It happened three years ago, at one of the local discount stores. It's one of those places that sells all sorts of electronics, computers, things like that. Anyway, Dora was standing next to this huge, flat-screen TV that was bolted to the wall. It was a monster of a thing, ya know? Like about forty feet long." Kellie spread her arms way out to the side, as if preparing for flight. "When Dora turned to look at something else, her shoulder accidentally bumped it. The whole thing came crashing down on her."

"Oh, no!"

"Yup. Knocked her right to the floor. Broken glass everywhere. She found out later the clerk who'd installed the dumb thing had been told to tighten the bolts." Kellie's face morphed into a scowl. "The fool had left the screwdriver right there, but then went off on a break in the lunchroom. He was yukking it up with his buds when that TV fell on Dora. When he heard the crash he raced back to the showroom, but of course it was too late. Someone said Dora was so delirious from the pain that she grabbed a piece of glass and tried to slash the guy's ankle. It's probably not true, but I wouldn't blame her if it was. Needless to say, the guy got canned. Served him right, for all the agony that poor dear has suffered."

With a somber look, Kellie held up her scissors and looked at Lara in the mirror. "Ready?"

Lara swallowed. "I'm ready."

She watched a strand of hair at least four inches long drop to the floor beside her.

"Um…so, is that why Dora has to wear a brace now?"

"You guessed it," Kellie said, her scissors making scary cutting sounds at the back of Lara's head. "The accident did a number on her. Gave her a permanent back injury. She ended up having to retire early from her job at the bank. Thank God she found a lawyer willing to sue. She ended up settling with the insurance company and got a decent amount, though I think she should've gotten more. At least the sweet dear doesn't have to work anymore. Once she's old enough to get social security, she should do okay."

Lara mulled that over. She didn't realize Dora had been through such an ordeal.

"Those cookies she supposedly makes?" Kellie said with a wry chuckle. "She gets them at the Shop-Along. She thinks they'll look homemade if she puts them on a paper plate and covers them with foil. I always pretend I don't know. I wouldn't hurt her feelings for the world."

"Well, it's the thought that counts, right?" Lara smiled at Kellie in the mirror. "She obviously means well. Does she live alone?"

Snip. Snip.

More damp curls floated to the floor.

"Yup. She lives in the same house she grew up in. Her mom died when she was real young, and her dad had to raise her and her sister by himself. 'Course I never knew him, but everyone who did said he was a real nice man. Dora's only sister had a bad heart. She died like, I don't know, seven or eight years ago?"

A thought tickled Lara's brain. Something she'd been meaning to ask her aunt.

"I was thinking," Lara told Kellie, "that Dora might make the perfect mom for a cat who needs a loving home. What do you think?"

Kellie was already shaking her head. "Dora supposedly has allergies galore. Pets are out of the question for her. Even her goldfish didn't work out, I heard."

Lara drew her eyebrows together. "She really does have her troubles, doesn't she?"

"She does," Kellie confirmed. "Back in the day, she did a lot of community theater. Just local stuff, but she really enjoyed it. She was kind of a wannabe actress, ya know? But after the accident, all that ended." With a fierce scowl, she snipped another lock of hair.

Lara's head was beginning to feel lighter. Her brain, on the other hand, was on overload. Kellie Byrd was a fount of information.

"Hey, enough of the sad talk," Kellie said. She smiled into the mirror at Lara. "By the time I get through with you, girl, you're gonna be *gaww*geous."

The door opened on a sudden *whoosh* of chilly, floral-scented air. It took Lara only a few seconds to place the source.

"Josette!" Kellie squealed. "I've been thinking about you, girlfriend. You doing okay?"

Josette Barnes stepped inside the salon and quickly closed the door. She went over and gave the stylist a quick air kiss.

"I'm doing just fab," Josette said in a silky voice. "Better than ever. How about you?"

Kellie shrugged and grinned. "My motor's still ticking. I guess that counts for something."

Lara couldn't resist turning slightly in her chair to stare at Josette.

The woman's dark hair had been swept into a messy topknot and secured with a lime-green scarf. She peeled off her black, knee-length coat to reveal a stunning plum-colored sweater over dove-gray jersey leggings.

Where are my manners?

"Hi, Josette." Lara gave her a tiny wave.

Josette's carefully made-up eyes popped open wide. "Oh. Lily, is it? I didn't recognize you. Hello, there."

"It's Lara," she said, smiling. "Kellie's giving me a trim, as you can probably tell." Lara glanced at the mounds of hair on the floor and sucked in a breath. *A major trim*, she thought nervously.

All at once, a look of panic came over Kellie. "Oh, Lordy—Jo, did you have an appointment this morning? I must have forgotten to write it down."

"No, no. Not to worry," Josette said, holding up her hands. "I didn't have an appointment. But I was hoping you might have time to touch up my roots and do a highlighting." Her face brightened. "I'm kind of, well…oh, Kel, I've met the most wonderful man! I've been dying to tell you all about him."

A new man?

How convenient that Josette's ex was so thoroughly out of the picture. Lara couldn't help wondering how soon that lump-sum alimony payment would be landing in the woman's stylish lap.

I'm being catty, she thought, chiding herself. Hadn't Aunt Fran told her that Josette was a kind soul?

Josette launched into her story of the man she'd met through a dating Web site. According to her, they'd communicated and exchanged pics for a few months, after which he invited her to meet him in his sprawling Connecticut home.

"I drove down early Wednesday," Josette said coyly. "Things went so well that I ended up spending the night there. Lucky thing I was prepared," she added. "If you know what I mean. The thing is, we really connected. Neither of us could believe how much we have in common!"

Kellie made the appropriate squeals of joy, and the two did a little dance.

Josette went over to the adjacent salon chair, draped her coat over the back, and plunked herself down. She crossed one leg over the other and twirled toward Lara and Kellie.

"Anyway," Josette went on, "I was floating on air when I left Connecticut Thursday morning. My beau had to fly to Washington on business, but I swear, I sailed up the Everett Turnpike in New Hampshire like I had wings on my car!"

A magical car indeed, Lara thought wryly.

Josette's story had a bit of whimsy, too, she couldn't help thinking. Was it pure coincidence that Theo had been murdered on the same night his ex-wife had driven out of state?

Surely the police had already questioned Josette. And wouldn't they also have checked with her new beau—whoever he was—to confirm her alibi for that night?

"Josette," Lara said gently, "you must have been so horrified when you got back that morning and heard about Theo."

Kellie's face froze. Josette's cheeks flushed into two ripe berries.

"Why…yes. Yes, I was. But as I've said to everyone, there was no love lost between me and Theo. I'm sorry someone saw fit to give him what he deserved, but it had nothing to do with me."

"Of course it didn't," Lara said. "I'm sorry. I shouldn't have said it like that. That's not what I meant at all."

Kellie breathed out a noisy sigh. "Hey, look, at this point I say we let the cops worry about finding Theo's killer. It's not our problem, right? We all got enough of our own troubles."

"I agree," Josette said. She smiled at Lara. "Actually, um, Lara, I've been meaning to stop by and see your aunt one of these days. There's something I've been wanting to talk to her about."

Hmm, that was a surprise. Especially since some of the locals had been calling Aunt Fran a crazy cat lady. Was this a ploy by Josette to change the subject?

"I'm sure she'd love to see you," Lara said. "Why don't you give her a call one of these days?"

"Thanks, Lara, I will." Josette said. She leaned forward slightly, and in that moment Lara thought the woman's eyes looked puffy, as if she'd been crying. "How long will you be staying there?"

"I'm not sure," Lara said truthfully. "At least for another few days."

Something flickered in Josette's eyes. Fear? Worry?

She's hiding something, Lara thought. *I just know it.*

Something else occurred to Lara. Josette had chattered endlessly about meeting her deliciously sexy new beau.

And never once told them his name.

Chapter 14

Sherry spewed a mouthful of coffee into her mug and began coughing violently. She snatched a handful of napkins from beneath the counter and smooshed them against her lips. "Sorry about that, Mr. Patello—didn't mean to spit on you."

The senior gent sitting at the counter—the same one who'd saved a seat for his friend Herbie the day before—gave the coffee shop owner an unsmiling nod. He shifted his mug a safe distance away from Sherry.

Sherry turned back to gape at Lara. "Oh, my *God*, Lara, are you kidding me?" she bleated. "Is that really you?" Sherry's eyes were the size of basketballs. "I am like, seriously blown away. You are a total babe, you know that?"

"Stop making such a fuss," Lara hissed at her. "It's only a haircut."

Lara bit off a grin. Inwardly she was beaming. Kellie's handiwork had been nothing short of miraculous. The jumble of overgrown curls Lara had brought with her to the salon were now shorter and softer, flouncing around her face in a swirl of gentle rings. Lara wasn't sure if she could keep it looking that way, but at least she could enjoy it for now.

She took a stool next to the elderly man. His homburg was parked on the opposite side, atop "Herbie's" stool. She smiled at him and then looked around the coffee shop. Her bestie had made such a production of her new "do" that she felt sure everyone must be staring at her.

Sherry, who'd obviously read her mind, laughed. "Don't worry. It's not even busy right now. Although," she said, sotto voce, "there is a delectable hunk of manliness over at the corner table whose tongue's been dragging on the floor since you walked in."

"Yeah, right," Lara said, refusing to be baited.

"I'm serious." Sherry swiveled her eyes toward the rear of the dining area. She poured a mug of coffee and set it down in front of Lara. "I'm surprised you didn't recognize him."

Shifting slightly on her stool, Lara sneaked a glance at the tables in the back. She caught a glimpse of straight dark hair and sharp cheekbones, peering over the rim of an open laptop. He smiled when she spotted him, but then quickly looked away.

A tiny flame ignited in the pit of Lara's stomach. Something about the face was familiar.

Never mind. She didn't need any distractions right now. She returned her attention to her coffee, grabbing a packet of half-and-half from a bowl on the counter and emptying it into her steaming mug.

"I only came in for a quick java and a mini-chat," Lara told Sherry. "I didn't get as much done yesterday as I'd hoped. I want to do a more thorough dusting and cleaning at Aunt Fran's, and see if I can figure out something with the cats. My gut tells me she hasn't tried overly hard to find homes for the ones she took in as strays."

"And my gut says you're right." Sherry pulled the coffeepot off the warmer and topped off Mr. Patello's mug. "It was different when she was working. But being housebound has really done a number on her, if you get what I'm saying. She's bonded so thoroughly to all the cats she took in that she can't bear to part with any."

Lara scrunched her face and rubbed her temples. There were no magic answers, that much was certain. It was going to take a lot more brainstorming to figure out a way to help her aunt and the cats. So far, she'd provided only a temporary solution.

"Lara, you know I'd take a cat if I could," Sherry said, her eyes sad. "But with Mom's allergies—"

"Sherry, you don't have to explain. I know all that," Lara soothed.

"I keep telling myself I'll get my own place one of these days." Sherry gave a halfhearted shrug.

"And some day you will," Lara assured her.

Sherry glanced at Mr. Patello, then closed her mouth. Lara knew she wanted to say more, but airing her problems within earshot of a customer wasn't exactly a wise thing to do.

Especially a customer who seemed to be hanging on Sherry's every word.

Mr. Patello turned abruptly toward Lara. "You girls talking about Fran Clarkson? The nut with all the cats?"

"Mr. Patello!" Sherry said sharply.

Lara stiffened at his tone—and at his words. "My aunt is not a nut, Mr., um, Patello, and I resent you calling her that. She is an intelligent, caring, and accomplished woman. And if you'd lived in this town for any length of time, you'd know that."

The man looked taken aback. "I…I do know that," he backpedaled. "Okay, I didn't mean to imply she was crazy. But in my book, anyone who lives with that many cats has to be a few degrees off her rocker." He tapped a gnarled forefinger to his head.

Then you need a new book, Lara wanted to shriek. Instead, she took a deep, calming breath.

"Mr. Patello," Lara said evenly, "do you even know how many cats my aunt has?"

The man flushed red behind his white beard stubble. "Well, no. Not exactly. But I heard it was somewhere around thirty."

Thirty! Who makes up such nonsense?

"It's eleven," Lara said, clenching her teeth. *Twelve if you counted Blue.* "And at least three of those eleven would have starved to death or worse, if she hadn't been there to take them in."

The man swallowed, his Adam's apple bobbing like a buoy over a fishing line. "Well, then, all right. I take back what I said about her. I wouldn't want to see any animal come to harm. I'm not an ogre, you know."

Lara placed her hand lightly on his arm. She felt like an ogre herself for getting angry at the old gent. "Mr. Patello, I apologize for the way I spoke. I shouldn't have raised my voice. It's just that it's hard to find good homes for that many strays. She's doing the best she can."

"You don't have to defend her," he said hoarsely. "I've known Fran Clarkson for a long time. She's good people." He rose from his stool and fumbled in his pocket for his billfold.

"Never mind, Mr. Patello," Sherry told him quickly. "It's on the house today."

Avoiding Lara's gaze, the man scooped his homburg off the adjacent stool, grumbled a thank-you, and hobbled out the door. Lara thought she heard him mumble the name Herbie, but that might have been her imagination working overtime.

Sherry blew out a long breath. "Like I needed *that* today."

"I'm so sorry, Sher," Lara groaned. "I really lost my cool, didn't I? I hope I didn't cost you a customer."

Sherry laughed. "No way. He's been a regular here for years. Believe me, he'll be sitting in that same spot tomorrow with his usual coffee and corn muffin, saving a stool for Herbie."

That made Lara feel a tad better. She took another long swig of coffee. "And in case you're wondering, Herbie used to be his dear friend. They had breakfast here together every morning, until Herbie died several months ago. Mr. Patello still saves his stool for him every day."

"Oh, the poor man," Lara said, feeling more than a little guilty. "Now I feel terrible at the way I spoke to him."

"Actually," Sherry said, "I thought you were pretty controlled. You apologized to him, but he did not return the gesture. Shame on him."

"You're right," Lara said. "Hey, listen, I've got to get going. I want to pick up some watercolor supplies. I didn't bring any with me when I packed the other day."

"Does that mean you'll be sticking around for a while?" Excitement rose in Sherry's voice.

Lara sagged. She felt so torn. "I'm not sure. I will for a little while, anyway. But don't get your hopes up. I still have to go back to Boston." She swallowed the last drop of the fragrant coffee in her mug.

"Yeah, I know." Sherry made a face and sighed.

"In the meantime, do you know where can I buy some art supplies? Is there an arts-and-crafts store near here?"

"You bet," Sherry said. "It's a good one, too. Mary Newman works there." She jotted directions on a napkin and gave it to Lara.

Mary Newman. Lara wondered how well acquainted Sherry was with the woman. She couldn't help thinking that Mary might know more than most people about her uncle's business dealings.

She took the napkin from her friend and perused it. "Great. This looks easy to get to. I've been gone for so many years that I've lost my bearings a little."

Tears suddenly filled Sherry's eyes. "I've missed you so much, Lara. I was happy when we connected again, but it's not the same as having you close by. Except for Theo getting offed, these past few days, having you back in town, have been so much like old times."

Lara felt herself getting misty. "I know, Sher. And honestly, I'm going to try to spend more time up here with Aunt Fran—and with you."

"Let's make it a plan," Sherry said. "And don't you *dare* attempt to pay for that coffee," she added, seeing Lara pull her change purse from her handbag.

"Okay," Lara relented. "But only for today. In the future I pay my bill, fair and square."

"Um, sure. Whatever you say." Sherry's gaze wandered to the customer who was waving at the two of them and heading toward the glass front door.

Lara turned, and felt her face flame.

"Nice to see you again, Tiger Lara," the man said, his wide smile reflected in his voice.

"Um...I..." Lara sputtered.

Sporty briefcase in hand, he grinned at her, pushed open the door, and then hurried across the street.

Lara looked at Sherry. "Huh?"

"OMG, I can't believe you didn't recognize him!" Sherry laughed.

But Lara *had* recognized him. The "Tiger Lara" was a dead giveaway.

Only one person had ever called her that.

Gideon Halley.

Chapter 15

Jepson's Crafts was housed in a flat-top, beige stucco building on Route Sixteen, close to the Moultonborough town line. The storefront itself was unimpressive, with hand-written signs advertising weekly sales taped haphazardly to the front windows. Lara couldn't imagine working in such a dreary place, especially when its purpose was to foster creativity. It didn't exactly smack of a cozy, artsy place to shop.

Oh, what the heck. If they had the items Lara needed, why should she care about the ambiance?

Customer parking, which consisted of a sea of cracked pavement with a Dumpster squatting in a far corner, was located behind the store. Lara was surprised at how many cars were in the lot. Jepson's must be a popular place.

The moment she stepped inside the store, she took back everything she'd been thinking. An explosion of colors greeted her. The store was well lighted and the aisles wide. Brightly painted shelves held an amazing array of arts-and-crafts supplies.

The black-and-white linoleum floor looked spotless, and the checkout counters were as high-tech as they get. Each aisle had a sign hanging above it, identifying in easy-to-read letters what could be found there.

Lara scanned the overhead signs until she saw the one she needed—Art Supplies. Since she planned to buy several items, she snagged a cart from the indoor corral.

Once she began shopping, she wanted to linger there all day. The selection was phenomenal, and the prices better than she'd hoped. After loading up with brushes, watercolor paints, a palette, and a pad of 140-pound paper, Lara aimed her cart toward the checkout that had the shortest line.

A slender clerk with stringy gray hair and plastic skeletons hanging from her earlobes rang up her order. The woman worked with sharp, efficient movements, as if she'd been trained to move the long lines ahead as quickly as possible.

Lara craned her head around, hoping to spot Mary. Finally, after paying for everything with the dwindling funds in her debit account, she said to the clerk, "I heard Mary Newman works here. Is she around today?"

The stringy-haired clerk nodded grimly. "She's here, but the poor thing's a mess." She moved Lara's bag to the end of the counter and began ringing up the next order. "You might catch her out back. I think she's on break."

Lara thanked the clerk and left. She didn't know what "out back" meant, so she headed out to the parking lot. By sheer luck—or providence, she thought—she spotted Mary near the Dumpster, close to where Lara had parked. Mary appeared to be disposing of some plastic grocery bags.

"Hi, Mary," she said, coming up behind her.

"Oh!" Clutching an open plastic bag, Mary jumped and swerved around. "Oh, it's only you," she said, closing her eyes for a moment. She tapped her fingertips to her heart. "You scared me, coming up behind me like that."

"Sorry." Lara thought her booted footsteps had made plenty of noise, but apparently Mary was in another zone—mentally, at least. "I thought you heard me."

Mary held up a white plastic bag. Two more like it rested at her feet. "I...I was throwing out some stuff," she said, tears filling her eyes. She dropped the bag on the pavement and began to cry.

Lara peeked at the bag. Inside were more of those magazines—*Confessions in Lace.* She could see the glossy cover of the mag on top.

"Mary, do you want to talk about it?" Lara kept her voice soft, nonthreatening.

Mary nodded, and the dam broke. She sobbed for at least a minute, during which Lara remained still.

Mary pulled a crumpled tissue from her jacket pocket and swabbed her eyes. "Will you help me get rid of these first?"

Lara hesitated. The magazines were definitely icky—in her opinion, at least. But what if Mary was destroying evidence? What if the mags had something to do with Barnes's murder? Could they contain clues as to the person who felt angry or desperate enough to kill him?

"Are you sure you want to dump these?" Lara asked her.

"I'm sure," Mary said firmly. "If you hold the Dumpster cover open, I'll throw these bags in. They're heavier than they look. It's hard for me to hold open the cover and toss them in at the same time."

Lara nodded and lifted the metal cover of the Dumpster. One by one, Mary picked up the bags and tossed them in, as far as she could throw them. "Thanks," she muttered to Lara. She shivered.

Lara eased the cover closed. "Shall we sit in your car and talk?" She hoped Mary hadn't already changed her mind about having a chat.

Mary glanced at her watch. "Okay, but I only have about eight minutes of break left."

They hurried over to Mary's SUV, which was parked close by. Once they were inside Mary locked the doors, then reached her arm around to the rear seating area. She lifted a silver laptop off the floor and set it down on the console between her and Lara.

"This is Chris's," she confessed. "Not his work laptop, but his home one. He doesn't use it much anymore. If he works from home, like during tax season, he brings his work laptop home with him."

"Does he know you took it?" Lara was sure she knew the answer, but she had to ask.

Mary bit her lip. "No. I found it in the bottom drawer in his desk at home, buried under some blank IRS forms. After Uncle Theo...died, I got to thinking about stuff. Chris has been acting strange for a while. I mean, don't get me wrong—our marriage is wonderful, and I know he loves me. But, well, he and my uncle weren't exactly friends. I'm scared that Uncle Theo might have gotten him involved in something that made Chris feel threatened."

And given him a motive for murder? Lara added silently.

"Mary, have you talked to Chris about it?" In Lara's mind, that would have been the logical place to start.

Mary's eyes grew moist again, and she shook her head. "Oh, God, Lara. I can't. He'd think I didn't trust him." All at once she froze and stared at Lara, as if seeing her for the first time. "I just noticed your hair," she said softly. "It's so pretty."

"Thanks." Lara smiled, and Mary looked a little more at ease.

"Lara, maybe you can help me," Mary said. "Can I show you something?" She opened the cover of the laptop.

Lara squirmed in her seat. This felt wrong—looking at Chris's personal computer. She didn't really know the man. Invading his privacy didn't seem like the best way to learn about him.

Although, she reasoned, what if Chris *had* killed Theo? What if one of the entries in his laptop gave Lara a clue she could take to the police?

But that wouldn't work, either. How would she explain it? Wouldn't a savvy defense attorney get the ill-gotten evidence tossed out in a trial?

Wait a minute. She was getting ahead of herself. This wasn't a trial, and so far she hadn't uncovered one iota of evidence. She looked over at Mary, whose fingers were nimbly skipping over the keys.

"You know his password?" Lara asked her.

Mary's face reddened. "He always uses the same one—MyMary82. That's the year I was born."

Very sweet, Lara thought. She wasn't sure the contents of the computer would prove quite as benign.

"Okay, look." Her hand trembling a bit, Mary turned the laptop to give Lara a better view. "This is Chris's e-mail program. Over the last few years, he's been sending Uncle Theo regular e-mails, about once a month. Each e-mail is totally blank, with a single Word document attached."

Lara's pulse spiked. "Ok*aaay.*"

"Now, watch this." Mary clicked open the Word document attached to the most recent outgoing e-mail. "What do you think?"

For a moment, Lara was baffled. The page was blank. "Am I supposed to be seeing something?" she asked.

"You tell me," Mary said with a sigh. "I've scrolled down, all the way to the end, but there's nothing."

Well, isn't this a puzzle, Lara thought. She wasn't familiar with many software programs—especially those that didn't relate to art or watercolors. She knew only the bare basics of Word. She had to agree that it was odd, though—Chris sending blank documents to Barnes.

Could it be a code of some sort? A signal between the two? Something only Chris and Barnes would be able to interpret?

Truth be told, Lara was grateful those documents had been blank. She barely knew Chris and Mary. She felt like a sleaze looking at Chris's personal stuff. What would he say if he knew Mary had divulged the contents of his e-mails?

"I'm so worried," Mary said, fear rattling her voice. "Uncle Theo—well, he wasn't always above board in his business dealings. At least that's what people said about him. But it wasn't his fault," she added quickly. "His father was a nasty man, a terrible role model. Anyway, he and Chris always used to clash. That's why I'm so scared."

"Scared of what?" Lara asked quietly, though she thought she knew. Mary was terrified that Chris might have killed her uncle. Lara felt sure that was it.

Her face pinched, Mary stared through the windshield. A sudden gust sent a handful of dried maple leaves scattering over the hood of her SUV. Lara shivered. She couldn't help thinking it was an omen of some sort.

"I'm scared Uncle Theo might have gotten Chris involved in something sh-shady," Mary stuttered out. "Oh God, Lara. I can't lose Chris, too!"

"Don't jump to conclusions," Lara cautioned. "You can make yourself crazy thinking things like that. I'm sure none of that happened."

"Honestly?"

Lara nodded. "Mary, I don't know what to make of the blank Word documents. But I'm also not the best person to ask. I used a word processing program when I was in art school, but since then I haven't kept up. I work mostly with paints and colors." *When I'm not washing dishes at the bakery.*

Mary swallowed, then sniffled. "I was afraid you'd say that."

"Although," Lara mused aloud. "If he sent the Word documents to your uncle as attachments, wouldn't they be stored somewhere else on his computer? He would've had to attach them from some other program or folder, right?"

"Right," Mary said glumly. "I already checked that. Whatever they were, Chris must have deleted them. They're not in his laptop anymore." With a childish huff, she slammed the laptop closed. "Never mind. I shouldn't have bothered you. I just thought you might—" She grabbed Lara's wrist. "Hey, wait a minute. I bet if you take this home with you, you'll be able to figure it out eventually. There has to be an answer! Someone just needs to take the time—"

"I'm sorry, Mary," Lara interjected, gently pulling her hand away. "But I can't do that. If Chris gave me permission, I'd help you in a heartbeat. I mean, I wish I could help. I can see how bad you're hurting. I…I just don't think this is the way to go about it."

And I have to go back to Boston. The thought made Lara's heart sink a little, though she wasn't sure why.

"I understand," Mary said hoarsely. "And believe me, I hate spying on Chris like this. It's not who I am. It's not who…we are."

"I get that. I really do," Lara said. "Chris loves you, Mary. That much is obvious. Why don't you talk to him about it? You'll feel a lot better afterward."

Mary's face got puffy with tears again. "I know you're right. I'm just not sure I can do that." She swabbed her wet cheek with the heel of her hand. "Lara, I have to go. My boss'll be looking for me. You probably noticed that this is a really busy store."

Lara didn't want to make Mary late, or get her in trouble. But there was so much more she wanted to ask. She settled for one question. "Mary, I found a slip of paper—part of a napkin, I think—that fell out of your car yesterday. It said 'Midnight Mary.' It's back at my aunt's, in case you need it."

A crimson stain crept up Mary's neck and into her cheeks. "I... Oh, right," she said. "I forgot I had that. But no, I don't need it. In fact, I meant to throw it away. You can toss it out." She started to open her door, then turned and gave Lara a pleading look. "I'll tell you who wrote it, but you have to promise you won't tell Chris, okay?"

Lara nodded. "Of course."

"You know Glen, the guy in our book club?" Mary's mouth twisted into an angry frown. "He's always trying to think of songs with the name Mary in them. Like, 'Along Comes Mary' and 'Mary in the Morning.' He writes them on slips of paper and passes them to me at book club. It drives me nuts. I hate when he does that."

"Have you asked him to stop?"

"Yes, many times. But he doesn't get it. He thinks it's funny. I'm... thinking of dropping out of the club. I love Dora, and Brooke is a darling. But Glen has to go. Or I will."

Lara's head was spinning into the red zone with all this new information. She scribbled a mental note to check out the song "Midnight Mary" when she got back to her aunt's. Those songs Mary mentioned all sounded like oldies. Glen was in his sixties, at least. They probably came from his era.

Now that she thought about it, Glen was another wild card. Barnes had evicted him from his apartment only hours before the murder. Didn't he have as much of a motive for murder—if not more—than anyone?

She felt Mary jiggling her arm. "You'll throw it away, right?" Mary was saying.

"Oh, um, the note? Sure—yes, I will. I'll throw it in the wastebasket as soon as I get back to Aunt Fran's."

But I won't empty the wastebasket.

Not until the cops figure out who killed Theo Barnes.

Chapter 16

On her way back to Aunt Fran's, Lara drove through the center of town. She found herself smiling at how familiar everything looked.

The block that housed Sherry's coffee shop had been there for decades. When she and Sherry were kids, the spot occupied by the coffee shop had been one of the last of the old-fashioned drugstores. Lara remembered saving her allowance each year to buy Christmas gifts for her family. The pharmacy had stocked so many knickknacks and tchotchkes that she could do all her shopping there, and buy the wrapping paper, too.

Over the years, the storefronts had changed, but the building still looked the same—light gray clapboard with white trim.

The only blight in the tiny downtown area was the dreary apartment house on the opposite side of the street—the one Theo Barnes owned, or rather, *had* owned. With a paint job, a touch of corrective carpentry, and a bit of landscaping, it could have made for some attractive living quarters. Lara hated to think what the inside was like, if the façade was that neglected.

As she drove past the town park, she was dismayed to see a large, dark-colored truck parked along the main drag. Its side panel identified it as the State Police Major Crime Unit vehicle.

Lara groaned.

Her stomach did a double-roll when she saw another truck parked next to the state vehicle. A cable-news van, its overhead dish looking large enough to receive transmissions from another galaxy, occupied two prime downtown parking slots.

Gritting her teeth, Lara steered her rental car up High Cliff Road. She was grateful there weren't any vehicles blocking Aunt Fran's driveway. Lara grabbed her crafts-store purchases and darted onto the porch steps and into the house. She found Aunt Fran sitting at the kitchen table, nursing a cup of tea and a slice of buttered toast.

"Lara!" Aunt Fran sputtered. "Oh my heavens. Your...your hair."

Lara smiled. She plopped her bag onto a kitchen chair and sat down next to it. "Like it?"

Aunt Fran's face lit up. "I do. I really do. Did Kellie do that?"

"Yup. She's a miracle worker, isn't she?"

"She certainly gave you a lovely hairstyle. I'm surprised you let her trim that much, though. She must have cut off at least five inches."

"Yes, she did," Lara said distractedly, distant memories coming at her like a comet.

When she was a girl, she'd fought constantly with her mom over getting her hair cut. "I'm sick of finding that hair all over the house," Brenda Caphart would shriek. "You're getting that mess cut off today, and I don't want to hear any arguments."

Lara would run to her room and sob. Only after a persuasive phone call from Aunt Fran would she give in and let her mom take her to a barber—never a salon—to chop off the bulk of the curls.

"You're a thousand miles away," Aunt Fran said. "And you look a bit pale. Are you all right, Lara?"

Lara shook herself back to reality. "I'm fine. I wasn't thrilled to see the crime scene van out there, though. Or the news truck."

Aunt Fran's smile was cryptic. "A reporter already tried to talk to me. I immediately locked the screen door and refused to let him inside."

"I suppose they have their jobs to do," Lara said.

With an odd twinkle of her green eyes, Aunt Fran said, "I kept telling him that I had no comment, but he still wouldn't leave. Then Munster came strutting into the kitchen and ran straight toward the screen door. Munster put his paws on the door and let out one long meow. You should have seen the man's face. His eyes widened, and he took a huge step backward. Poor fellow almost fell off the porch."

"Wait a minute. *Munster* scared him?" Lara couldn't wrap her brain around that. The darling kitty was a bundle of love wrapped in a striped orange bow.

"Yes, and...now that I think back to it, it was really quite strange. Before Munster came into the kitchen, the reporter kept peering through the screen, trying to see past me. I don't know what he saw, or thought he saw, but the oddest look came over him. I suspect he harbors a fear of cats."

"You're probably right," Lara agreed, feeling sure it was something else.

"Did you get what you needed at the crafts store?"

"Yes! I've been missing my watercolors, so now at least I have a small supply." Lara held up her bag from Jepson's.

Aunt Fran's smile was guarded. "Does that mean you're going to stay longer than you planned?"

Lara wanted to say yes. She wanted to say she was going to stay forever. *Oh, Lord. Where did that come from?*

All at once, a depressing thought struck her. Maybe Aunt Fran would have been better off if Lara hadn't shown up at all. Once Lara returned to Boston, who was going to step in and help her?

"I...I'm not sure, Aunt Fran. Everything is so, you know, up in the air right now."

Lara glanced at her aunt's now-empty plate and mug. She quickly cleared the table and washed the dishes in the sink.

After tidying the kitchen, Lara fetched the grooming supplies she'd put away the night before. Aunt Fran joined her in the large parlor while she gave Twinkles a thorough brushing.

Dolce was next. Lara had to pry his sleepy form off her aunt's lap, but once she started grooming him he closed his eyes and purred with bliss.

"You've made some wonderful feline friends these last few days," Aunt Fran noted. The hint of sadness in her voice pierced Lara's heart like an arrow.

Lara lifted Dolce and kissed his nose, then returned him to her aunt's lap. She should have been pleased by her aunt's declaration, but instead it felt like a guilt trip.

She managed to corral Cheetah and Lilybee—Bootsie's kittens—and give them each a gentle brushing. Their spotted tummies were so adorable she couldn't resist planting noisy kisses on them.

"I wish I could nab Callie and Luna," Lara told her aunt. "How did they end up here?"

"They're darling, aren't they? They've only been here a few weeks. I found them on my porch one morning, stuffed inside a cardboard box with holes punched in the top. It was obvious they'd come from a bad situation—they were terrified when I first brought them inside. I suspect some kind soul rescued them and dumped them here, knowing I'd care for them. But they're still very young. In time, they'll come around. The one I'm not sure of is Ballou."

Lara grinned, picturing the handsome black kitty with the white 'stache. Deep down, she felt sure Ballou would eventually emerge from his shell. It was going to take time, and a lot of patience. It would be up to Aunt Fran to work at socializing him after Lara left.

"What happened to Ballou's ear?" Lara asked. "Do you think he lost the tip in a fight with another cat?"

Aunt Fran smiled. "No. It means that, at some point, he was trapped, neutered, and released. I was actually relieved when I saw that."

"Really?" Lara had never heard of that. "Who do you think did it?"

"There's a group that operates in Carroll County, helping feral cats. The vet nicks off the tip of the ear so that if anyone finds him, or wants to take him in, they'll know he's been neutered. And vaccinated."

Lara was confused. "Then...how did he end up here, with you?"

"It's an odd story," Aunt Fran said. "Ballou showed up here one raw, rainy day this past spring. The rain was coming down in buckets, and the poor darling looked drenched to the bone. He must have been desperate, because he came onto the porch to get out of the deluge."

"It would break my heart to see that," Lara said. "Do you think he sensed there were cats in the house?"

"He might have. Anyway, I put a bowl of dry food and some fresh water on the porch for him, but he panicked and took off the moment he saw me. Something told me he'd be back, though. Sure enough, about fifteen minutes later I caught him gobbling the food from that bowl."

"How did you lure him inside?"

"That was the strange part. I didn't have to lure him at all. I opened the door wide and spoke softly to him in a singsong sort of tone. He lifted his head and seemed to sniff the air. I think he felt the warmth coming from the kitchen. But he also seemed to be staring at something behind me. And then, like a shot, he dashed inside. I only saw him for a moment, because he quickly disappeared."

"Huh," Lara said. "Except for that one encounter I had, I never see him. I wonder where he hangs out in the house." She picked a blob of cat hair off her sweater. "I'm surprised he hasn't tried to go back outside."

Aunt Fran leaned back in her chair. She gave Lara a mischievous smile. "I think he spends his days in your room, Lara. He feels safe under your bed."

My bed, Lara thought. She realized with a jolt that Aunt Fran still thought of the spare room as Lara's.

"What? No," Lara insisted. "I'd have seen him."

"Not necessarily."

Aunt Fran was right. Since Lara had arrived on Wednesday, she hadn't spent a lot of time in her room. And when she had, she'd mostly been asleep.

"All your other cats are neutered, right?" Lara said.

"Of course they are. Except for the kittens. They're not quite ready yet."

Lara wondered if Aunt Fran was worrying about how to pay for it, too. One more thing they'd have to talk about before Lara hightailed it back to Boston.

For a while they sat in cozy silence. The feeling of serenity should have given Lara comfort, but instead it made her sad.

She suddenly realized what was missing.

"Hey, Aunt Fran, aren't the kids coming today?"

"Not today," her aunt said. "Their mom has the day off, so she's picking them up after school. She promised to take Darryl shopping for a Halloween costume."

"Oh." Lara smiled. Darryl was such a great kid. She hoped he found the perfect costume. A giraffe would suit him nicely.

Next on Lara's agenda was litter-box duty. She emptied and cleaned each one, then added fresh litter. She scrubbed the areas around the litter boxes, where odors clung. The sharp smell she'd detected when she first entered the house on Wednesday was slowly, but surely, dissipating.

Lara was dumping a bag of trash in the outside barrel when she spotted movement in her aunt's grassy field. It was the crime scene techs, trekking back to their van. One of them carried several paper bags, and the other juggled lighting equipment. Both wore protective gear, including booties that made them look like invaders from outer space.

She was glad to see that the media truck had left.

Arms crossed against the chill, she glanced out over the field. The ugly yellow tape was still in place. It skirted the far side of her aunt's land, almost to the edge of the brook.

Apparently, the techs weren't yet done collecting evidence. Which meant they'd probably be back on Saturday. Or maybe they'd just wanted to discourage any nosy types who might think schlepping over a crime scene was a fun new form of entertainment.

A speck of movement at the bank of the brook caught Lara's eye. Was that— Yes! It was Blue.

This time, she intended to keep the cat in her sights.

Lara bounded across the yard, circling the shed, which was imprisoned by yellow ribbon. The sacks of tulip bulbs still sat where Brooke and Dora had left them, near the brick walkway. The techs had extended the crime scene tape to include her aunt's shed and a large section of the vacant lot. The route around the barrier would be circuitous, but she was determined to catch up with the elusive Ragdoll cat.

The path around the tape was rocky as she picked her way downhill. The last thing she needed was a sprained ankle. When she finally reached the foot of the hill, she hoofed it along the edge of the brook.

She smiled when she spotted Blue. This time she had her cell in her pocket, so she'd definitely get a pic of the cat. The thought inspired her to move her feet along even faster.

Lara was almost at the far side of the lot, close to the bank of the brook, when suddenly she felt herself pitching headlong into space. She landed facedown on the cold ground. What the— She shuddered. Was this déjà vu all over again?

Something had caught the tip of her boot and sent her flying. This time it was something hard, metallic.

Lara pushed into a sitting position. Bits of dirt stuck to her jeans, but she ignored them. She looked all around. She knew it was silly, but she was terrified that another body might pop into her line of vision.

Eventually she breathed out a sigh. *No corpses today,* she thought soberly.

The only thing she saw was a length of metal piping, about eight inches high, jutting out of the ground at an angle. That's what she'd tripped over!

And then she spied movement, barely ten or twelve feet away. A feline face peeking through the grass.

Lara felt her irritation dissolve and her face crack into a smile. Moving almost in slo-mo, she pulled her cell out of her pocket and aimed the camera. Through the phone's display, she saw two furry ears sticking up through the weeds, above a pair of bright blue eyes. She zoomed in—a feature she loved about her phone—and snapped two photos in quick succession.

"Gotcha this time, Blue," Lara murmured.

She tapped the "photos" app on her phone.

Hmm. No sign of a cat in either pic. Had she taken them from too far away? Or had Blue ducked lower into the grass when she'd sensed her cover had been blown?

Why are you so mysterious, beautiful girl? Why are you such an escape artist?

Lara looked back at the spot where she'd seen Blue. The cat was no longer there. Using her fingers, Lara enlarged the first pic, and then the second. But the furry ears and shining blue eyes she was sure she'd seen were not in either photo.

Frustrated and annoyed, Lara brushed off her jeans. She rose to her feet and trod over to examine the metal rod she'd stumbled over.

The rod was solid and about half an inch wide. She tried to jiggle it free, but it wouldn't budge. Who had planted it there, and why?

The sky was growing darker, charcoal swatches melding with the clouds. It was the type of sky she loved to paint when she was in a sullen mood. Lara shivered. In her haste to catch up with Blue, she hadn't even gone inside for her jacket. The October chill was beginning to seep into her bones.

Her aunt, no doubt, was wondering where she'd gone off to. With an exasperated sigh, Lara climbed the hill again, going around the back side of the shed toward the porch. She turned and glanced once more over the grassy lot. Then she scooted back inside to the warmth of her aunt's home.

Chapter 17

"Once again, Lara, you've outdone yourself," Aunt Fran said. "That lasagna was one of the best I've ever tasted."

Lara grinned, then wiped the blob of marinara sauce she felt drizzling down one side of her mouth. During her marketing excursion the day before, she'd bought the ingredients for a spinach lasagna. She decided to take a shot at making it. She'd watched Gabby do it several times, and thought she could remember the steps.

The dish came out even better than she'd hoped. Loaded with creamy ricotta and fresh mozzarella, it was tasty and rich and downright delicious. If she did say so herself.

Right now, though, Lara didn't want to think about Gabby. She felt guilty enough for ditching her bakery job, even temporarily, with so little notice.

"I'm *so* glad you liked it," Lara said. "And it's even better left over, so we can have it tomorrow, too."

Lara realized she'd just committed herself to staying at least another day, if not longer. She sneaked a look at her aunt, who wore a pensive expression.

Time to reroute the conversation.

"Aunt Fran," Lara said, "when I went outside to put the trash in the can this afternoon, I thought I saw...a cat in the field."

Aunt Fran's face twitched. "Really?"

"Yup." Lara swallowed. "Anyway, I decided to see if I could follow it. I traipsed around that yellow tape, down the hill, all the way to the rear of the lot. And then, like a klutz, I tripped over a metal rod that was sticking out of the ground. That thing was solid! After I fell, I tried to pull it out of the ground, but it wouldn't budge."

Aunt Fran narrowed her eyes. "Where was the rod?"

"It's hard to describe," Lara replied. "Not too far from the brook, about twenty, maybe thirty feet from the far corner of the field."

Her aunt's lips tightened. She dabbed them with the tip of her napkin. "I suspect you tripped over a length of rebar," she said, her soft tone belying the fury in her voice.

"Rebar?"

"It's used in marking boundaries," Aunt Fran explained. "And it might account for the noise I heard one night a while back."

Lara jerked forward. "What noise?"

"About a month ago, not long after I'd fallen asleep one night, a roaring noise, like a loud engine, jolted me awake. At first I thought I'd imagined it. But then I heard it again, even louder. As quickly as these bad knees would take me, I hobbled to my bedroom window and looked outside. At first, I didn't see anything. But then I spotted two round lights in the darkness."

"Headlights?" Lara guessed.

"Exactly." Her aunt's face looked flushed.

"You'll have to clue me in, Aunt Fran. I'm not sure where you're headed with this."

"Lara, I think someone was trying to remove the boundary marker on my land. Someone with a truck, who could tie a length of chain around the front end and pull the marker out of the ground."

"But that's, that's…despicable! Who would do that?"

"I don't know." Aunt Fran frowned. "But whoever it was, I feel sure he was hired by Theo." She pushed aside her empty plate, her hand trembling.

Ah, now the light was dawning. "Okay, so tell me if I'm getting this. If Theo could remove the marker and set it in a different spot, it would make your lot appear smaller—"

Aunt Fran nodded. "And his own parcel larger."

"And then," Lara went on, feeling her ire rise, "when he hired a surveyor to plot out his own property, he'd have *proof*, so-called, that his lot line extended way beyond where it actually does."

"That's right." Aunt Fran's smile was grim. "Now you're catching on."

"But would that fool a surveyor?"

"No, I don't think so," her aunt said. "They're professionals. I'm sure they'd know if a boundary marker had been disturbed. Plus, to make the ruse work, Theo would also have to move the corresponding marker at the front of the lot. The whole idea is insane."

Lara sat back, stunned. She didn't like the implications. It was all too…diabolical.

"Did you report it to the police?"

Aunt Fran shook her head. "No, though I probably should have. At the time, it didn't seem serious enough for that. For all I knew, it could have been just some rowdy kids out there with a few too many beers in them." "I suppose," Lara said doubtfully.

Lara's thoughts were swirling. A part of her was relieved that her aunt hadn't reported it. The police already had Aunt Fran on their suspect list—mainly because of the proximity of the murder scene to her property line. And because of her ongoing dispute with Barnes. If they'd known about the truck incident, they might have taken a closer look at her, grilled her a bit more harshly.

The thought made Lara shudder.

"I could use a cup of hot tea," she said, rising to clear the dishes. "How about you?"

"I'd love one," Aunt Fran said.

Lara stuck the dishes in the sink to soak and put on the kettle. A minute later she delivered two mugs of steaming tea to the table and sat down with her aunt.

"So," she said, "do you suspect anyone in particular of trying to move that boundary marker? You said it would have been someone with a truck, right? Or access to one?"

"Exactly. No one in particular comes to mind, but I feel certain Theo was behind it." Aunt Fran stirred her tea absently. "He had a way of making people feel obligated to him. One of his employees could have done it on the threat that he'd lose his job if he didn't."

A furry form surprised Lara by springing onto her lap. Munster rubbed his orange face against hers, his tail almost dangling in her tea.

"Hey, I don't need you stirring my tea, or getting scalded," she teased him, pulling him out of harm's way. She pushed her mug farther back. The cat issued a loud purr and settled in her lap.

"I feel sorry for anyone who worked for Barnes," Lara said. "Didn't you say Heather Weston did at one time?"

"Yes, she did clerical work for him. Hated it. And you might be interested to know that he once tried to retain your old friend Gideon Halley to represent him in a suit against one of his lumber suppliers."

Lara felt her cheeks grow warm. She wanted to protest that Gideon wasn't her old friend—only a former classmate. But that would be a lie.

Tiger Lara. She'd almost forgotten Gideon's childhood nickname for her. He'd gotten it from *Peter Pan*, in which a character, a loyal friend to Peter, was named Tiger Lily. Lara's red hair had prompted the nickname. It sure beat Carrot Top or Red Baroness, which is what other kids called her.

Should she tell her aunt that she'd seen Gideon at the coffee shop earlier? No, it wasn't important, she decided. It wasn't likely she'd see him again, so why bother?

"Tell me about the claim," Lara said.

"It was a frivolous one, and Gideon politely declined to take the case. Theo never forgot it. He bad-mouthed Gideon all over town, told everyone what a sleazy lawyer he was. When he realized he was only making himself look foolish, he finally stopped. Gideon took it all in stride, of course."

"Hey, anyway," Lara said, anxious to change the subject. "What I started to tell you before is that...well, the cat I saw in the field today was Blue. That's why I was so determined to follow her." She didn't know why she was hesitant to say the cat's name, but there it was. She'd said it.

Aunt Fran's jaw slowly dropped. She reached over and placed her hand over Lara's wrist. "Lara," she said quietly. "When you were a little girl, do you remember seeing Blue?"

"Of course! That's why I couldn't believe she was still here. Aunt Fran, it has to be her. She knows me. She recognizes my voice."

For a long moment, her aunt held her gaze. Her voice was gentle. "Lara, I want you to listen to me. When you were a girl, you were the only one who ever saw Blue. We—your mom, dad, and I—simply assumed she was your imaginary feline friend. She comforted you the way any child's imaginary friend would."

Lara felt a jagged lump lodge in her throat. "Wait a minute. Are you telling me you never saw her?"

Aunt Fran sat back in her chair. "That's right," she said. Lara started to object but her aunt held up a hand. "Think about this. Do you remember ever feeding her? Or brushing her?"

"I—" Lara began, but then stopped. "I guess I just assumed you did all that. I was a kid, Aunt Fran. Adults took care of stuff like that."

Didn't they?

Her aunt's smile was achingly sweet. "But you fed my other cats, didn't you?" she pointed out. "Every day after school you gave them a treat. You made sure their water was fresh."

Okay, wait a minute, Lara thought. *This is crazy. Blue was never imaginary. She was a real, flesh and blood feline.*

She tried to remember a time when she'd held Blue, or stroked her lush fur.

She couldn't, except...well, there was that one night, when Lara was seven or eight, she'd given her mom some lip. In exchange, she'd lost her TV privileges for a week. Furious at her mom, she'd thrown a minor hissy, for which she was sent to bed early.

Lara had cried herself to sleep that night. At some point during the wee hours, she'd been awakened by a soft form pressing against her foot. When she'd sat up and squinted into the darkness, she'd realized that it was Blue. Lara had reached out to her, but the cat had remained still, calming Lara with her presence. Almost immediately Lara had drifted back to sleep, and in the morning Blue had been gone.

But she'd been there. She *had*.

She felt Munster stir. The cat yawned, hopped off her lap, and then padded over to check out the food dishes.

Lara pasted on a smile, but she knew it went flat. "You know, maybe you're right. Maybe it was Bootsie I saw with Darryl."

Aunt Fran nodded, but the worry lines in her kind face deepened. "You've been under a lot of stress, Lara. You uprooted your life to drive up here and help me. Look at all the work you've done in only a few days. Maybe it was too much all at once."

"I wanted to do it," Lara said testily, feeling her throat tighten. "Like I said before—I'm only twenty-seven. A little work isn't going to—"

A *ping* from her cell phone interrupted her.

Lara scooped up her cell. "It's Sherry," she said. "Excuse me for a sec." She tapped the text and read it, feeling the blood drain from her face.

Lara set down her cell phone and looked at her aunt. "Aunt Fran, you're not going to believe this. Glen Usher is dead."

Chapter 18

Lara read the text aloud to her aunt:

"'Police found Glen Usher dead in his car. Medication overdose. Possible suicide, cops not sure. Poor guy.'"

"Oh my," Aunt Fran said, touching her fingertips to her lips. "Poor Glen, indeed."

"I didn't know him at all," Lara said. "But I feel really bad about this. I can't help putting some of the blame on Barnes. He was the one who tossed Glen out of his apartment." She sent a quick text back to Sherry and set her phone on the table.

"That much is true," her aunt said, looking somewhat dazed by the news. She shook her head. "Keep in mind, though—Glen's had a long history of ill will with just about everyone in town. Wherever he went, he quickly wore out his welcome. Oh, listen to me—I'm already speaking of the poor man in the past tense."

But he is past tense, Lara thought, then scolded herself. What a terrible way to think of a person.

All at once, she felt immensely sad. She'd been in Whisker Jog barely three days. In that short span of time, two people her aunt knew had died— one violently. Lara was beginning to feel as if she'd brought bad luck to the entire town, not only to her aunt.

Her thoughts going back to Glen, she remembered what Mary had said about him.

"I forgot to mention this," Lara told her aunt, "but when I was at the crafts store today, I talked to Mary Newman. Let me tell you, that is one person who did *not* care for Glen Usher. In fact, she told me she wanted him thrown out of the classics book club. From what she said, it sounded like Glen had a major crush on her. He used to pass little notes to her with song titles written on them." She explained what Mary had said about songs with the name Mary in the titles.

Aunt Fran sat back in her chair. She looked troubled. "That bothers me, Lara. Passing silly notes might seem like an innocent thing. But if Mary told him to stop and he didn't, then he was crossing a line."

"I agree," Lara said. "I don't think she wanted Chris to find out, either. I think she was afraid he'd punch Glen in the teeth or something."

Aunt Fran was silent for a long time, then she pushed off her chair and took hold of her cane. "You know what's sad? Glen was actually a smart man. But somewhere along the way, his emotional growth got stunted. He never learned to be an adult or take on adult responsibilities. It was truly a waste of a good mind." Her eyes brimming with tears, she picked up her mug and started to inch toward the sink.

"Leave that, Aunt Fran." Lara quickly drained her own mug. "I'll wash it with the dishes."

"I'll do the dishes," her aunt said abruptly. "I'll have to do them after you're gone, won't I?"

Lara felt something akin to a boulder drop inside her stomach. "I…I know. Of course, that's true. But while I'm here, can't I do the chores? It'll give you a chance to rest your knees."

Aunt Fran turned and dropped back into her chair. She set down the mug and then covered her face with one hand. "Oh, God, I'm so sorry, Lara. I didn't mean to snap at you. I must sound like an ingrate."

"No, you don't," Lara said, fighting back her own tears. She went over and slipped an arm around her aunt's shoulders. "We're both on edge. My future is in limbo. A killer is still out there. I don't know how to help with the cats. I—"

"Lara, stop," Aunt Fran said. "Stop right now. You've done more for me in the few days you've been here than anyone has ever done for me. I will never be able to thank you for pulling me out of the dark hole I'd sunk into."

"But I've hardly done anything," Lara whined. *And there's so much more to do.*

"That's not true." She pointed at Lara's chair. "Sit for a minute. Listen." She held up one finger. "Can you hear it?"

Reluctantly, Lara sank back onto her chair. "What am I supposed to hear?"

"You tell me."

Lara was puzzled. What was her aunt talking about?

She closed her eyes, took in a deep breath. And another. She felt her aunt's gaze on her, but she kept her eyes shut.

After a minute or so, Lara realized something. Compared to only a few days ago, the house had the feel, the essence, of a real home. The cats were more relaxed, more at ease in their surroundings. Their coats were brushed, their dishes clean.

It was as if they knew they didn't have to compete for attention.

The sound she heard was peace. The contentment of a happy household.

Lara opened her eyes and looked at her aunt. "I think I get it," she said, her voice a choked whisper. "It's the way things are supposed to be."

Her aunt nodded. "That's right. And it's because of you."

Lara started to shake her head in protest when a slight movement caught her eye. A furry black face with a white 'stache was eyeing them from the doorway to the large parlor. His sleek body was taut, ready to flee at the slightest sound. How long had he been there?

The expression on her aunt's face told Lara she'd spotted him, too.

"I see it, but I can't believe it," Aunt Fran whispered.

Lara remained as still as she could. Aunt Fran's face shone with a mixture of awe and delight.

Minutes passed, and then Aunt Fran sucked in a breath.

Ballou took a step forward, then another. He'd crossed the threshold into the hallway adjacent to the kitchen.

"He wants to come in here," Lara said in a soft voice.

Aunt Fran nodded, her eyes fixed on the cat.

Still wary, Ballou moved a few steps closer to the kitchen. He craned his sleek black head around, peering toward the food bowls near the sink.

"I think he's hungry," Aunt Fran whispered.

Lara felt her heart race. She wanted Ballou to feel safe here, to know that he was loved. This was real progress.

Ballou made an odd *brrrpp* sound, then padded slowly into the kitchen. He shot a look at his human companions—just to be sure they planned to stay put. One wrong move and he'd probably flee the scene. But apparently he felt reassured, because he licked his lips and moved toward the nearest food bowl.

Lara and Aunt Fran both clapped soundlessly as they watched the cat gobble from the bowl of kitty kibble. The look of joy on her aunt's face warmed Lara's insides.

After he finished eating, Ballou licked one paw in preparation for a post-dinner bath. And then, as if suddenly remembering where he was, he turned, looked at the humans, and bolted from the room.

"He's going back upstairs," Aunt Fran said, laughter in her voice. "Oh, that just made my day. You're a miracle worker, Lara. I honestly believe that."

Lara smiled, but she didn't feel like a miracle worker. "I didn't do anything, Aunt Fran. He probably got used to my scent from secretly sleeping in my room—if that's what he's been doing. He must've been hungry enough to risk eating in our presence. By now he has to know we're not going to hurt him."

Aunt Fran sobered. "Look at us. Rejoicing over Ballou's progress when poor Glen died alone in his car. I wonder how long he'd been there."

"I don't know. Sounds like Sherry didn't know much, either. By tomorrow I'm sure the news will be all over town."

"Medication overdose," Aunt Fran said pensively. "I'm afraid it does sound like Glen might have taken his own life. The way he lived—he didn't have much of a future, poor fellow."

"Did he have any family?" Lara asked.

"None that I know of. His folks died when he was young. I don't think he had any siblings. Glen was the quintessential loner."

Lara insisted on doing the dishes. This time she wasn't taking no for an answer. She shooed Aunt Fran into the living room to watch TV for a while.

After the dishes were washed, Lara replenished the cats' food and water bowls. Fatigue was beginning to tug at her. If she flopped into her favorite chair in the large parlor, she'd probably conk out.

Instead, she went about the task of scooping the litter boxes. She was getting so that she could do it in her sleep. Tomorrow she'd change and wash all the boxes, leaving them freshly scrubbed for Aunt Fran.

Her aunt had obviously tried to place the boxes in strategic locations in the house. Not easy, especially since the cats avoided the small parlor. In addition, the layout of the lovely old Folk Victorian was deceiving. The rooms were small, if charming, leaving not much space to spread around the litter boxes.

For the second time that day, Lara walked a bag of trash out to the barrel next to the house.

The October sky was cloudy, the moon hidden. Dampness clung to the air.

The sharp, sudden cry of a small animal rent the air. It came from the vacant field, not far from where she'd tripped over the rebar. Lara felt her pulse spike.

She prayed it wasn't a cat she'd heard. Was Goldy still missing? As far as she knew, no one had reported spotting her. Lara reminded herself to check her tablet once she got back inside the house.

She was scurrying up the porch steps when she heard the cry again. She turned and stood stock-still. Wendy had said that the cat knew her name. Lara cupped her hands around her mouth and called, "Goldy."

Her only response was the toot of a car horn somewhere in the distance.

Lara sagged. She called Goldy's name several more times. Finally, she trudged back inside and heated some water for cocoa.

Chapter 19

Aunt Fran was watching a program on PBS—something about the Egyptian pyramids. Dolce lay curled in her lap, snoozing.

"I wondered where you were," Aunt Fran said.

Lara explained what she'd been doing outside. "I put on some water for cocoa. You'll have some, right?"

"I'll pass," her aunt said. "I don't need to be up all night."

"Right. Gotcha."

After a few minutes the kettle whistled. Lara made herself a cup of instant hot chocolate and returned to the large parlor. She held the mug close as she sipped the chocolatey liquid. With cats all around, she didn't want to risk scalding any of them. Munster, especially, was famous for coming out of nowhere and leaping onto her lap.

Callie and Luna were nestled in their favorite spot on the carpeted tree. When Lara looked up, she noticed one of them observing her curiously. It was Callie—the more long-haired of the pair.

"Talk to her," Aunt Fran said quietly.

Smiling, Lara spoke to Callie, keeping her voice soft and singsong. "Sweet Callie," she murmured. "Will you let me hold you one day?"

Callie perked her ears, then leaned against her sister, Luna. *Not today*, she seemed to be saying.

"She will, one day. I feel sure of it." Aunt Fran closed her eyes and leaned her head back, setting the remote on the edge of her chair. "I'm going to rest my eyes for a few."

Lara smiled and slid the remote off the chair arm. Her aunt looked so peaceful. Lara turned down the sound on the television, taking a moment to study her aunt. Even at—what was she, fifty-six?—she still looked so youthful, so attractive. As a younger woman, Aunt Fran had reminded Lara of the actor Audrey Hepburn. Slender, with stunning green eyes, high cheekbones, and the warmest of smiles.

Sometimes Lara forgot that her aunt had been married once. From the few pictures Lara had seen, Brian Clarkson had been lanky and athletic, with straight blond hair and a mischievous grin. Her aunt was twenty, a junior at UNH, when she and Brian had eloped during spring break. Brian, who'd already earned his master's, was teaching middle school in a town near the UNH campus.

The happy couple had been married only eight months when Brian stopped one day on his way home from school to help a stranded motorist. It was one of those icy, snowy, blustery days, when the windchill made it feel like twenty below. Brian had stepped out of his car on Route 108 and had begun trudging toward the disabled vehicle. He never made it. A tow truck, whose driver claimed he hadn't seen Brian until it was too late, slammed into him, killing him instantly.

Her aunt never talked about Uncle Brian, at least not in Lara's memory. Lara's dad was the one who'd told her the sad story, when she'd asked once why Aunt Fran had a different last name.

Did Aunt Fran ever think about her husband? Did she ever ponder what her own life would've been like if Brian's hadn't been tragically cut short?

Surely she did, at least once in a while. Oddly, there were no photos of Brian displayed in the house. Lara suspected Aunt Fran had tucked them away in a private place, along with the shards of her broken heart.

Lara was itching to get her hands on the art supplies she'd bought earlier in the day. The watercolors were calling to her, begging her to paint Blue.

She looked over at her aunt, who was dozing peacefully in her chair. Lara gulped back the dregs of her cooling hot cocoa, delivered her mug to the kitchen sink, and dashed upstairs. She retrieved her Jepson's bag from her closet, where she'd tucked it for safekeeping. At the last minute, she remembered to grab her tablet, too.

The kitchen table was the perfect place to spread out her art supplies. Lara set up her palette, brushes, and two cups of water. She carefully tore a sheet of 140-pound paper from the pad she'd bought. Luckily, she'd remembered to buy masking tape, which she used to line the edges.

If she'd tried, she couldn't have stopped the grin she felt forming on her face. Using one of her pencils, she made a light sketch of Blue's head and chest. Next, she dipped a fine-tipped brush into water and drew the outline of the cat.

From there, she filled in the colors, using a blend of black and brown paint to depict Blue's chocolate-toned face. It took several tries to get the hue just right, but she was pleased with the way it came out.

Blue's eyebrows and body were a lush cream color. Lara had bought a small tube of white paint, and she squeezed a tiny amount onto a sheet of scrap paper. She gradually added touches of gray and brown, until she got the shade she wanted. When she painted at her studio apartment in Boston, she used a tile to blend colors. For now, she'd have to improvise. It hadn't been practical to buy a full set of watercolor supplies, especially since she had no idea how long she'd be in New Hampshire.

To depict Blue's stunning eyes, Lara dipped her brush in the aquamarine paint. She tried several color blends, using miniscule amounts of yellow and green to enhance the blue. She'd have preferred having a photo to work from, or even the real cat.

Yeah, right.

Aunt Fran didn't believe there was a real Ragdoll cat. And Lara was beginning to wonder if Blue existed only in her imagination.

Lara worked until her eyes watered. She was more tired than she realized. After she finished, she sat back and examined her results.

She'd captured the gorgeous feline perfectly, right down to the serene, inscrutable expression in her azure eyes. Nonetheless, she wasn't totally thrilled with the result.

Lara jumped when she heard the tap of her aunt's cane on the linoleum floor behind her. Aunt Fran came around the adjacent side of the table and sat down. She set aside her folded newspaper. Her sharp eyes perused every square inch of the painting.

"Well done," Aunt Fran said in a guarded tone. "It's nice to finally see one of your watercolors."

"Thank you," Lara said. "I was going a little crazy without my art supplies. It feels good to put color to paper."

"What kinds of things do you normally paint?" Aunt Fran asked. "I assume you don't always paint cats."

"You're right." Lara smiled. "Although I do try to incorporate cats into my watercolors, even if they're not the focus of the painting." She looked over at her tablet. "Here, let me show you some examples."

Lara pulled her tablet over and brought up a file she'd labeled "Gallery." The file contained three of her watercolors that the owner of an art gallery on Marlborough Street in Boston had agreed to display. "They're a bit pedestrian for my clientele," he'd told her smugly, "but you never know—they might appeal to a collector who goes for that sort of standard Boston backdrop." He'd given her a patronizing smile and hung the watercolors in a far corner of his gallery, away from most of the foot traffic.

"This is the first one," Lara explained to her aunt. "You probably recognize it—it's Boston's City Hall. Some people hate the design. Over the years, there's been a ton of controversy over it. But I've always loved the stark lines of raw concrete, and the wide plaza that seems to stretch endlessly." Lara felt herself getting animated. "Anyway, this is my favorite part." She pointed to the lower right corner of the painting, enlarging it on her tablet.

Aunt Fran beamed. "Oh, Lara, I see what you've done. It's marvelous. Absolutely enchanting."

At the lower edge of the painting, a family of three dressed in Puritan garb—father, mother, and young daughter—gazed in sheer wonder over the vast brick plaza. They looked as if they'd emerged through a time warp into modern-day Boston. The child, a girl of about seven, had one arm clasped around a striped orange tabby. Her other hand was encased firmly inside her mother's.

"I wanted to convey the awe that the early settlers would feel if they saw Boston today. It's a concept I've been toying with for a long time. That's why it's so important to get their expressions right. I want all their hopes and fears and dreams to be reflected in their eyes."

She swiped her finger over the tablet and brought up the other two watercolors. Each depicted a different Puritan family—plus cat, of course—one peering up at the towering glass face of the John Hancock Tower, the other gazing over the reflecting pool at the Christian Science Center.

"So, what do you think?" Lara said gingerly.

Aunt Fran's eyes filled. "I think," she said softly, "that my niece is a supremely talented artist with a shining career ahead of her. I'm simply blown away by these paintings."

Lara pushed back her own tears. She was surprised at how much her aunt's praise meant to her. "Thank you. That means a lot. Problem is, no one's shown any interest in these particular paintings. At least as far as I know. Anyway, I have scads of other watercolors. Sometimes people text me pictures of their kids, or dogs, or families, and I paint from those. I've sold a bunch of them online, but the shipping is kind of a pain. Some customers want to buy them framed, so I have to arrange for that, too. *Plus*, I have to work at the bakery to keep my rent affordable."

Aunt Fran looked somber. "And then you have to contend with a grumpy aunt with bad knees and a house teeming with cats. It's too much."

"Grumpy aunt?" Lara shrugged with exaggerated nonchalance. "I'm sorry, but I don't have one of those. To *whom* might you be referring?"

Her aunt smiled, but her eyes were serious. "I think, Lara, that it's time we discussed your return to Boston. Don't you agree it would be best for both of us if we set a date? That way there aren't any ifs or maybes."

Lara pushed aside her tablet and sighed. When she'd driven to Whisker Jog on Wednesday, she'd figured it for a two-day trip at best. She hadn't intended to fall in love with her hometown again. She hadn't intended to get so attached to her aunt—and to the cats.

And she hadn't anticipated finding Blue, who seemed to pop in and out of the scenery like a prop in a play.

She leaned her elbows on the table, cupping her chin in both hands. All her best efforts at giving the house a thorough cleaning had been stalled by one thing or another—mainly Barnes's murder.

Tomorrow is the day, she decided. If she could whip the house into some semblance of order, she'd feel that much better when she had to leave.

Beyond that, she didn't have much of a game plan. Maybe she needed to choose a weekend every month to spend with Aunt Fran and keep the house in decent shape? That way Aunt Fran could plan, too. During each visit, Lara could buy a month's worth of groceries and cat supplies, and get the house all spiffed up.

In the morning, she'd propose it to Aunt Fran.

Unfortunately, her aunt's knee problems weren't going to resolve themselves. Somehow, she had to persuade her aunt to have the surgery she needed.

Lara was packing up her watercolors when she spied a portion of the headline in the newspaper her aunt had brought into the kitchen.

"Aunt Fran, may I see that paper?"

With a baffled look, her aunt gave it to her.

Lara unfolded it and stared at the caption over the article above the fold: *TRUCK ROLLOVER CAUSES MAJOR JAM.*

She read the article quickly, interested only in the major points. On Thursday morning, a trailer truck had jackknifed across the Everett Turnpike in Nashua, creating a massive traffic backup. The driver had escaped with minor injuries, but the traffic jam had extended over the Massachusetts border for nearly twenty-two miles.

An aerial photo of the traffic backup showed a stretch of cars at a standstill behind a semi that rested diagonally across the highway.

Thursday.

That was the same morning Josette Barnes claimed she'd *sailed up the Everett Turnpike like she had wings on her car.* If that were true, her car would've needed *real* wings, not metaphorical ones.

Lara gave her aunt a brief account of what Josette had told her and Kellie at the beauty salon.

"I don't know, Lara. I hear what you're saying, but I simply can't see Josette killing Theo. The woman doesn't have murder in her bones— I'm sure of it."

Maybe, Lara thought. But the story Josette had related of her magical night with her "beau" was beginning to seem more like a fairy tale than a true account.

"I forgot this part," Lara added. "She told me she'd been wanting to talk to you about something. That she planned to stop by some day and see you. Do you have any idea what it might be about?"

"Not a clue," her aunt said. She looked at Lara and smiled. "I guess I'll find out when she gets here."

Lara tapped her fingers on the table. "What about Glen Usher? Could he have had, well, 'murder in his bones,' as you put it?"

Aunt Fran's face clouded. She shook her head. "Glen was more like a child than an adult. Intelligent, yes. But emotionally he was disorganized and immature. I can't imagine him arranging a secret meeting with Theo. It would've taken planning, and Glen wasn't a planner."

Lara sat up straighter in her chair. "Then I've made a decision. I'm not leaving Whisker Jog until Barnes's murder has been solved." She reached over and squeezed her aunt's hand. "I'm not leaving you here with a killer on the loose."

Chapter 20

There was something about the clusters of lilacs on the wallpaper that made Lara smile every time she walked into her bedroom. Well, her bedroom in Aunt Fran's house. The periwinkle flowers, trailing along slender green stems against a pale yellow backdrop, summoned a host of warm memories.

How many nights had she slept in this room as a kid? One hundred? Five hundred?

She chuckled when she saw Izzy and Pickles. The pair lay sprawled atop her chenille bedspread, their furry calico forms stretched to maximum length. Izzy looked up sharply at her, then began licking a paw. Lara pictured a thought bubble above the cat's head. *Don't even think of dislodging us 'cuz it ain't happening.*

Lara laughed. "Don't worry, you calico cuties, I'm not going to kick you off the bed. But you have to leave a little room for me, you know."

She toed off her boots, plunked the bag with her watercolor supplies on her bureau, and scooted onto the bed with her tablet. Remembering that her cell was in her jacket pocket downstairs, she made a mental note to charge it before morning.

Lara managed to twist her body around the cats until she found a comfortable position. "Come on now, guys. We have some Googling to do."

It took only seconds to bring up a link to the "Midnight Mary" song. As she'd guessed, it dated back to the sixties. The lyrics intrigued her.

The song was about a teenage boy in love with a girl named Mary. Mary's father disapproved of him, so he and his beloved Mary had to meet secretly. They always met at the same place—and apparently always at midnight.

It made Lara wonder—did Glen fantasize about secretly meeting Mary Newman? She was a lovely woman, if a bit naïve. Had he spun daydreams in his head about being with her? Had he believed he had a shot at wooing her away from her husband?

Aunt Fran claimed Glen wasn't a planner, but Lara had her doubts. What if the note had been Glen's cryptic way of asking Mary to meet him at midnight? Since the note didn't say where, it suggested that Mary knew the meeting place.

The thought sent a chill down Lara's spine.

And yet...Lara couldn't imagine Mary having anything to do with Glen. She'd already expressed her distaste for him. What had she said? *Glen has to go. Or I will.*

A weird thought sneaked into Lara's head. What if Mary had agreed to meet Glen at midnight, but sent her uncle Theo instead? According to Aunt Fran, Barnes had adored his niece. Could Mary have recruited her uncle to put a good scare into Glen? Tell him to quit bothering Mary or else?

Possibly.

If it were true, it meant Glen had come prepared. Whoever had met Barnes that night behind the park bench had already filched the hoe from the side of Aunt Fran's shed. Why would Glen do that if he'd thought he was meeting Mary?

Lara yawned. She needed to sleep on all those unanswered questions. Her feline-covered bed was calling. Tomorrow promised to be a busy day.

She noticed that the battery power on her tablet was running low. Before she stuck it into the charger, she took another peek at Sherry's Facebook page. Unfortunately, no one had reported seeing Goldy, the missing cat.

Poor baby. Please be safe.

* * * *

After breakfast with her aunt the next morning, Lara set about doing a thorough cleaning of all the rooms. Aunt Fran's trusty Hoover was old, but it sure sucked up the dust and cat hair.

Lara even ran the vacuum-cleaner attachment over all the curtains, both downstairs and up. She wanted to launder, press, and rehang them, but she'd have to tackle that task when she could devote an entire day to it.

By twelve thirty, she was tired, achy, and hungry. Her jeans were dusty. Her hair felt grimy.

"I don't know about you, Aunt Fran," Lara said, flopping onto a kitchen chair, "but I am officially starving. How about I pop down to the coffee shop and pick up a few BLTs for us? I'm in the mood for some of Daisy's creamy potato salad, too. Unless you'd like to join me and pay Sherry and Daisy a visit?"

Aunt Fran had spent the morning going over old invoices and correspondence that had collected on her desk. She'd hoped to dispose of most of it, keeping only what was current. Lara was pleased to see she already had a large stack ready for the recycling bin.

"Honestly, I'd love to come with," Aunt Fran said. "But my internal engine is sputtering a bit today. I think I'll stretch out and read for a while. Would you mind getting mine to go? You can sit and visit with Sherry for a while and enjoy your lunch there first."

Lara wanted to protest, but saw that it would be futile. Besides, she didn't want to press her aunt into doing something that would put extra strain on her knees.

Her dwindling debit account was another matter. By now it was hovering close to the danger zone. She had a small savings account from which she could borrow, but crossed her fingers that it wouldn't come to that.

"Okay. That sounds like a plan," Lara agreed. She rose from her chair and went over and plopped a light kiss on her aunt's cheek. "But I won't stay long, I promise. I just need a little break, okay?"

"I think you've done enough work today," her aunt chided lightly, a smile on her face. "When you get back from lunch, why don't you do more of your watercolors? I can tell you're itching to get back to it."

Lara glanced outside the kitchen window. "Not a bad idea," she said. "It does look nice out today. Maybe when I get back, I'll bring my pencils outside and do some sketching. I often sketch a scene before I paint a watercolor of it."

She grabbed her jacket from the front hall closet. Something tickled her brain—something she was supposed to do. She reached into the pocket and groaned. *Darn.* That was it—she'd forgotten to charge her cell. And she'd even made a mental note to do it!

With only a 12 percent charge left on the battery, it wasn't worth taking it with her. "That's what I get for leaving it in my pocket," she grumbled to herself.

Lara went into the kitchen, where she'd left her charger. She plugged the phone into the wall socket and set the cell phone on the Formica table.

Her aunt smiled at the phone. "Do I need to watch it?"

"No." Lara crinkled her brow and smiled at her aunt. "Aunt Fran, you don't have a cell phone, do you?" she asked.

Her aunt held up her hands and shrugged. "No, I don't. I figured it was one more thing I didn't need to pay for."

Hmm, Lara thought. Aunt Fran lived alone with two bad knees and a slew of cats as roommates. What if she fell and couldn't reach her landline? Who would call 9-1-1?

It was something she should probably talk to her about before she headed back to Boston.

She went upstairs to her room, where she removed her grimy jeans and her ancient, pill-dotted sweater. She dumped them both in a pile for the wash and pulled out a fresh pair of jeans. From her suitcase, she dug out a clean top, which just happened to be a floaty lavender tunic with flared sleeves and a lacy-edged hem.

She knew it was silly, but it made her feel better to gussy up a bit. She brushed her hair and put on her dangly parrot earrings.

Lara twirled once in the mirror. Not exactly the height of fashion. But it was better than what she'd been wearing when she'd been cleaning the house.

She strode along the sidewalk toward the coffee shop, the sky a crisp blue under a bright lemon sun. The distant hills, their brilliant autumn glow mostly a faded memory, still made for an impressive backdrop.

Her pace slowed as she reached the building that housed the coffee shop. Something caught in her throat—a mixture of pain and joy. She choked back a sudden rush of tears.

I wish I could stay longer, she thought. *But I have a job. I have obligations.*

She sucked in a lungful of air, hoping to cleanse away the melancholy. Then she smiled—was that a whiff of Daisy's sugar cookies she detected? She increased her stride a bit.

When she passed before the façade of Kurl-me-Klassy, she halted. She spotted the bubbly Kellie Byrd through the storefront glass, fussing over the head of a petite, white-haired woman. Lara knocked lightly on the window and waved to the stylist.

Kellie jerked her head toward the window. When she spied Lara, she opened her mouth and closed it again. Only after several seconds did she nod and offer a halfhearted wave. She turned back to her elderly customer without another glance.

Lara frowned. Had Kellie just given her the cold shoulder?

No, she'd probably imagined it. She pulled open the door of the coffee shop, her mood lifting instantly.

"There she is!" Sherry shrieked from behind the counter.

Lara cringed. She adored Sherry, but sometimes her friend could be a bit too boisterous with her greetings.

"Hey," Lara said, sliding onto a stool at the counter. She was grateful to see that the cranky Mr. Patello was absent today, as was his friend Herbie.

"Everyone's been talking about Glen," Sherry hissed, leaning toward Lara. She poured her a cup of coffee and shoved a bowl of half-and-half packets at her. "What do you want for lunch?"

"BLT on toasted wheat with a side of potato salad. Pack up another one exactly like it for Aunt Fran. And don't skimp on the potato salad."

"Yeah, like I would," Sherry said tartly.

"So, what are the police saying?" Lara prodded.

Sherry shook her head. This time she spoke quietly. "They think Glen might have overdosed on his own heart medication. *On purpose.* No one's exactly come out and said it yet, but I heard Chief Whitley muttering something to the state police guy when they were paying for breakfast this morning."

"But…don't they still need autopsy results?"

"Of course, they do. But I heard the state police guy say they wanted to wrap this one up fast. Having an unsolved murder on the books is bad for the cops, bad for the town. If they can pin it on Glen…?" She lifted her shoulders in a theatrical shrug.

"Wait a minute. Are you saying the police think Glen killed Theo?"

Sherry nodded. "Yup. I'm almost positive that's what they were saying."

Lara still felt skeptical. "I can't believe they want to just *pin it* on someone, Sher. I mean, wouldn't they want the real murderer caught?"

Sherry leaned forward and spoke out one side of her mouth. She reminded Lara of a spy from the 1940s. "Here's the thing. They found a note in Glen's car. I don't know what it said, but I think it was a confession. It was written on one of our napkins—he did that all the time. He was always walking out with handfuls of them, poor slob. He was kind of a hoarder, you know? His car always looked like an explosion in a candy factory, with wrappers and half-eaten junk all over the place."

A napkin? *Interesting*, thought Lara. The "Midnight Mary" note had been written on a napkin. Or torn off from a napkin, anyway. It was still in her wastebasket back in her bedroom. She'd have to check it out when she got back to her aunt's.

Her coffee was cooling. She plunked a container of half-and-half in it and stirred, her thoughts jumping around in her head like grasshoppers.

Had Sherry heard the police correctly? Had Glen written a napkin note confessing to Barnes's murder?

Glen definitely had motive. Barnes had tossed him out of his dreary apartment with barely a day's notice. How humiliating to be living out of his car, especially when he was nursing a bad crush on Mary.

Of course, there was always another possibility. What if Sherry had heard it all wrong? It was easy to misinterpret something when you were eavesdropping on a private conversation. If that were the case, the police would still be looking for the killer.

Lara was mulling this over her first sip of coffee when she felt someone's gaze on her. She looked up to see a man sitting in the far corner of the coffee shop grinning in her direction.

Oh, God. It's him—Gideon Halley.

Should she acknowledge that she saw him? Or should she pretend she couldn't see that far?

Or should she act like an adult instead of a teenager and wave to her old friend?

She flashed a smile and waved to Gideon. He held up one finger, signaling that he was coming over to see her. Within seconds he'd closed his laptop, stuck it in his sporty canvas briefcase, and wended his way over to Lara. He looked spiffy in a business casual sort of way. Neatly pressed charcoal chinos, crisp tan shirt under a hunter-green sweater. Was that a typical fashion ensemble for a country lawyer?

Lara felt her heartbeat rev up.

Gideon slid onto the stool beside her, his chocolate-brown eyes beaming. "My word, it's good to see you again," he said, his voice deep and resonant.

"You saw me yesterday, remember?"

"I know, but I didn't have time to greet you properly. Lara, you look fantastic."

Lara felt her mouth widening into a clownish grin. Could she look any dopier? "It's great to see you, too, Gideon. How've you been doing these days?"

"Doing great," he said. "Hey, can I give you a hug?"

A flash of warmth flooded Lara's face. "Um…well, sure, why not."

Gideon reached over and slipped an arm around Lara, his briefcase clutched in his hand between them. The hug was quick, but warm and sweet. "Hey, sorry I couldn't stop to chat yesterday, but I was running a tad late for a client meeting and had to hustle back to my office."

"No problem," Lara assured him. "So you're a lawyer now?"

"Yep," he said, without elaborating. "Tell me, what brings you back to Whisker Jog? Visiting your aunt?"

"Exactly." She saw no reason to mention the cats. "It's been a long time since I've been up to New Hampshire. I'm starting to get reacquainted with everything."

Gideon sat for a moment and stared at her. It almost seemed as if he couldn't take his eyes off her. "Lara Caphart, as I live and breathe," he finally said. "Or do you have another name these days?"

Was that a clever way of finding out if Lara was married? Oh, who was she to talk? She'd already sneaked a peek at his left hand. Bare, she was pleased to note. Not that it mattered.

"No, it's still Caphart." Lara took a swig of her coffee to hide her smile.

"You live in Boston now, right?"

"Correct. And don't go giving me that down-home, country-boy act, Gideon Halley," Lara said with mock severity. "Word on the street is that you're one heckuva sharp lawyer."

Gideon made a comical face. "Well, if it's all over the street..." He laughed.

Sherry sidled over and set Lara's luncheon plate in front of her. "Hi, Gid."

"Hi, Sher."

Sherry turned and scooted away before Lara could beg another coffee refill.

"Hey, look," Gideon said, "I can see I'm interrupting your lunch, and I have a client meeting at two to prepare for."

"On Saturday?"

He shrugged. "A lawyer's work is never done." He tugged at his left sleeve and glanced at his watch. Unless Lara was seeing things, it was a vintage Superman watch. "Are you...going to be in town for a while?" he asked her.

Lara felt herself droop. "I'm not sure. I'm trying to help Aunt Fran with a few things. I'm playing it loose, as they say."

"Okay, how about this? If you're still here on Monday, do you think you could squeeze in a lunch date with me? Well, I don't mean a date exactly," he added quickly, a faint blush tinting his cheekbones. "Just a—"

"I'd like that," Lara said, saving him from stumbling over his words. Some sharp lawyer he was. "We can catch up and chat about old times. I'll have to let you know, though."

"Oh, good. Great!" He looked oddly relieved.

Lara gave him her cell-phone number. Gideon handed her a business card and went on his way.

Sherry appeared magically at the counter, coffeepot in hand. She gave Lara a top-off.

"Were you eavesdropping?" Lara accused, trying to sound miffed.

"Get a grip," Sherry said, and then giggled. She looked all around, then leaned closer to Lara. With her other hand, she plopped a brown paper bag on the counter. "I think somebody liiikes you," she sing-songed.

Lara balled up a napkin and tossed it at her. "And I think somebody needs to mind her own business. You never told me you and Gideon were so buddy-buddy."

Sherry shrugged. "Hey, the man eats here at least twice a week. You want me to ignore him?"

"No," Lara groused. "I...assume the man in question is unattached?"

"As free as a young robin," Sherry confirmed. "At least, as far as I know." She squelched a smile, but then her expression turned sober. "Lara, let's get serious. Not kidding around anymore, okay?"

"Um, okay."

"How important is it that you go back to Boston? I mean, we have some wonderful art galleries in New Hampshire. I'm sure you'd be able to show your work in one of them. And think of how happy it would make Fran if you stayed in Whisker Jog."

"Are you trying to lay a guilt trip on me?"

If she was, it was working. More than Lara wanted to admit.

"That would be my normal M.O.," Sherry admitted. "But I've given it a lot of thought, and...you know what? I have to call it like I see it. You've been *so* in your element these past few days. You bop around to the stores like you've never been away. And I don't have to be at your aunt's house to see how much of a difference you've made in her life. It shows in your face. And you already found a hairstylist who does a great job with those ridiculously gorgeous curls you're always whining about."

"Yeah, well, I appreciate the compliment, but I'm not so sure Kellie wants me as a customer any longer. When I waved to her this morning through the window, she looked less than thrilled. She waved back, but it was like someone had to twist her arm to do it."

"Really? That's weird. Definitely strange for Kellie."

Sherry excused herself to help a customer who wanted to pay his tab. "Thank you, and have an awesome day!" she warbled to the man.

She turned back to Lara and lowered her voice. "Okay, where was I? Oh, yeah—Kellie. I'm, like, ninety-nine percent sure Kellie didn't snub you. Why would she?"

"Well, yesterday when Kellie was cutting my hair, Josette Barnes came in. I kinda sorta asked Josette if she was shocked about getting back to New Hampshire Thursday morning and finding out Barnes had been murdered."

Sherry winced. "She thought you were accusing her of offing him, right?"

"Not exactly. But she acted like I was trying to extract information from her."

"Were you?"

Lara thought to herself, and then groaned. "Oh God, I probably was. It just seemed like way too much of a coincidence that the man she despised was murdered on the *one* night she was out of town. Doesn't that strike you as weird?"

"I hear you," Sherry said. "But if I were you, I'd lay off with the questions. Josette's a sweetheart, in spite of being a ninny and marrying Theo Barnes. Let me tell you, she deserves every penny of that lump-sum alimony payment she'll be getting. I hope she gets it real soon."

"There's something else," Lara said. "Kellie told me she was being kicked out of her space by the end of the year."

"Yeah, we all are." Sherry gave her an incredulous look. "Mom and I told you about it, remember?"

"I remember. At the time, though, I didn't know Kellie. I gathered from what she said that she's seriously ticked off about having to relocate. She told me she hasn't found another place yet. It's stressing her out."

Sherry shifted her gaze around the coffee shop. Only two of the tables were occupied, and a sole diner sat reading a tabloid at the other end of the counter.

"Lara," she said in a low tone. "Maybe it would be best if you stopped asking questions. People can get the wrong idea, you know?"

"Wh...what?" Lara sputtered. "I can't believe you said that. First of all, I didn't ask Kellie anything. She volunteered the information. Second of all, I—"

"Calm down, Lara. I'm only saying that you're not with the cops, so let them do their *thang*, as they say, and find the killer on their own—if they haven't already. In my humble opinion, they have."

Lara stared down at her untouched BLT. She jabbed a fork into her potato salad and shoved it into her mouth.

Sherry waited while she swallowed. Finally, she heaved out a sigh. "Listen, Lara, I'm not trying to give you a hard time. Just think about what I said, okay? About Boston? The other stuff doesn't matter. The cops'll sort it all out."

Lara ate the rest of her lunch in silence, while Sherry busied herself rounding up dirty plates and utensils. She couldn't stop thinking about everything Sherry had said.

The other stuff does matter, she thought. It mattered that a man had been murdered. It mattered that no one had been arrested for the crime.

Unless Glen really had been the killer. In which case the matter should be closed.

If the police could prove Glen had murdered Barnes, it would wrap things up in a neat little bow. Her aunt would escape the cloak of suspicion. And Lara could focus on finding a way to help her care for the cats.

The cats.

Lara was going to miss them terribly after she left. Even if she paid her aunt monthly visits, she'd be thinking about all of them while she was in Boston. She'd miss their comforting presence. She'd wonder if Ballou was making progress. Sure, Aunt Fran would give her updates. But it wouldn't be the same as seeing it with her own eyes.

Lara's thoughts bounced to Blue. She wondered what Sherry would say if she told her about the reappearance of the blue-eyed kitty.

Best not to mention it, she decided. Not until she could somehow prove that her own eyes hadn't been playing tricks on her.

"You have this mysterious little smirk on your face," Sherry said. "Are you mulling over the possibilities of staying in Whisker Jog?" There was an unmistakable leer in her voice.

Lara swallowed the last chunk of her potato salad. "I was thinking about a lot of things," she said, avoiding eye contact with her friend.

At that moment, Daisy emerged from the kitchen clasping a white paper bag. She scooted around the counter to give Lara a hug. "These are for you, sweetie." She winked at her. "And there's plenty more where these came from, if you get my drift." She exchanged a sly look with Sherry.

"In other words, you're bribing me with cookies not to leave town, right?" Lara peeked into the bag and saw three pumpkin-shaped cookies coated with thick orange frosting.

Pumpkins. Why did that remind her of something?

"Oh my gosh, I bought a pumpkin for Aunt Fran the other day. I was going to carve it or paint a cat on it and put it on the front steps. I must've left it in the car!" Lara opened her tote and pulled out her wallet. "I'm paying today, for both lunches."

Sherry accepted the cash with a frown. "I'll cut you if you even attempt to leave a tip."

"Okay," Lara said, biting off a giggle. "But remember—you can't stay in business giving free food to freeloading friends."

"Thanks for the advice, and for the alliteration," Sherry said dryly. "I'll paint a sign that says that and hang it in the window."

They both glanced toward the coffee shop's front window. The "lost cat" signs were still taped to the glass—a grim reminder that the missing Goldy was still unaccounted for.

"No hot tips on Goldy's whereabouts?" Lara asked glumly.

"No. I was praying someone might recognize her from my Facebook post with the sketch you drew, but so far, *nada*." Sherry furrowed her brow. "I'm scared for her, Lara. That Wendy gal is going to be devastated if Goldy never comes home."

"I know. I'm scared, too, but let's not give up hope. Goldy still might turn up."

Daisy snagged a larger bag from underneath the counter and stuck Lara's cookies inside, along with Aunt Fran's takeout lunch. They all hugged, and Lara left.

Outside, Lara paused on the sidewalk. She was pondering her conversation with Sherry when a massive black car suddenly swerved out of a parking space, barely ten feet from where she stood. The car lurched toward the sidewalk, then quickly corrected its course. Lara squeaked out a cry and jumped back. She watched with dread as the car zoomed past her and sped toward the yellow light.

For one scary moment, she was sure the car was going to splatter the pedestrian who'd started to cross at the intersection. Luckily, the woman spotted the car in time. She skedaddled out of the way with only a second to spare, her short legs doing a broad jump to reach the curb.

Lara breathed out a sigh of relief, her heart fluttering in her chest. For several seconds she stood there, trying to calm herself as she watched the offending car fade into the distance. If she didn't know better, she'd think the vehicle had jet propulsion.

"Jerk!" yelled a fiftyish, heavyset man who'd been heading into the coffee shop. "Typical out-of-stater, right?" he growled to Lara. "Drives like he don't have a brain in his head." The man shook his fist at the receding black car and then disappeared into the coffee shop.

Out-of-stater.

The man had been right. Lara distinctly saw Massachusetts plates on the car as it motored like a demon through the light. She wasn't a car person, but if she had to guess, she'd say it was one of those big old Lincolns. Something out of the 1990s.

A thread of unease wound through Lara. She wasn't sure why, but she couldn't help thinking that the driver of the black car had been watching her before he took off. Unfortunately, through the car's tinted windows, Lara hadn't been able to get a glimpse of his face.

It was a man, though. She'd been able to tell that much from the profile. Lara shivered. She scurried over to the woman who'd come close to being picked off by the speeding car.

"Are you okay?" she asked. "That guy almost hit you!"

The pedestrian, a plump senior dressed in an orange tweed coat, cursed under her breath. "Yeah, I'm fine," she grumped, hoisting her purse onto her shoulder. "But did you see that creep? Nearly made vegetable soup out of me."

Given the colors in the woman's coat, it was an apt analogy. "Did you get a look at the driver?" Lara asked her. "We should probably report it to the police."

"Nah. Even if they catch him, what are the cops gonna do? Give him a slap on the wrist and send him home to his mommy?"

"The driver was young?"

"Yeah, a young punk. Dark glasses, crap hanging from the mirror. You know the type. Lots of 'em around these days. Too many, in my opinion."

Lara rubbed the arm of the woman's coat. "If you're sure you're all right—"

"Yeah, yeah. Thanks, anyways." The woman waved her off and started down the sidewalk. Then she turned and said, "Hey, thanks, lady. At least someone cares about us old people."

Lara smiled to herself. For sure, the woman was a character.

Forcing the black car out of her mind, she hurried back to Aunt Fran's.

Chapter 21

Lara slid the slender knife out of the fleshy face and set it down on a newspaper. *Messy job*, she thought, wiping her hands on a paper towel. *But it had to be done.*

"There, what do you think?" she asked her aunt. "Should I add a few more whiskers?"

Aunt Fran laughed. "Oh, no. It's perfect the way it is. Honestly, I've never seen such an adorable pumpkin. Look at that sweet face—you even made the cat smile."

"I wanted a happy cat, not a scary one," Lara said, examining her handiwork. "I don't like perpetuating the notion that cats are scary in any way." She lifted the pumpkin and picked off a stray dot of pulp. "Shall I put it out on the porch step?"

"Sure, go ahead. It'll be the best pumpkin in town."

"Halloween's in a few weeks," Lara said. "If I get to the store before I leave, I'll pick up some of those mini-lights that run on batteries. You definitely don't want to be sticking a lighted candle in there."

Aunt Fran's smile faded, and she looked away. She began using the newspaper to wrap up the guts of the pumpkin.

Lara knew what her aunt was thinking. By the time Halloween rolled around, Lara would be back in Boston. Gabriela would be doing a booming business with her orange-tinted cannoli and spider-web cakes. The bakery would be bustling, and Lara would have dishes piled up to the moon to wash. Her old life would reclaim her, made better by having reconnected with her aunt.

So why did the thought depress her?

Only three of her paintings—the ones she'd shown to her aunt—were hanging in an actual gallery. She still had her online business selling commissioned watercolors. She didn't get rich from it, but at least it gave her some pin money. If she dabbled more in social media, maybe she could gain more recognition for her work, which could translate to more customers. A win-win all around, if it worked.

The big problem was her living expenses. Even with the reduced rent she paid Gabriela, her budget was barely manageable. Boston was an expensive city in which to live.

Lara stepped outside, onto the porch. She set down the pumpkin on one side of the top step. *It really is cute*, she decided. She almost wished she'd gotten a second one.

She folded her arms and looked out over the yard. Dried leaves shifted in the breeze. A gray squirrel darted up the trunk of the maple tree.

But something was different. What was it?

The yellow crime scene tape—it was gone! Oh, what a relief. Was that a positive sign for the investigation? Had the police concluded that Glen Usher was Barnes's killer?

The sun was dipping lower. In another hour, it would be dark.

Lara headed inside. Aunt Fran was nowhere to be seen. *Probably resting upstairs*, she thought. For about the zillionth time since she'd arrived in town, she felt a surge of guilt wash over her.

The pumpkin innards were on the kitchen counter, wrapped loosely in layers of newspaper. Lara wasn't sure what her aunt wanted to do with them, but they'd make good eats for the small animals in the field. She carefully picked up the newspaper, put on her jacket, and then located her tablet, which she'd stuck in her tote that morning.

Her favorite spot in the crook of the big rock was calling to her. She needed to clear her mind, to sit alone with her thoughts where it was quiet and peaceful and serene.

But first she had to get rid of the pumpkin remains. She went over and stood at the crest of the hill, almost directly above the spot where she'd found Theo Barnes.

Lara unfolded the newspaper and shook it briskly over the downward slope. Chunks of pumpkin fell out in seedy orange globs. She grinned. The mice and chipmunks, if any were around, were going to have a literal field day.

She crushed the layers of newspaper into as tight a ball as she could, then carried it over with her to the rock. She dropped to the ground, pressing her shoulders into the rocky alcove. It took a bit of shifting, but eventually she found a comfortable position. With her legs stretched out in front of her and her tablet in her lap, she felt as if she'd found a bit of heaven. She tucked the newspaper under one knee to keep it from blowing away.

Firing up her tablet, she went directly to Sherry's Facebook page. She crossed her fingers, praying that someone had posted a sighting of Goldy.

A long string of comments appeared. Mostly they were heartfelt wishes that the missing cat would find her way home. Lara scrolled through all the comments, disappointed that no one had reported spotting the cat.

She studied the sketch she'd made of Goldy, enlarging it on the screen. Wendy had been thrilled with the likeness, Lara remembered. So much so that she'd expressed the opinion that Goldy would surely be found.

If only, Lara thought bleakly.

She leaned her head back and closed her eyes. Only a moment later, she felt a slight stirring in the air. When she opened her eyes, her heart did a pole vault over her ribs.

Sitting beside her on the right, staring at the sketch of Goldy, was Blue.

Lara stayed very still, almost frozen in place. "Blue," she whispered, in the tiniest of voices.

The gorgeous Ragdoll met her gaze, then returned to studying the image on the laptop. Blue's coat was fluffy and full, not tangled or matted. She looked as if she had been enjoying regular brushings, as well as hearty meals.

Lara's hand twitched. She desperately wanted to reach out with one finger and touch Blue's furry face.

She resisted the urge.

It struck her, now, that she'd never touched Blue. Even as a girl, whenever she'd tried to hold Blue, or even pet her, the cat suddenly wasn't there. It was her presence, more than her corporeal form that Lara had always felt.

How did I never notice that?

And then she heard a sound that warmed her to the core. The softest of rumbles.

Blue was purring.

That was new. Totally new.

It lasted only a moment. At the far corner of the field, near the spot where Lara had tripped over the rebar, a disturbance in the meadow caught her attention. A furry head poked through the grass, then sank out of sight. Something about the shape was decidedly feline.

Either that or Lara's mind had truly gone over the edge.

If it was Goldy, Lara needed to find her. The poor lost kitty would no doubt be ravenously hungry. Had she been prowling the field for a mouse?

Lara wished, now, that she'd thought to bring along some cat treats before she came outside.

Blue was still at her side when Lara set aside her tablet and rose from the ground. She gazed out over the meadow, thinking she spied movement again. When she looked down, Blue was gone.

Chapter 22

Dinner that evening consisted of warmed-over spinach lasagna, a hastily tossed salad, and some rolls Aunt Fran had located at the back of her freezer. The mood was subdued. Even the cats sensed it. Munster, who typically hovered at Lara's feet during meals, munched from one of the kibble bowls on the other side of the kitchen.

"So, it's definite then, right?" Lara said. "The police know that Glen killed Theo?"

While Lara had been outside with her tablet that afternoon, Aunt Fran had received a call from Chief Whitley. The police were officially concluding their investigation of Barnes's death. A note scrawled on a napkin and found in Glen's car had pretty much wrapped things up. There were still papers and miscellany from Barnes's home that they had to go through, but apparently that was just routine cleanup of the case.

"I wish I could see that confession note," Lara said without thinking. "Something about the whole thing reeks like a dead fish to me."

Aunt Fran gave her a quick look. She set down her fork over her half-eaten meal. "What are you saying? You think the police are wrong?"

Lara winced inwardly. She'd never told her aunt about the "Midnight Mary" note—it was still in her bedroom wastebasket.

What Lara would really like to do was to compare it to Glen's so-called napkin confession. Assuming he'd written it himself, the printing on the confession should be similar to the lettering on the note Lara had. But how could she persuade the police to let her see it?

She couldn't. Not unless she showed them her "Midnight Mary" note. Even then, they might say she was crazy. Either that, or they'd find it suspicious that she hadn't turned over the note to them. Although, at the time, Glen was still alive. The note didn't appear to be related in any way to Barnes's murder.

"I don't know, Aunt Fran," Lara finally said. "Something about the whole thing doesn't ring true to me." She poked at a lasagna noodle with her fork.

"I tend to agree. It's almost impossible for me to picture Glen bringing that hoe down on the back of Theo's head."

With a sigh, Lara pushed aside her plate. "Maybe I'd better tell you something."

As succinctly as she could, Lara explained the situation with the note on the torn napkin.

"I don't see that you've done anything wrong, Lara," her aunt said in her defense. "The note with the song title on it was between Mary and Glen. It had nothing to do with Theo."

Yeah, but what if Mary recruited her uncle to deal with Glen? And what if Glen then lashed out with a deadly blow after Theo read him the so-called riot act?

It was making her head hurt.

"You're probably right," Lara said, grateful for the moral support. "But now I'm wondering about the handwriting, or rather, the printing, on the confession note. The note with the song title on it is printed in pencil, in bold block letters. I would love to know what that confession looks like."

With a concerned look, Aunt Fran reached across the table and took Lara's hand. "Lara, stop beating yourself up. You picked up a discarded note in a parking lot. Period. It doesn't mean it was your obligation to solve a murder."

"I know."

It suddenly struck Lara that the common denominator in all of this was one person: Mary Newman.

Could the sweet, sensitive, adoring niece of the victim be a cold-blooded killer? Was it possible that Mary's blubbering over her uncle was nothing more than an act?

There could be any number of reasons why Mary might've wanted her uncle dead. Had the police examined Theo's estate-planning documents to find out who stood to inherit his assets? Did he have life insurance?

Mary had admitted she suspected her husband of being involved in something shady—something she thought her uncle had gotten him into. Lara wasn't sure how those erotic magazines came into play, but Mary had sure been anxious to get rid of them the day Lara had spotted her by the Dumpster at Jepson's.

What if Mary *had* killed her uncle? Glen might have seen her late that night—either as she was driving through town after the murder, or sneaking through the park after she'd killed Barnes. Mary knew he had a juvenile personality. He might have told her he'd seen her that night, and assured her it would be their little secret. At that point Mary would have known he was a liability.

It would've been easy for Mary to write a note on a napkin and leave it in Glen's car. If she'd knocked on his car window, he'd surely have opened the door for her. She could have smiled and played coy, saying she wanted to talk to him, then somehow managed to spike his coffee with his own heart medication.

Oh, Lord. That was all too much for Lara's brain to handle. She was an artist, not a cop. It wasn't her problem. She hadn't driven to New Hampshire to solve a murder. She'd come to help her aunt and the cats.

"Lara, I can see the wheels churning beneath that lovely new hairstyle," Aunt Fran said. "What are you thinking about?"

Lara rubbed the space between her eyes with her fingers. "What do you think about Mary Newman?" she asked. "She acts like such a delicate flower, but I suspect there's a vein of steel in her. Is it possible she killed her own uncle?"

Her aunt's brow furrowed. "I suppose, when you analyze it, she might have had motive. But really, Mary?"

"Do you think she's Theo's sole heir?"

"Probably. But remember what you told me—that Josette gets a chunk of his estate, too. The remainder of the alimony she's entitled to. Anything Mary inherits will be reduced by that amount."

"But I'll bet Theo was loaded," Lara said darkly. "Whether he earned it by honest means or not, I suspect he left behind a pretty hefty estate."

"Lara," her aunt said quietly. "Why are you doing this? I'm the first person to speak out when I see an injustice. And maybe there is reason to believe Glen didn't kill Theo. But you have to remember something—we don't know everything the police know. Whatever information we have is limited. Please, let them do their jobs, okay?"

The plea in her aunt's voice tore a hole in Lara.

The sudden roar of an engine made them both jump. A car had pulled into the driveway, its motor growling like a bear.

Lara leaped off her chair. She peeked outside, and her insides curdled. In the ambient light, she saw the outline of a behemoth car idling in the driveway. It looked like the one that had nearly picked off a pedestrian that afternoon near the coffee shop. Her own car, the rental, was parked on the opposite side. She'd purposely kept it out of the way in case any more police vehicles decided to pay a visit.

Lara thought about flipping on the porch light, but then nixed the idea. It might attract the interloper's attention—the kind of attention she definitely didn't want.

"Aunt Fran," Lara said, trying to keep her voice from rattling, "I don't want to alarm you, but there's a car here, and I'm pretty sure it's the same one I saw this afternoon after I left the coffee shop. The driver almost ran a woman down, and I witnessed it. Maybe you should go in another room while I get rid of him."

And hope he's not here to get rid of me.

Aunt Fran scraped back her chair. "Absolutely not," she said, latching onto her cane. "I won't put up with anyone coming here and threatening my niece." She rose, went to the window, and stood next to Lara. "Should I call nine-one-one?"

Lara felt her heart hammering. "No, honestly, Aunt Fran, this guy could be a nutcase. I really wish you'd go in the parlor and let me handle it."

Her aunt started to protest when the unwanted visitor suddenly doused his headlights and shut off his engine. Lara's mouth felt like a wad of cotton. Instinctively, she pushed her aunt gently to the side, away from the door.

The driver's-side door to the monster car opened, then slammed shut. A man got out. For a few moments, he paused and looked around, as if confused. Then he started walking toward the porch steps, clutching something in his hand. It looked like a box of some sort, tied with string or twine.

At least it isn't a gun, Lara thought. Unless there was a gun in the box.

Something about his shape was maddeningly familiar.

And then she got it.

Now he was climbing the steps.

Her blood reaching the boiling point, Lara flipped on the porch light and whipped open the door. The man jumped back and let out a startled squeal.

"Luca Calabrese! Get your butt in here so I can kill you."

Chapter 23

Luca stepped gingerly over the threshold, his expression a mixture of fear and defiance. "Okay, I know what you're gonna say, and I'm sorry! I'm sorry I scared you. I'm sorry I almost ran over that old lady." He glanced at Aunt Fran and blushed. "No offense."

"I don't know who you are, young man," Aunt Fran said in a voice that would send Godzilla packing. "But you need to sit right there, lower your voice, and explain yourself." Using her cane, she pointed at her vacated kitchen chair.

Luca clutched the box—a pink bakery box—to his black leather jacket and backed into her chair, dropping onto it sideways with a thud. He tossed back the lock of raven-black hair that dangled over his right eye.

"So you admit it," Lara said, seething. "You nearly ran down an elderly pedestrian." She'd save the stalking part for later. "By the way, Aunt Fran, this is Luca, my landlady's grandson. Luca, this is my aunt Fran."

The young man looked visibly rattled. For one crazy moment Lara thought he was going to burst into tears. "I didn't mean to," he muttered, pouting. "I just got so, like, freakin' ticked when I saw you huggin' that guy at the coffee shop."

Lara felt her jaw drop. Aunt Fran gave her a curious look.

"You were watching me? Through the glass?"

"Not exactly. Well, yeah, kinda, but not at first. I was gonna go in and ask someone for directions. I couldn't find the sign for High Cliff Road. Anyhow, I was halfway through the coffee shop door when I saw that guy with the briefcase huggin' you. Freaked me out, like, totally. You never said you had a boyfriend in New Hampshire." He gave her a hurt look. "Anyhow, I went back to my car and sat there, kinda just watchin'. When you popped out of the place, I was afraid you'd see me so I took off. I know I was going too fast. I...wasn't thinkin', I guess. Is that old lady okay?" he said, in a meek tone.

If Lara hadn't been a proponent of nonviolence, she'd have smacked him. Up one side and down the other.

"First of all, who I choose to hug is none of your business. *None.* Do you read me?" She pointed a finger between his eyes. "And by the way, that man asked for permission to hug me. He's an old friend I hadn't seen in ages."

Lara saw her aunt suppress a smile. Had she suspected it was Gideon who'd hugged her at the coffee shop?

"Okay, okay. I hear ya." Luca flushed to the tips of his ears and then plopped the pink box on the table. "Before I forget, Nana said to give you these. They're the macaroons you like, the ones with the sliced almonds."

"Tell her thank you," Lara said, itching to dig into the box. "But I'm not finished with you. Do you know that women do not appreciate being followed? Did you know stalking is a crime?"

Luca groaned. "Come on, Lara. You can't seriously call that stalking. I brought you cookies, didn't I? Besides, I was only doin' what Nana told me to do."

Very deliberately, Lara sat down opposite Luca and stared him down. "Are you telling me that Gabby asked you to drive all the way up here just to give me cookies?"

"Nah. She told me to drive up here to give you this." Luca unzipped his leather jacket and pulled out a large white envelope, folded in two. He tossed it on the table in front of Lara. "Nana thought it might be important, so she told me to bring it to you. And she said to tell you that she misses you, but to take all the time you need. All she cares is that you're comin' back."

That annoying lump filled Lara's throat again.

"Well, tell her thank you," Lara said raggedly. She looked at Aunt Fran, who was leaning on her cane, her sharp gaze focused on Luca.

Luca gave a quick nod and moved to the edge of his chair. Lara could see he wanted to bolt. "I better go. I told my buddy I'd have his car back by seven, so I'm, like, already—whoa! Hey there, little guy! Where did you come from?"

The look of surprise on Luca's face was nothing short of comical. Munster, who'd been lurking under the table, had apparently decided to check out this stranger.

"That's Munster," Aunt Fran informed him. "It appears you've made a friend."

Luca took Munster's head gently in both hands and gave him a good rub. "Dude, you are like, some cool cat. Aw man, I wish I had a cat like you." Lara smiled and shook her head. Luca loved cats?

Munster settled in Luca's lap and issued a steady purr. Lara felt her mood soften. "Hey look, Luca, I appreciate your driving all the way up here with the letter."

Luca shrugged. "Yeah, whatever. Nana thought it might be important. But would you do me a solid, Lara? Don't tell her about me almost runnin' down that old dame, okay? Otherwise I'll have to hear about it for the rest of my frickin' life."

"I won't, but I want you to think about what you did, Luca. That could've turned out bad. Seriously bad. You were lucky that woman had a little oomph in her step. She made it to the curb in the nick of time."

"I know." His face paled. "If you find out who it was I almost creamed, I promise I'll send her the biggest box of chocolates I can find, okay?"

Lara stuck out her hand. "Deal."

Luca shook her hand weakly, then stood with Munster clinging to his jacket. "Sorry, Munster, but I gotta split, okay?" He set the cat gently on the chair he'd vacated.

Aunt Fran had tottered over to the fridge and was fussing with something on the counter. "Wait just a minute, young man," she ordered. She handed him a bottle of water and a brown paper bag. "I made you a peanut butter and jelly sandwich for the road."

His eyes lit up. "Sh…oot, that's my fave. Thanks! Nana's always making me sandwiches with salami and prosciutto and stuff like that. I never get to just be a kid anymore."

And that said it all.

As for Aunt Fran—Luca had frightened them both half out of their wits, and she still sent him on his way with a snack.

Lara stood at the screen door, peering into the darkness. She watched as Luca backed his car carefully out of the driveway. This time he was driving about seven miles an hour.

"Well, at least I got my adrenaline rush for the day," Lara said wryly.

Her aunt sat down again. "He seems infatuated with you. How old is he?"

"Twenty-four. Going on sixteen." Lara rolled her eyes at the ceiling.

"Now, first things first." She snapped the string on the pink box and opened the lid. Inside was a batch of plump, golden-brown cookies graced with sliced almonds. Lara snatched one up and invited her aunt to do the same.

"God, how I've missed these," Lara said. "I swear, since I started working at the bakery, almond paste has become one of my favorite food groups."

Aunt Fran tested a cookie. "Delicious," she pronounced after she'd swallowed a bite.

"Okay, back to business," Lara said around a mouthful of her second cookie. She picked up the envelope and peered at the label. "Huh. It's from a Wayne Lefkovitz. Louisburg Square, Boston."

"Someone you know?"

"No, I have no idea who he is." Lara pulled on the tab and ripped it open. Inside was a one-page letter, printed in an elegant font on a sheet of pale gray stationery. Lara read it once, then once more—just to be sure she hadn't misread it. A twinge of excitement rushed through her.

Her aunt read her face and smiled. "Good news?"

"It's...unbelievable news. Remember the pics of the three watercolors of Boston I showed you? Well, this man apparently saw them in the gallery where they're on display. He wants to buy them, but only on the condition that I paint three additional watercolors with the same theme. He wants to choose which Boston landmarks he'd like me to paint. Apparently he's a private collector with his own personal gallery." Lara jiggled in her chair. "Aunt Fran, look at what he wants to pay me!" She held up the letter for her aunt to read.

"Oh, Lara, this is fantastic news," Aunt Fran said, skimming the contents of the letter.

In his letter, Lefkovitz mentioned that he'd located Lara's address through her Web ste, since the gallery owner had refused to give him her contact info. Lefkovitz urged her to call him as soon as possible so that they could discuss details.

"I'm impressed that this guy took the time to write a letter and overnight it to me," Lara said. "He could just as easily have shot me an e-mail through my Web site."

"Personally," Aunt Fran said, "I think it's a sign of good old-fashioned courtesy."

"I'm going to call Mr. Lefkovitz and assure him that I will accept his offer. He seems anxious for me to start work on the paintings."

While she was thrilled about this latest development, she knew it added one more twist to her already jumbled plans.

* * * *

Lara climbed into bed that night, her mind like a clothes dryer tossing around ideas until they fell into a muddled heap. Izzy nestled into her neck, while Pickles tucked herself behind Lara's legs. She was floating into dreamland when a faint *brrrpp* drifted from under her bed.

Aunt Fran was right, she thought. Ballou had been finding refuge there. "Good night, Ballou," she called softly. "Always remember, you're safe here. Safe and loved."

Chapter 24

Feline cleanup was getting faster and more efficient with every passing day. Lara now had the litter box scooping/scrubbing detail down to a science, and could zip through it in under an hour.

Today was Sunday. The house smelled so much better than it had when Lara had arrived on Wednesday. She'd decided that, later today, she'd experiment with making her own air fresheners. If she could get her hands on some inexpensive cardboard cutouts and scented oils, she could make some that would look adorable—and smell nice at the same time. It would mean another excursion to Jepson's for supplies, but she didn't mind. It was her debit card that was screaming, *No, please! Not again!*

She had enough gas in her rental car to get back to Boston. That, at least, was a relief.

Shortly after she'd read Wayne Lefkovitz's letter the night before, she'd given the man a call. He'd been delighted to hear from her, and was anxious to give her a deposit on the newly commissioned artwork. Their verbal agreement firmly in place, he also promised to purchase her first three paintings from the Marlborough Street gallery.

Was her career finally taking off? Was her artwork going to gain some recognition? The idea thrilled Lara. It motivated her to get back to her painting, something she'd neglected for the better part of the week.

But something else was germinating in her brain.

That morning, when she'd cleaned the litter boxes in the closed-in porch at the back of the house, it had struck her that the space was rarely used. Aunt Fran preferred the large parlor—or the spot in front of her bay window in her bedroom—for relaxing with a book or watching television.

It is a shame, she thought. The porch had insulated windows and screens on one side, with a perfect view of the yard and the meadow beyond. It was ideal for enjoying summer breezes during the balmier months. In the colder weather, the heat that came from the old-fashioned floor grate infused the room with a cozy warmth.

The porch contained a folding card table and chairs, along with a vintage pullout sofa. It was a refuge of sorts for old furnishings that didn't fit anyplace else. The walls needed a paint job—a task that could be done in a day. The windows had plain white shades, and were devoid of curtains or valances. The dull, gray carpeting—the kind that used to be called indoor-outdoor—was worn in several spots.

But it had possibilities.

What if Lara fixed up the porch and turned it into a casual sitting area? On designated days, maybe between one and four, visitors could stop by and have tea and snacks while they visited with the cats. If her aunt served the refreshments free of charge, it wouldn't be a true eating establishment, like many of the new cat cafes that were springing up.

It would simply be a shelter. Stop by. Enjoy some treats. Bond with cats.

Adopt a cat.

Lara sighed. She knew it wouldn't be that easy.

Right now, Aunt Fran was deeply attached to all of her cats. Nonetheless, Lara felt sure she would allow the kittens, at least, to be adopted into loving homes. With the early days of winter nipping at their heels, it wouldn't be long before other cats that needed rescuing would come along. Feral or not, every cat deserved care and love.

Lara had to give it more thought, she knew, before she sprang the idea on her aunt. She'd first have to check the state laws for establishing a shelter. They'd also need to work with Aunt Fran's veterinarian to provide neutering and shots. Establish adoption fees. Devise a way to evaluate those who applied to adopt. They'd need a ramp to make it accessible to everyone. And a separate parking area to be set out.

Oh boy. It was a lot, now that she analyzed it. Would it be biting off more than they could chew? Could Aunt Fran handle it when Lara wasn't there?

Lara would be in Boston, but maybe she could find her aunt some help. Lara still intended to visit at least once a month. Instead of lugging art supplies back and forth, she'd buy more and leave them at her aunt's. If she could persuade Gabby to give her more flexible bakery hours, she might squeeze in an extra day in New Hampshire here and there.

The kicker was the generous fee she'd be getting from Wayne Lefkovitz. His offer had stunned her. It would be the most she'd ever earned from her artwork.

She could use a chunk of it to renovate the porch, and to pay any legal fees needed to establish the shelter. Lara grinned. She just happened to know a lawyer in town who might be willing to help.

But she needed to think. She needed to plan.

It couldn't be done all at once.

Grinning as if she'd discovered a vein of platinum in her aunt's yard, she scurried up the stairs to fetch her art supplies and her tablet.

* * * *

Lara considered setting up her workspace on the back porch, but then instantly rejected the idea. Munster, ever the considerate helper, would no doubt want to inject his artistic notions into her work. She pictured him jumping onto the table and sticking his paws in all the paints. For sure, he'd try his paw at painting something. He might even be a better artist than Lara, which would be truly embarrassing.

Chuckling at the mental image, Lara carried the card table from the back porch into the small parlor. She'd spent so many hours in that room when she was a girl. The cats, for some reason, rarely went in there, so it would be the perfect place to paint.

Aunt Fran had been unusually quiet at breakfast. She'd asked Lara if they could attend the Sunday noon service at Saint Lucy's, and, naturally, Lara had agreed. After that, her aunt had excused herself and headed upstairs to shower and get ready for church. Lara suspected she needed some private time, so she'd left her alone.

Today, Lara wanted to paint another watercolor of Blue. The first one had been good, more than acceptable. But today, after studying it in a different light, she found it lacking. She decided to start fresh.

New day. New painting.

She still wasn't sure the fluffy Ragdoll was *her* Blue. If she were honest with herself, she'd say it was unlikely. The new Blue was probably a descendant of the original one—a genetic doppelganger with ancient memories passed down from her kitty mom.

Lara set up her paints and brushes and got to work. She made a quick sketch of the cat, then began to fill in with color. It was coming along nicely until she began painting the ears. She wasn't getting the color right.

Darn! She wanted a rich chocolate brown, but the shade wasn't right—it was edging toward charcoal. She'd mixed in too much black.

From the tube of white paint, she squeezed a dot onto her blending plate. Normally, she would paint over the area she wanted to fix with the correct color. But because the spot where she'd used the wrong shade was so dark, she chose to lighten it first with white.

Lara was blending strokes of white paint into the too-dark ears when her hand halted. What was bugging her about it?

The white paint. She was using it to cover a darker color.

She was using it to hide the *wrong* color.

No. She was using it to hide the color she didn't want anyone to see.

Heart racing, Lara glanced around for her tablet. She'd left it on the red table where Darryl always read. She fetched it, and immediately brought up a Word document. The content didn't matter—she only needed it for experimentation. This one happened to be a recipe for linguini alfredo that Gabby thought she might want to try making one day.

She wasn't quite sure how to do it, but she wanted to change the font color—from the standard black to, well, any other color. Ah, the icon for font color was right there on the toolbar at the top of the page.

Lara used the "Control" key to highlight the text, then moved the mouse up to "Font Color." She clicked the mouse on "Red." The linguini recipe changed to red. She repeated the task, this time clicking the mouse on "White."

The linguini recipe disappeared.

Yes!

She knew the text wasn't really gone. The white text against the white background had made the recipe invisible.

This time she highlighted the text and changed it to "Automatic." The recipe reappeared in its original form.

She was sure, now, that that was what Chris Newman had done. He'd hidden whatever was in those documents by changing the font to white.

Lara closed the document and set aside her tablet, her mind racing. Should she tell Mary Newman what she'd learned? She had Mary's cell number.

What if Chris were my husband? Lara asked herself. *Would I want to know what was in those documents?*

With a sigh, Lara dug her cell out of her pocket. She sent a text to Mary, explaining what she'd figured out about the font.

It would be Mary's decision.

Chapter 25

Lara stretched her arms high over her head and then massaged the back of her neck. She was getting stiff from sitting for so long.

She hopped off her chair and headed for the kitchen. After pouring a glass of milk, she made up a little plate of Gabby's scrumptious macaroons. Bootsie strolled up next to her and rubbed against her leg. Her face breaking into a smile, Lara bent and stroked the kitty's head.

It was going to be hard, leaving the cats. In the span of a few short days, she'd gotten so accustomed to their comforting presence. How was she going to sleep without Izzy and Pickles wrapped around her like a furry tortilla shell?

Munching on a cookie, she couldn't help wondering if Mary had read her text yet. Lara prayed that whatever was in those documents would help ease the woman's fears.

Lara set down her milk. Cookies in hand, she strolled out onto the front porch. The day was turning out warm for October—almost sixty degrees. The sun was blindingly bright. She cupped one hand over her eyes and peered toward the shed. She pulled in a breath.

Something was out there.

And then she saw her. Blue was padding toward the house at a leisurely pace. She had a cat-that-swallowed-the-cream look, if Lara ever saw one.

Even more amazing, another cat was tagging along behind Blue. Lara almost choked on her cookie. It was Goldy—the missing cat!

As quietly as she could, she went back inside and nabbed some kitty treats from the kitchen. It took only seconds, but by the time she'd gone back outside, Blue was gone.

But Goldy was still there. The cat stared at Lara, and then gave out the most pathetic meow Lara had ever heard.

"Oh, sweetie, you're hungry, aren't you?" Lara asked softly. She descended the porch steps almost on tiptoe, fearful of spooking the cat.

Goldy backed up a step when she saw Lara ambling slowly toward her. Lara continued to speak soothingly, her voice almost a lullaby as she approached the cat.

And then she was there, and in the next instant Goldy was gobbling from her hand.

Lara gently wrapped her hands under the cat and lifted her to her shoulder. "I can't wait to call your mom," she told Goldy. She cuddled the cat to her chest.

She carried Goldy into the house and then into the small parlor. She quickly made up water and food bowls for her. While Goldy dived into the kibble, Lara called Wendy.

"I have a wonderful surprise," she told Wendy. "Goldy is here with me, and she's eating up a storm."

Wendy broke into sobs. "Oh, my God, thank you. Thank you! I'm going to name all my future cats—and kids—after you!" She promised to be there within ten minutes, as soon as she threw on some clothes.

Lara felt her eyes brim with tears.

Wendy made it in about eight minutes, cat carrier in hand. Her face tear streaked, she scooped Goldy into her arms and pressed her face into her fur.

"I don't know how to thank you," Wendy snuffled.

Lara laughed. "I don't want thanks. I'm as thrilled as you are that she's back. Just take good care of her, okay? Try to keep her indoors."

"That's a promise," Wendy said firmly.

They hugged, and Wendy nearly floated out to her car with Goldy.

Lara swiped at her eyes. She knew who deserved all the credit for bringing Goldy home.

A little Ragdoll cat with the bluest eyes she'd ever seen.

* * * *

A banging at the door jolted her.

Probably Wendy again, wanting to ask me something, Lara thought. She was so happy for the woman that she swung open the door without first peeking outside. Her knees morphed into rice pudding when she saw who it was.

"Oh, um, hi C-Chris," she stuttered, her pulse entering the final lap of the Indy 500.

Chris Newman stared at Lara through the screen. His face was pinched, his glasses tilted slightly on his nose. "I need to talk to you. May I come in?" *He's asking permission. That's a good sign, right?*

"Well, um, sure, although we're getting ready for church." Only a partial fib.

"This won't take long. I need to explain something."

It sounded innocent enough. Although...hadn't she read that the Boston Strangler drank coffee with one of his victims before he killed her?

Lara tried to keep her voice even, but she felt her hand tremble as she let him step inside. She stayed close to the door to prevent him from inching farther into the house. "What did you want to tell me?" she asked. Her voice came out like a squeak.

Chris's face crumpled, and his eyes got watery. "I caught Mary with my laptop this morning. Apparently, she'd gotten a text from you." Lara took a step backward, but he held up one hand. "Don't worry, I'm not mad. I'm glad it all came out. It's actually a relief to talk about it."

Lara swallowed. "To talk about what, Chris?"

"Those stories—I never wanted anything to do with them. Theo forced me to write them to make up for messing up his tax return!"

Lara spewed out the breath she'd been holding. "I'm sorry, Chris, but I still don't understand. What stories are you talking about?"

"The stories in that disgusting magazine." He gave Lara a bewildered look. "You saw them, right? Mary told me you did."

"I-I saw her throwing some stuff in the Dumpster in the crafts-store parking lot. I guess I caught a glimpse of one of the covers, but I never looked inside any of the mags." *The cover was revealing enough.*

His face a mask of anguish, Chris dropped onto the same chair Luca had occupied the night before. Lara considered renaming it the "hot seat."

"The stories," Chris said miserably. "They're erotic. Stories of men and woman falling in lust and love, getting torn apart, and then ending up back in love. You know, the ole happy-ever-after garbage but with more, you know, hanky-panky." His ears reddened. "It's the type of crap you see on TV soaps, only in much more salient detail. The mag claims the stories are true, but that's a crock. It's all a load of crap dreamed up by writers like me."

Lara strained her brain to remember what the Web site had said. *All adult true accounts of love lost and found.*

"If you hated writing those stories, then why did you agree to do it?" Lara asked quietly.

"The error I made on Theo's tax return was a bad one. I failed to account for a massive business deduction that never should have slipped past me. As soon as I realized it, I filed an amended return, but at that point the IRS wasn't so quick to accept it. Theo had been audited in the past—before my time—and always ended up with penalties. Bottom line—Theo had to pay an extra six grand he shouldn't have had to pay. Not this time, anyway."

"That doesn't sound fair," Lara said.

Chris shifted nervously. "It wasn't. I was still fighting the IRS on his behalf when he—" He hung his head.

Lara still felt mystified. "Chris, are you saying Theo was, well, sort of blackmailing you?"

"Not sort of. He *was* blackmailing me," Chris said. "Theo knew I always wanted to be a published writer. He took advantage of that. He forced me to write those stories because they pay extremely well. I never saw a dime, of course. Theo submitted them under a pen name he created for himself, and *he* kept the royalties."

"But what could he have done to you if you didn't comply?"

Chris looked at her as if she were denser than a block of wood. "Oh, only ruined me," he said acidly. "Most of my clients are friends or business acquaintances of Theo's. One bad word about me from him and I'd have lost most of my business." Chris gave her a rueful smirk. "I can't survive doing tax returns for people who get excited over a fifty-dollar refund."

A category that included Lara. If she was lucky enough to get that much.

She had to ask. "Okay, I get that. But how does Mary fit into all this?"

"She doesn't. That's why I feel so awful. I made her worry about me for nothing. Every time one of those stories was published, Theo insisted on giving me a copy of the magazine. I didn't want them, any of them. He did it to torture me. And yet, there was this tiny voice in my brain that kept whispering, *Be proud—you're a published writer.* Well, anyway, I stuffed them in my desk drawer at home, under the laptop I was using to write them." He rubbed his hands over his forehead. "Poor Mary. I never thought she'd look in that drawer. She's always so respectful of my privacy."

Lara was beginning to feel bad for the guy. Oddly, she believed him—about the magazine articles, anyway. As for Theo's murder…

"Chris, I'm sure the police have asked you where you were the night Theo was…killed."

"Oh yeah," he said darkly. "I went into the station for an interview with one of the police detectives. I told him the truth—I was home with Mary that entire night. We'd stayed up late watching a Chevy Chase marathon. Mary loves that guy." He gave a quick smile. "Bottom line, Mary was my alibi and I was hers. Except we didn't need alibis, because we're both innocent." Lara slowly let out a breath. "I believe you, Chris."

"Of course, there's one thing that still worries me. I'm sure by now the police have gone through Theo's belongings, including the contents of his computer. If they find those stories in his email inbox—" he fretted.

"If they find the stories, all you can do is tell the truth. Tell them exactly what you told me."

Chris gave her a flat smile. "I guess you're right," he agreed with a sigh. "I just don't want any of this to reflect on Mary."

"I heard that the police think Glen Usher was the one who murdered Theo," Lara said. "I imagine they're going to be closing the case very soon."

"I heard that, too. The police are finishing up loose ends, but by tomorrow I expect they'll make a formal announcement." Chris's eyes blazed. "Glen Usher had a thing for Mary, you know. She thought I didn't notice, but I'd have to be blind not to." He laughed. "I guess she figured I'd pop him in the nose if I found out."

Or spike his coffee with his own heart medication?

"I'm glad we talked, Chris," Lara said. She'd be even gladder when he left.

"Yeah, me too. But I want you to understand something, Lara. Those stories I wrote—there was nothing illegal about them."

"I get it, Chris. You don't need to explain. So tell me, what kinds of stories do you really want to write?"

His eyes sparkled behind his wire-rimmed glasses. "Sci-fi," he said. "But specifically, the type of stuff they used to write in the fifties, when space exploration was so new and thrilling. Sometimes I wish I lived back in those days. But anyway, I'd actually like to publish my own magazine one day with those kinds of stories. In the meantime, I submitted a short story to a sci-fi mag—one of the popular ones." He shrugged. "I know it's a long shot, but until I get a rejection, I'm keeping my hopes high."

"Chris, I think that's great. Even if you get a rejection, you'll submit it somewhere else, right?"

He nodded, and then hesitated for a moment as if he had more to say. Finally, to Lara's relief, Chris left.

Lara closed the door behind him. She peered through the glass and watched him climb into his vehicle and take off.

Something was bothering her. What was it?

She retrieved her macaroons from where she'd plunked them on the counter. Biting distractedly into a cookie, she tried to figure out what was sticking like a needle under her skin.

Munster strolled out of the large parlor, paused in the kitchen doorway, and peeked his head around. Deciding it was safe to enter, he padded over to Lara and stretched up a paw to her, begging for a snack.

"Macaroons aren't good for you," she scolded playfully, even as she picked off a teensy crumb from her cookie and gave it to him. "That's all, though. They have too much sugar for..." She frowned, her thoughts coalescing.

That was it! That's what was bugging her.

Not a single cat had come into the kitchen when Chris was there. Munster, the usual greeter, had been conspicuously absent.

It meant nothing, of course.

Except that Munster, the most sociable cat in the house, wanted nothing to do with Chris Newman.

Chapter 26

Lara pulled into the parking lot of Saint Lucy's just in time to see Brooke, Darryl, and their mom clamber up the steps of the white-steepled church.

"Thank heaven we came early," Aunt Fran said. "Otherwise we'd have had to park in the hinterlands."

Lara bounced her gaze all around the extensive parking lot. She was relieved when she nabbed a space close to the church entrance. "Is the noon service always this crowded?"

"It is. There's an early service at eight thirty, but mostly older folks like me attend that one. Since a lot of people sleep in on Sunday, the noon service is perfect for them."

Aunt Fran had donned a pantsuit that morning. The jacket was hunter green, the pants navy. On her lapel was a feline-shaped brooch—the eyes two tiny, shining emeralds. While the ensemble was attractive, it hung too loosely on her.

Lara had been forced to wear her best pair of jeans, since she hadn't brought along any "dress-up" threads when she packed for New Hampshire. Luckily she'd had time to wash, dry, and press the jeans, along with one of her better tops. She decided she looked presentable enough for church.

Her hair was another matter. After she'd washed it early that morning, the curls, although shorter, had sprung back with a vengeance.

It's only hair, she told herself. *And you'll always have to live with curls, so suck it up.*

"You'll have a chance to meet Pastor Folger," Aunt Fran said. "He's been here for over nine years now. As pastors go, he's quite popular. He comes off as a fuddy-duddy, but in reality he's far from it. Modern in his thinking, he listens without judging. He's great with young people, something we're in dire need of these days."

Lara gulped. She hadn't been to a church service in a while. "Looking forward to it," she said, pasting on a big grin.

She helped her aunt out of the car and up the granite steps into the church vestibule. Two scarred pine benches sat on either side of the small foyer. A wooden cross hung over the entryway to the church. A rack of brochures and booklets hung over the bench on the left. Above the opposite bench was a statue sitting on a marble shelf that was carved into the wall. Saint Lucy, Lara presumed.

"Lara!" Brooke spotted her the moment she entered. Darryl crept up behind his sister and waved.

"Hey, Brooke," Lara said. "Hi Darryl. I missed you Friday."

Darryl gave her a shy smile. "Mom took me to buy a Halloween costume. You know what? I got a new book," he said, beaming. "It's about leopards."

Heather Weston came up behind Darryl and placed a hand on his shoulder. "Good to see you again, Lara."

"Hi there, Heather. It's great to see you, too."

Heather hesitated, then said, "In the few days since you arrived in town, Darryl has begun reading so much better. I can't help thinking there's a connection." Her brown eyes twinkled. "Can you tell me your secret?"

Lara knew she was only half-serious. Heather couldn't possibly know anything about Blue.

"Well, Darryl loves to read," Lara said, avoiding the question. "And he loves animals. Put those two together, and you have a winning combination!"

The boy nodded vigorously. "Yup. I'm getting more books about animals from the school library now. Those books with pirates and zombies have too much fighting. I don't want to read that junk anymore."

Heather laughed and rolled her eyes. "Live and learn, right?" She greeted Aunt Fran with a warm hug. "This is the lady I'm forever grateful to. Taking on my monsters every day after school."

Brooke rolled her eyes. "Yeah, like we're real thugs, Mom. Our mug shots are hanging in the post office."

"They're far from monsters." Aunt Fran smiled at the kids. "You know how much I enjoy having them."

"Brooke, before I forget," Lara said. "Your *Pickwick* book is at the house. You must've left it there either Wednesday or Thursday."

"It is?" Brooke shot a guilty glance at her mother. "I was sure it was in my bag."

Heather looked sternly at her daughter. "If you didn't know it was missing, that means you haven't been reading it, doesn't it?"

"*Noooo.*" Brooke gave her mom a contrite look. "Yes," she groaned. "It's so boring!"

"You have a book report due in a week," Heather reminded her. "Fran, if you're going to be home today, can we stop by later in the afternoon for it?"

"I'll help you with it, Brooke," came a voice from behind them.

They all turned at once to see Dora Pingaree, attired totally in black, clasping her hands at her waist. Gray bags hung beneath her puffy eyes. She looked as if she hadn't slept all night.

Lara's heart broke for the woman. Was she in terrible pain today? Lara suspected that the black attire was in remembrance of both Theo and Glen.

"Dora!" Brooke greeted her book-club friend. "I didn't see you come in!"

Dora smiled wanly at the group. "So great to see everyone. Lara, I see you're still in town." Her tone held a note of surprise.

"Still here," Lara said, avoiding her aunt's gaze.

The vestibule began to fill.

"I know *Pickwick* is a long book," Dora said, sliding her arm through Brooke's. "But the writing style is so filled with humor and wit and delightful descriptions. We'll break it down into sections...." Her voice trailed off as they entered the church together.

Aunt Fran leaned close to Lara. "If you don't mind, I'll think I'll sit for a few. Pastor Folger should be along anytime. I'd like to be sure you meet him before the service."

"Absolutely." Lara escorted her aunt over to one of the pine benches and sat beside her. When she looked up, she saw Mary Newman and Josette Barnes striding into the vestibule. The two couldn't have looked more different. Mary was outfitted in charcoal gray, from her prim chapel veil to her flat, sensible shoes. Josette, on the other hand, was a study in fashion—flaunting a lime-green cape over a form-fitting, burnt-orange sweater and black leggings.

Mary spotted Lara, and a look of embarrassment flashed in her eyes. Lara wondered if Mary had told her aunt Josette about Chris and his published stories.

Josette held out a gorgeously manicured hand to Aunt Fran. "Fran, how have you been?"

"Quite good, actually. And you?"

"I'm excellent." She slid a quick look over at Mary. "I mean, you know, under the circumstances," she said more quietly. She bent her head lower.

"Fran, I've been wanting to talk to you about something. Can I stop by some day this week?"

"Anytime." Aunt Fran smiled. "Give me a quick call first so I'll be properly dressed."

"Will...you be there, Lara?" Josette said.

If one more person asks me that...

"Probably not," Lara said. "But I'll be making frequent visits to New Hampshire, so I'm sure I'll see you again."

"Well, that's...great." Josette's smile looked ironed on. "Anyway, I'll catch you later, Fran." She pushed Mary a bit forcefully toward the doorway to the nave.

Aunt Fran grew quiet. Lara squirmed on the bench, then noticed a man in long black vestments and a white collar moving purposely toward them.

Lara rose.

"Good morning," the man said. "I'm Ernest Folger. And you must be the niece I've been hearing so much about. Welcome to Saint Lucy's." His smile warm and kind, Pastor Folger's pale blue eyes twinkled from a round, rosy face.

"Yes, I'm Lara. I'm very pleased to meet you, Pastor." She grasped his outstretched hand.

Pastor Folger turned to Aunt Fran and greeted her in a deeply respectful manner. It was clear that they'd been friends for years. Lara took an instant liking to the man. Everything about him seemed genuine.

"I hope we'll be seeing more of you, Lara," he said, winking at Aunt Fran.

Here we go...

"I hope so, too," Lara said. She amazed herself by realizing that she meant it.

The pastor's eyes narrowed, and his mouth curved into a frown. "As I'm sure you know, we've had two unfortunate deaths this past week. One by his own hand, which makes it even sadder. Although..." He shook his head slightly and tapped a finger to his lips.

Lara waited for him to finish his sentence, but the pastor apparently thought better of it.

"Regardless," he said with a deep sigh, "I'll be praying for both their souls today. And Lara, please don't judge our lovely town by what can only be called a tragic anomaly."

"No, Pastor, I won't."

He bade them both good-bye and went into the church. Lara and her aunt rose to follow him, just as a latecomer rushed into the vestibule. She stopped short when she saw Lara. "Oh. You're still in town."

Sheesh, is everyone in town gossiping about me?

Lara bit off a retort. "Hi, Kellie," she said to the stylist. Through eyes that were now slits, Kellie Byrd studied Lara's coiffure. "I see your hair got all the curls back. Didn't you blow-dry it this morning?" Reminding herself where she was, Lara ignored the accusatory tone. "I don't normally blow-dry my hair, Kellie." She gave the woman as courteous a smile as she could manage. "As for the curls, I'm afraid they go whichever way they want without much direction from me."

Kellie suddenly noticed that Lara's aunt was standing slightly behind her. "Oh, um, hi Mrs. C." Her face going tomato red, she mumbled an apology and gave her an awkward hug. "See you after the service," she sputtered and dashed off into the church.

Lara and her aunt followed her. Aunt Fran tipped her chin toward the altar, indicating that she wanted to sit in a pew near the front.

As they walked along the main aisle, the oddest thought struck Lara.

If Glen Usher *hadn't* killed Theo Barnes, then the main players in the suspect pool were all right here, right now.

And of all places, in the church.

Chapter 27

"I thought Pastor Folger made a thoughtful tribute to both Theo and Glen," Aunt Fran said.

"He did," Lara agreed. She helped her aunt into the front seat of her rental car, then scooted over to the driver's side.

The pastor had spoken highly of both men. It was clear that he'd dug deep to find warm hearted stories about each of them. The smiles and tears of most of the parishioners had been a testament to his way with words.

"Oh, flippity floop," Lara said. "Aunt Fran, I left my jacket in the pew. It was so warm in there I had to take it off. Be right back, okay?"

"Take your time," her aunt said.

Lara was grateful they'd escaped after the service without having to stop and gab with anyone. Considering the way some people had been asking her how long she'd be sticking around, she was beginning to feel persona non grata.

She hurried up the steps and into the vestibule. The church was quiet, almost eerily so. Now that she was alone, she took a moment to admire the arched, stained-glass windows. They towered toward the vaulted ceiling on both sides of the nave. She remembered, ages ago, Aunt Fran telling her that the windows had been created from hand-stained glass, a method only the most skilled artists could master.

Unfortunately, she couldn't linger. Her aunt was waiting in the car. She trotted down the aisle as quietly as she could. She didn't want her footsteps to echo in the church. She snagged her jacket off the bench where she'd left it.

Her jacket folded over her arm, she'd almost reached the vestibule when the clatter of high heels sounded in her ears, followed by an urgent female voice. A second voice shushed the first one, and the two chattered in hushed tones.

Yikes!

Whoever it was, they'd apparently come out of the tiny restroom at the back corner of the church.

Panic squeezed Lara's throat. Her breath felt glued inside her lungs. She was torn between the desire to hear what they were talking about, and the more instinctive need to flee.

No contest.

Lara's frantic gaze landed on the thick, floor-length curtain hanging over the confessional closest to her, on the left. On tiptoes, she dashed inside the darkened booth and sat on the little bench. Her heart slammed her chest so hard she was sure her blood vessels were going to burst. It felt like a remake of Poe's story of the heart buried under the floorboards!

"I didn't want to tell anyone before," a woman's voice burbled, "but I can't keep it inside any longer!"

Lara recognized the voice—Josette's.

"It's okay, honey. We're all friends here," Kellie Byrd said in a subdued voice.

"I know," Josette blubbered. After a long pause she said, "I can't believe I'm admitting this, but, remember I told you about spending the night in Connecticut with my new beau?"

Lara pictured Kellie nodding.

"Well… Oh God, it was all a lie! I *did* drive to Connecticut that afternoon, and Aaron and I *did* have dinner at his place, but—" She started to bawl in choked sobs.

"It's okay, Aunt Josette. Don't be embarrassed. You can tell us."

Mary Newman!

"I know. Okay, here goes," she went on after a noisy snuffle. "That night, after we had dinner, Aaron tol-told me he didn't really think we were a good match. He told me I should leave right away so I wouldn't have to drive back to New Hampshire in the dead of night. It was so…humiliating!"

"What a jerk!" Kellie bleated. "I mean, come on, what kind of guy does that, ya know? A creepazoid, that's what kind!"

"Kellie, we're in church," Mary admonished.

"I know, I know. Sorry," Kellie said. "But Jo, why didn't you get a hotel room somewhere, so you wouldn't have to drive all that way home at night?"

"I-I thought about it, but then I couldn't bear the thought of staying that close to Aaron. I wanted to just get home where I could cry my heart out."

Kellie sighed. "I hear ya."

"It— The thing is, I lied to the police, and now they're going to find out. They asked me for Aaron's phone number so they could contact him. I had no choice—I had to give it to them!"

"But you didn't do anything wrong, Aunt Josette," Mary insisted.

"Jo, did you call Aaron to let him know what happened?" Kellie's voice.

"No. Why?"

"Because if you explain your situation to him, maybe he'll agree to confirm your story. It's not like you're guilty, right? Why can't he just tell them you spent the night there? It's the least he owes you."

"Oh God, Kellie, I can't ask him to lie to the police! Isn't that a crime?"

A long moment of silence ensued. Lara wanted desperately to suck in a long breath, but she was terrified to move. The confessional was getting stuffier. She wondered when anyone had last used it.

"Ladies, we're all forgetting something," Mary said in a hushed tone. "The police think Glen killed Theo, and I happen to agree with them. No one needs to lie."

Lara heard the shuffle of feet. What was happening? She prayed the trio was leaving.

"Come on, let's go get some coffee," Kellie put in. "Someplace where we can talk privately."

"You mean someplace where that nosy niece of Fran Clarkson's won't come bouncing in, don't you?" Josette asked. "She as much as accused me of murder, you know."

What? No I didn't!

"I don't know what her problem is," Kellie said with a caustic snort. "Maybe she killed Theo and wants to throw the police off her track, ya know?"

"Lara's okay," Mary said softly. "She's been very kind to me."

Bless you, Mary.

The clatter of shoes fading into the distance told Lara the women were leaving.

Thank heaven!

A quiet fell over the church. Not a single sound echoed off the walls.

Lara slowly peeled back the musty-smelling curtain and stumbled out of the confessional. She was light-headed from being closed in so long. Okay, it was only about three minutes, but still—

Her jacket was still draped over her arm. She swung it over her shoulders and shrugged it on.

"Lara?"

"Oh!" She jumped at the voice.

"I'm very sorry. I didn't mean to startle you," Pastor Folger said. He'd padded up the main aisle so quietly she hadn't heard him.

Lara tapped her heart. "My fault entirely," she said. "I left my jacket here and had to come back for it."

The man smiled, his eyes filled with compassion. "I do sincerely hope you won't be a stranger. It's been good for your aunt, having you here."

"I know." Had he and Aunt Fran spoken privately? "Pastor, may I ask you something?"

"You surely may," he said, steering her with an outstretched arm toward the vestibule. "What can I help you with?"

Lara followed his lead. "How well did you know Glen Usher?"

"I've known him since I moved to this parish nine years ago. Not terribly well, but he wasn't an easy man to know. In spite of that, we had many a talk over the years. I wish I could have done more for him." The pastor gave her a pensive look. "Why do you ask?"

"I had the feeling you're not totally convinced that Glen actually—well, you know, took his own life."

The pastor nodded, his eyes crinkled in obvious sorrow. "You're very perceptive, Lara. It was out of character for him. Taking another man's life in the heat of anger is entirely different from taking one's own. Quite frankly, I'm not sure Glen committed either sin."

"Have you told the police that?"

Pastor Folger gave her a benevolent smile. "I've shared my thoughts, but I don't have an iota of proof. Only a gut feeling, if you will. I simply have to trust in the police to do their jobs properly."

Lara mulled over his words. "Pastor, why do you think Glen was, well, the way he was? It was almost like he never grew up."

A shadow fell over the pastor's face. "From what I gleaned, Glen's parents had him later in life, and then both died when he was barely a teen. With no other family, he ended up in a group foster home. There was no one left in his life to put him first, so he floundered. Do you see what I'm saying?"

Lara swallowed. "I think I do. And thanks so much for listening."

An insightful, caring man, Lara thought.

She hurried out to the car. The woman who'd always put Lara first was patiently waiting.

As she had been for the last sixteen years.

Chapter 28

Aunt Fran gave Lara an amused smile. "I can't believe you sat in that confessional, *literally* hearing Josette's confession. The irony is almost comical."

"I know, right?" Lara set a mug of tea on the table in front of her aunt. "I felt kind of weird doing it, though, even if Josette did call me nosy and said I practically accused her of murder. The problem is, I'm now on the fence about Josette. I think I'm adding her back to my suspect list."

Aunt Fran's eyebrows shot up in surprise. "You have a suspect list?" She ran a hand over Dolce's head. The cat closed his eyes and purred in her lap.

"Well, yes, an informal one. Nothing I can take to the police." She sipped her tea and plucked a macaroon from the plate of cookies she'd set out.

"I understand what you're saying, Lara. And yet, all the evidence points to Glen. Even if none of us can picture him killing Theo, and then killing himself, the police believe his confession clinches it."

"It might, and it probably does," Lara said. She ran a hand through her hair, feeling the curls slither through her fingers. She shared the pastor's feelings about Glen with her aunt.

"That's…interesting," her aunt said. "Pastor Folger usually has excellent instincts." She shook her head. "But I think, at this point, we should leave it in the hands of the police. If Glen actually wrote a confession and left it in his car—"

"I know, I know," Lara interrupted. "Something about it just seems off to me. I can't get it out of my brain." She picked a sliced almond off her macaroon.

Maybe it was time. Her old life—her real life—was calling to her. Not very loudly, she admitted. In fact, it had dwindled to a bare whisper. But it was there and had to be dealt with.

"Aunt Fran, you know I'm going to have to go home soon. Maybe as early as tomorrow." *Except I'm not sure anymore where home is.*

Her aunt looked down at Dolce. "I know."

"But listen, this morning, when I was cleaning the litter boxes, I had some thoughts about how to get you some help with the cats. *And* find homes for the kittens. Hear me out, okay? And try to keep an open mind."

She explained her idea about transforming the back porch into a meeting place for people and cats. Lara would do all the initial cleaning, painting, and decorating. If Gideon Halley was willing, they'd retain him to do the necessary legal work, including obtaining a license, to give Aunt Fran's home official status as an animal shelter.

"And what if," Lara said, fresh ideas skipping through her head like baby goats, "we recruited some vet tech students to volunteer on different days. Once we're set up, we can do some fundraising to help cover neutering and veterinary care. Oh, Aunt Fran, the more I think about it, the more I love the idea. Plus, I can start painting more watercolors to sell, with the proceeds going to the shelter. I'll bet Sherry and Daisy will even display them in the coffee shop and sell them on consignment."

For a long moment, her aunt was silent. Finally, she rested her elbows on the table and folded her hands. "Lara, it sounds like a wonderful plan, honestly it does. I'm impressed, and truly grateful, that you've put so much thought into it. But I'm simply not sure it's doable. You'll be in Boston most of the time. Even if we find volunteers, it might not be enough. And we'd have to work closely with Amy Glindell, my vet, to arrange for neutering, shots, exams."

"I know all that," Lara said. "I understand there'd be a lot of glitches to work out." Frustration was making her tone rise. "All I'm asking is that you think about it. Picture it in your mind. Imagine how it could be if we actually did make it work."

A tiny gleam danced in Aunt Fran's eyes. "I will think about it. I promise," she said.

"But wait! There's more!" Lara said, grinning this time. "Since we didn't plan anything for dinner, why don't you let me treat us to a pizza later? I'll pick it up. We'll order it with globs of whatever toppings you like."

"Now that's an offer I can't refuse," Aunt Fran said with a laugh. "But you've been spending too much money. I insist you let me treat this time."

"No," Lara said firmly. "This one's on me."

Big words from someone with a fast-shrinking debit account.

She had about sixty dollars left to draw from—not enough to keep her going for much longer. But, she reasoned, once she signed the new contract with Wayne Lefkovitz and collected the initial deposit, she'd be in better financial shape than she'd been in in a long time. There should also be a few checks in her mailbox when she got home from clients who'd custom-ordered.

"I just did some fuzzy math in my head, Aunt Fran. Let me take care of the pizza this time, okay?"

Her aunt didn't argue. "You got it."

The one thing Lara hadn't factored in was transportation. Any future trips to New Hampshire would require her renting a car each time. She'd have to look into a cheaper way to travel back and forth.

For now, she was content to pull a Scarlett O'Hara and think about it tomorrow.

* * * *

They finished their tea, and Lara put away the cookies in a sealed container. Aunt Fran announced that she was going up to her room for a while to relax and read.

As they were leaving the kitchen, Lara glanced toward the small parlor. The door stood open about three inches.

Her mouth went desert dry. Hadn't she closed the door?

She retraced her actions in her mind. She'd worked for a while on the watercolor of Blue, after which she'd called Mary Newman. Then she had taken a break and gone into the kitchen for some cookies. That had been around the time she'd spotted Goldy in the yard with Blue.

After that, everything had happened quickly. Wendy had arrived to retrieve her cat, and then Chris Newman had shown up. Once he'd left, Lara was too agitated to paint. She'd thrown some things in the wash, then busied herself tidying the house, which included taking a few measurements on the back porch. While she'd waited for her aunt to come downstairs, she'd sat in the large parlor and brushed three of the cats.

But she was sure she'd shut the door to the small parlor. She hadn't wanted to tempt any curious felines into investigating her watercolors.

She distinctly remembered pulling the door closed.

Had someone sneaked into the house while she and Aunt Fran were at church and opened the door?

Lara reached out with her left hand and pushed the door open wider. She peered into the room, and her stomach dropped to her knees.

Resting on the chair she'd sat in when she was painting earlier in the day was Brooke's dreaded book—*The Pickwick Papers.*

And sitting atop the book was Blue, her gaze snaring Lara's with a questioning look.

Lara closed her eyes. She took in a deep breath. Her head felt like a helium-filled balloon floating to the ceiling.

When she opened her eyes, Blue was still there. At least, now, Aunt Fran would see her, too.

Aunt Fran leaned on her cane and peered through the doorway. "Oh, look at that!"

Yes!

"I didn't realize you'd dragged that old card table in there." Her aunt smiled. "I guess it makes a good worktable for you, doesn't it?"

Lara felt woozy.

Please tell me you see the cat. Please tell me I'm not crazy.

"It-it does, yes. I painted for quite a while this morning."

"I can't wait to dive into the new book I'm reading," her aunt said, looping one arm through Lara's. She moved away from the doorway to head upstairs. "It's one of those sagas that begins during World War Two and jumps back and forth to the present."

"Sounds really good," Lara said, taking the hint. Aunt Fran was clearly anxious to go to her room and read.

Lara's heart suddenly sank. In her mind, she saw the Aunt Fran she'd known as a child. She'd had pep in her step, to coin a cliché—an endless supply of energy. Now, thanks to a horribly debilitating condition, she'd aged far beyond her years.

No matter what Lara did to help the cats, nothing short of surgery was going to fix her aunt's knees. If Aunt Fran wanted a shot at a normal life again, she'd have no other choice.

Her spirits low, Lara helped her aunt get settled upstairs, then went back into the small parlor. This time Blue was nowhere to be seen.

But good ole *Pickwick* was still there.

She snatched up the book that seemed to travel the room on its own. "Gotcha now!" she said with a wicked laugh. The laugh of a madwoman?

The book bore traces of the soda Brooke had spilled, although this book had escaped with only a few purple blotches staining its edges.

It was a clear, sunny autumn day. Maybe if she lugged the book outside to her favorite spot against the curved rock, she could flip through it and try to figure out what was happening. Was something hidden inside the book? Something that made it levitate?

Maybe Charles Dickens himself would stop by and drop off a clue.

"Yeah, sure," she told herself, tapping her head with a finger. "And then I'll jump into a spaceship and visit Mars for the afternoon."

She slipped on her jacket and headed into the backyard. The air felt crisp and clean, tinged with the seasonal scents of apples and dried leaves. She sucked in long breaths. Her lungs needed a good airing out, especially after being trapped in that confessional, for—oh, gosh—at least three solid minutes.

She trod over to the curved rock and stared out across the meadow. Everything looked peaceful, with no sign of Blue. For a long time Lara stood there, turning things over in her head.

She dropped to the ground and snuggled against the curve of the rock. Her legs stretched out before her, she began flipping through *The Pickwick Papers*. She wondered why Brooke had opted for the hardcover of the lengthy classic instead of choosing a paperback.

As she flipped through the beginning pages, she realized that the volume contained some wonderful illustrations—delightful depictions of the Dickensian characters the author's works were known for.

Fishing through the pages, Lara found herself giggling at the names. Mr. Blotton. Doctor Slammer. Miss Bulder.

The more she skimmed the volume, the more the prose sucked her in. Nearly every sentence was a charming concoction of old-fashioned verbs and clever humor. She didn't think it was boring at all.

Nonetheless, she understood Brooke's reluctance to finish reading the volume. The size of the book alone was intimidating.

Riffling casually through the book, Lara was nearing the halfway point when she noticed some writing in the margin of one of the pages. Large block letters, scrawled in so heavy a hand they'd nearly torn their way through.

MAKE HIM PAY!

SUE HIS BUTT OFF!

Lara frowned. Harsh words, coming from a young teenager. Why would Brooke have written something like that?

Wait a minute. What had Brooke told Lara that day, when Lara asked her what the book was about?

A band of lame old dudes who roam all over England ...

Something like that, anyway. But there was something else.

Some ditzy landlady sues dumpy old Pickwick for not marrying her....

Lara felt a tingling in her stomach. For someone who'd proclaimed the book boring, Brooke had sure gotten riled over it.

Did Brooke have anger issues? Could they be related to her feelings toward her absentee dad?

Going back to the book, Lara turned another page. Her insides roiled with nausea.

Graphic images of a realistic-looking heart had been etched into the margin with a ballpoint pen. The blade of a knife, superimposed over it, suggested the kinds of torture the illustrator would like to inflict on it.

Her heart smacking her ribs, Lara turned the page again. This time she nearly vomited.

The organ in question had been slashed to threads, images of blood drops flying everywhere. The artwork was mediocre, but the message as clear as glass.

Lara closed the book hard.

She couldn't keep this to herself. Brooke's mom had to know so she could get her daughter some help.

She set the book down on the grass. When she pulled her hand away, her sleeve caught the corner of the cover. She nabbed a glimpse of the owner's name, written inside in the upper right corner.

And in one horrifying instant, the tumblers fell into place.

It wasn't Brooke who'd scribbled in the book, because the book wasn't Brooke's.

A shuffling noise behind Lara made her gasp. She whirled her head around and saw someone moving toward her at a surprisingly fast clip.

"Hey, there! What are you doing out here all by your lonesome? Catching up on your reading?"

"Um, not really," Lara said, in a voice that came out like sandpaper. "I'm just enjoying what's left of this lovely afternoon."

Dora Pingaree laughed, not an ounce of mirth in her tone. Her right hand was tucked slightly behind her. "I guess you should enjoy it while you can," she said flatly. She moved closer, until she stood barely three feet from where Lara had left the *Pickwick* book.

Lara tried to swallow, but it felt as if a giant hair ball was lodged in her throat.

"I should have known you'd look inside the book," Dora said coldly. "If that stupid, clumsy girl hadn't spilled her drink, it never would have ended up in her bag. By the time we got through wiping the grape soda off all the books, the school-bus driver was tooting for her out front. She snatched up all her books and stuffed them into her backpack. I didn't realize she'd taken mine, too." Dora's smile chilled Lara to the bone. "Not until you mentioned it in church today."

Chapter 29

Lara felt her insides gurgle. She didn't know what Dora was hiding behind her back, but felt sure it wasn't anything good.

"Oh, heck, Dora," she said with a laugh, trying to act clueless. "Anyone can spill a drink. I do it all the time. I'm the klutziest—"

"Shut up. You talk too much. This is all your fault. None of this would've happened if you hadn't shown up in town."

A shard of anger ripped through Lara. "*My* fault? How do you figure, Dora?" Every muscle in her body tensed. She wanted to leap to her feet and face the woman, but something told her to bide her time, and wait for the right moment.

"You brought Fran to the coffee shop for lunch. She hadn't been there in a rat's age." Dora stared hard at Lara, her eyes blazing with rage behind her tinted glasses.

"Your point is?" Lara said, willing herself not to tremble.

"My *point*, missy, is that I was on a fast track to becoming Mrs. Theo Barnes. Didn't you see him kiss my hand that day? Didn't you see him kiss my *left* hand?"

"I… I guess I did, Dora. I didn't know it meant that."

"And then he saw your aunt," Dora spat out. "He loved her once, you know, and she loved him."

"I know all about that," Lara said. "But it was a long time ago. My aunt had no feelings left—"

"I told you to shut up. You don't get it, because you don't listen and you think you know everything. Theo wanted your aunt's land, but she refused to sell it to him. She was doing that to hurt him, to get back at him for the way he treated her when they were engaged." She glared out over the meadow as if poisonous weeds were sprouting from it.

Lara tried to swallow, but her throat felt frozen. "That's...not the way I heard it, Dora. Theo wanted to build condos on the parcel." She lifted one hand toward the pristine meadow. "Think of all the small animals that would've been disrupted—"

"God, you are a chatterbox. You know nothing about progress, do you?" Her right arm twitched behind her. "If your aunt had done the right thing and sold him the land, she could've made a pretty penny. Enough to feed all those creepy cats she keeps taking in. How does she even live in that place with all those things?" Dora wrinkled her nose.

Lara tamped down a retort.

"That day, when I heard Theo tell Fran that his proposal still stood, I knew what he was doing. He wanted one last shot at getting her to marry him, even though he'd practically proposed to me. And mark my words, Fran would've caved. No one could resist Theo's charms."

"You misunderstood him, Dora. He was talking about his proposal to buy the land, nothing more."

Dora's face fell, and she shook her head back and forth. "No, I—"

"Admit it, Dora. You got it wrong." She lowered her voice. "Is that why you asked Theo to meet you near the park bench that night?"

The woman tottered, but quickly regained her composure. "I wrote him a note on fancy paper, pretending I was Fran. It was easy to copy her handwriting. I'd saved all the notes she'd written me over the years. I knew Theo would come if he thought it was her." She gave out a demented laugh. "But when he saw me there, waiting on the bench, he got really mad. He knew I'd tricked him."

Lara slowly let out a breath. "Did he hurt you, Dora?"

Tears filled Dora's eyes. "He shoved me away when I told him I wanted to marry him. I told him I'd love him so much more than Fran ever could. I wanted a *ring*, Lara. For the first time in my life, I wanted to be a wife!" She sucked in a furious breath. "You know what he said? He said I must be smoking dope if I thought he'd ever marry an old bag like me." Her right arm jerked again. This time Lara saw what she was holding—a knife. A long, scary-looking knife.

Bile crept up Lara's throat. Her vision blurred.

"He had no right to treat you that way, Dora. Let's face it, Theo was not a nice man. You'd have been miserable married to him."

"Like you'd know," she spat out. "I don't see a man hanging off your arm." She swiped at her eyes with the hand holding the knife.

Fear clutching her in a vise, Lara looked toward the house. She saw no sign of movement.

Maybe if she could catch Dora off guard, she could knock the knife out of her hands. "H-how did you ending up killing him?"

"He was so mean to me. He didn't like being tricked, so he threatened to blackmail me."

Blackmail?

Something poked Lara's memory.

Oh, God. That was it.

She should have seen it sooner, but she'd been too paralyzed by dread to snap the final piece into place.

Dora was moving like a normal person, without any sign of her injury. Lara shuddered. Dora's bad back had been an act. All along, she'd had everyone fooled.

"You mean about the accident, Dora?"

"I couldn't have him screwing things up for me. Everyone gives me special favors and free stuff. So what if I have to wear that awful brace when I'm in public? It's a small price to pay for the sympathy I get. And for the insurance settlement—which wasn't bad, all things considered."

She smiled, and Lara saw the insanity dancing in her eyes.

Lara plastered on a grin she felt sure made her resemble a clown. "Dora, I have to admire you. You truly are a clever one. I'd never have thought of letting a TV fall on me." She gave out a chuckle of fake admiration.

"Who told—" Dora twisted her lips into a scowl. "It doesn't matter. That clerk deserved it. Like a slob, he'd left that screwdriver right there on the shelf after he tightened the bolts. I'm pretty handy with tools. I knew I could make that TV fall on me and act like I'd wrecked my back."

"But...you had X-rays, didn't you? Or an MRI?"

"Of course. Nothing showed up, so I played the pain card. At the hospital, I screamed with agony. They kept me longer than they would have, gave me all sorts of medication. They finally sent me home, shrieking from the constant pain." She gave out a malicious laugh. "They prescribed a back brace, said it should help over time."

Lara wanted to throw up. How could she have ever thought Dora was a decent human being?

"Once I was home, I called one of those ambulance chasers who advertise on TV. He managed to squeeze a settlement out of the insurance company. It wasn't a fortune, but it'll keep me going for a while. I think the fools settled just to get rid of me. I was one of those nuisance cases."

At the corner of her vision, Lara thought she detected a shadow flitting past her aunt's bedroom window. "You said Theo threatened blackmail. How did he find out?"

Dora's face pinched with fury. "I got careless. A few months ago, he drove by my house when I was getting into my car. It was obvious I was moving with the agility of an athlete. After that, he'd drop snide little comments whenever he saw me, just to let me know he knew. That's another reason I wanted to marry him. A husband can't testify against his wife, right?"

"I don't think it works that way, Dora."

"Shut up! What do you know?"

"Dora, didn't it ever occur to you that a man who treated you so callously couldn't seriously have wanted to marry you? Don't you think you deserved better?"

Dora stuttered backward as if she'd been slapped. She quickly regained her balance and shook her head. "No, you don't get it. I— Theo and I had always been friends. Good friends. Don't you see? Those little comments meant nothing. He was teasing, that's all."

Her mind is flip-flopping all over the place.

Lara's hand inched toward the *Pickwick* book. "Is that why you drew these horrible pictures in here? Because he *teased* you?"

A single tear trailed down Dora's cheek. She gave a childlike shake of her head. "No. That…that day, when I drew those things—it was the day I saw him kissing that witch who works at the library. They thought no one saw them, but I did. They were making out like teenagers in the periodical room." She squeezed her eyes shut, as if she could see it in her mind. "I wanted to rip her face off, but I kept my cool and ran out of the building. I knew Theo didn't care about her. He was only toying with her until we could get married." Another tear flowed down her cheek.

She's delusional, Lara thought.

And then, as if a switch had been flipped, Dora began to laugh—a· sound that made Lara's limbs turn numb.

"You really don't get how clever I was. That night, when I tricked Theo into meeting me, I'd already taken your aunt's hoe from the shed and laid it under the bench. I knew that if it came to it, I'd have no problem killing him. If the police found the hoe, they'd blame it on Fran. One way or the other, I'd win. He'd either agree to marry me, or he'd die. Don't you see, Lara? He made the choice himself."

Lara clutched her stomach, willing herself not to heave. Dora was insane. How had no one ever seen it?

"Nobody won, Dora. Can't you get that? A life was taken for nothing."

Dora acted as if she hadn't heard. "When Theo started to leave that night, he laughed and said I'd been aptly named, that I was a 'dumb Dora.' I...I got so angry. He started to walk behind the bench to go to where he'd parked his car on the street. I— I grabbed the hoe from under the bench and slammed it on the back of his head. *Bam!* He went down like a rock—never knew what hit him."

Lara flinched.

"Too graphic for you?" Dora taunted. "Afterward, I hung the hoe back where I'd found it in the shed. It wasn't until the next morning I realized I'd made a mistake. I hadn't wiped my prints off the handle."

"Hence the ruse about wanting to help my aunt plant her bulbs."

Dora laughed. "Exactly. In case the police found it, I had to come up with a reason why my prints were on that hoe. That's why I recruited that silly girl to do some planting with me. I knew she'd jump at the chance to help Fran."

Lara stifled a gag. It sickened her to think of Brooke having been anywhere near Dora.

Dora looked down at Lara as if she were a worm. "Now that I've got the police believing Glen was the killer, I have to get rid of you. I can't have you hanging around to screw things up for me."

Glen? Oh God—not him, too.

Dora took a step closer and kicked the *Pickwick* book. "You were going to turn this in to the cops, weren't you? To show them how crazy I am."

In a voice that rattled, Lara said, "What happened, Dora? Did Glen see you that night?"

Dora stared out over the park, as if reliving it in her head. "Unfortunately for him, yes. Theo had evicted him, so he was living in his car in the library parking lot. Apparently he'd gone into the park to, shall we say, use the facilities? He'd just finished when he saw me crossing through the park to get to my car."

And the next morning Lara had discovered Theo's body.

"He could put you at the scene," Lara said tonelessly. "I'm surprised you waited as long as you did to...get rid of him."

"I had a private little chat with Glen the next morning. I assured him I would take care of his needs, even hinted I might let him have a room in my house if he promised to keep it clean." She laughed. "As if."

Dora's eyes took on a mad sheen. "It was almost too easy. I brought him a coffee and a sub sandwich after the downtown shops had closed. No one was around. His car was behind the library. I still had a full bottle of my sister's meds—she died years ago from heart disease. I knew Glen took something similar for his heart, so I simply added it all to the coffee. I wore gloves, of course. It was brilliant, when you think about it. He never saw the confession I wrote on the napkin. I brought it with me and slipped it under the front seat."

Her limbs stiff and tingling, Lara pulled up her knees and started to rise. She couldn't sit there any longer and allow herself to be slaughtered.

"Don't you dare move," Dora hissed, waving the knife at her. "It'll be easier to dispose of you if you're sitting on the grass."

Lara shot her gaze toward the house. She didn't dare scream. If Dora caught Aunt Fran looking out the window, she'd no doubt kill her, too. Even if her aunt called 9-1-1, they might not get there in time.

She sat down again, her legs bent slightly at the knees. "Dora, I feel so bad about all this." Determined to keep Dora talking, Lara shook her head with as much fake pity as she could dredge up. "I can see you've gone through some tough times. You didn't deserve all the bad luck you've had."

Dora looked uncertain. "Don't pretend you feel sorry for me. That makes me very angry."

An icy knob of fear settled inside Lara's chest. "Okay, I'm sorry. But I can't help thinking what a lousy hand you were dealt. I mean, your mom died when you were young, and then you lost your dad and your sister. I can't imagine how devastating that must have been."

Dora's lip curled into a snarl. "My sister was a self-righteous prude, always tattling on me to Daddy for every stupid thing. From the time we were kids, he loved her more than he loved me. You think I care that she's dead?"

Any hope Lara had for reasoning with Dora fizzled. The woman was deranged and had been for a long time. She hadn't acted only in community theater. Her entire persona as a sweet but eccentric middle-aged woman with a debilitating injury had been a clever and convincing performance.

Dora's right arm twitched again, and she brandished the knife. "This time I'll remember to wipe off my prints," she said, a maniacal glint in her eyes. She moved toward Lara. "You have about ten seconds to say a final prayer, Lara. Better make it a—"

A flash of fur suddenly leaped out from behind Lara. With the speed of a rocket, Blue launched herself at Dora, her claws sinking into the woman's horrified face. Dora reeled backward, her feet scrabbling to keep purchase on the ground.

Momentarily frozen, Lara stared in shock. Then the knife flew out of Dora's hand, and Lara jumped up off the grass and kicked it away. From somewhere near the house, Lara thought she heard someone shouting her name.

Dora's screams ripped through the air, shrill enough to make Lara's ears hurt. "Help me—something's attacking me! Please…get it off me!" She raked her fingers over the cat as if an army of wasps were stinging her.

Footsteps clomping across the yard echoed in Lara's ears. In the next instant, Blue sprang off Dora and vanished into the meadow.

In a heartbeat, Lara was on Dora, shoving her backward onto the ground. She dropped onto Dora's abdomen with a thud, pinning her with her weight. Too spent to do more than wriggle her arms, Dora flung out a string of obscenities.

"Lara!"

The sound of her name made Lara whip her head around toward the house. She sagged with relief when she saw Chief Whitley and one of his officers sprinting in her direction.

"You okay, Lara?" the chief said, his brow furrowed with concern. He dropped onto one knee next to Dora and produced a pair of handcuffs.

The other officer placed a pair of powerful hands under Lara's arms and lifted her firmly but gently off Dora. He set her carefully on the grass.

"Yes, I… I think so," she said, a sob escaping her. She pushed her hair out of her eyes. "Dora tried to kill me with a knife. She killed Theo and Glen."

"She lying!" Dora bellowed, her face scratched and bleeding. "She used voodoo on me. She's a witch! She's a killer."

Whitley looked at Lara and shook his head. "Stay still, Dora. Your face is all scratched and bloody. We're gonna take you to get checked out, but then we're arresting you. I'm going to read you your rights now, so be quiet."

He issued the standard Miranda warning, Dora injecting a filth-laced comment at every pause.

"She did it!" Dora looked at Lara with pure hatred swirling in her gaze. "She played some kind of trick on me. I'm telling you, she's a witch!"

The truth struck Lara hard in the chest.

Dora never saw Blue. She felt her weight and she felt her claws, but she never saw her.

Whitley looked at Lara with an odd expression. It wasn't hard to read his thoughts. *We get it. She's nuts.*

"Lara!"

This time it was her aunt calling to her. Aunt Fran was hobbling across the lawn toward them, her cane smacking the ground with each hurried step.

Lara raced to her and threw her arms around her. She squeezed her aunt harder than she had since was eleven years old.

Aunt Fran pressed a shaky hand to Lara's cheek. Her thin form quaked. "Thank God I saw you out here in time. I was upstairs reading when my geranium pot suddenly flew out of the alcove and shattered on the floor. I was so shocked I went to pick it up, and that's when I looked out the window. I guess you had a guardian angel looking out for you."

I did, she wanted to say. *A feline guardian angel.*

"It's okay, Aunt Fran. I'm fine now."

And she really was.

She was finer than she'd been in a very long time.

Chapter 30

"For the love of all that is holy, Fran, will you get this cat off my neck?"

Sitting adjacent to Chief Whitley at her kitchen table, Aunt Fran gave out an amused chuckle. "Lilybee obviously likes you, Jerry. Otherwise she wouldn't be chewing on your shirt collar."

With one large hand, the chief of police peeled the kitten gently off his shoulder. "Here. Go to your mom. I'll bet she has some nice tuna fish or something she can feed you." He handed Lilybee to Fran, who promptly set the kitten on her lap and stroked her white fur.

Lara giggled. She'd been doing a lot of that since the pall of murder had been lifted.

Three days had passed since the police had hauled a screaming Dora into the squad car and charged her with the murders of Theo Barnes and Glen Usher. Lara cringed every time she recalled Dora's bloodied face.

While it wasn't for public consumption, the chief had confided to her and Aunt Fran that the deep scratches on Dora's face had been self-inflicted, as evidenced by her bloody fingernails. It was one more sign in a long list of indicators that Dora had been mentally unstable.

The chief filled them in on a few things. "That day, when you called nine-one-one, Fran, I was actually on my way up here to see you. We'd started going through the contents of Theo's house—cleaning up loose ends and the like. The note you wrote asking him to meet you that night was tucked into one of his desk drawers."

Aunt Fran looked flummoxed. "But I never wrote Theo a note."

"We know that now. But at the time, it sure didn't look good. I hate to admit this, but I was dragging my feet coming here to ask you about it. The last thing I wanted to do was take you down to the station for questioning."

He shot a wary look at Munster, who'd emerged from the large parlor and was ambling straight toward him. Whitley held up a large hand as a barrier. "Your call came in right about then," the chief continued. "Strange timing, huh? I still can't get over how odd it was."

"Strange, but very lucky," Aunt Fran said.

"When I got here and saw Dora raking the skin off her face—" He shook his head. "I gotta say, I've never seen anything like it. I know it's late in the season, but...did you see a bee or a wasp go after her, Lara? Something that would've made her dig into her face like that?"

"No, nothing like that." Lara willed herself not to squirm in her chair. "But her mind was ricocheting all over the place. One minute she hated Theo, and then the next she wanted to marry him. What do you think's going to happen to her, Chief?"

"Right now, she's undergoing a psych eval." The lines in the chief's forehead deepened. "My guess? She'll be found competent to stand trial. I don't think Dora will be seeing the light of day any time soon."

Lara felt her throat tighten. "It's such a waste. She did it all to herself, that's the sad part. She was her own worst enemy."

"She was a good actress, I'll give her that," Whitley said. "I'll give you another little tidbit, but it's not to leave this room. Dora has already scored fairly high on the narcissistic personality chart."

That didn't surprise Lara, but her aunt was looking pale.

"I guess I was oblivious," Aunt Fran said. "I'd known her so long that I'd thought of her as eccentric, but not dangerous."

"That's because you look for the best in everyone, Fran. You always have. It's one of the things I—" Whitley's face reddened, and he gave her a crooked grin. "Well, you know what I mean." He reached over and covered her thin hand with his huge mitt.

Lara saw a warm glow spread over her aunt's face.

I knew it!

Outside, a car door slammed.

The chief quickly withdrew his hand. "That must be Chris."

Moments later, Chris Newman's face peeked through the screen door. "Morning, everyone," he said when Lara opened the door. She let him in, but said nothing. She couldn't help noticing that he avoided eye contact with her aunt.

She nodded at the chair she'd dubbed the hot seat. "Coffee?"

"No thanks, Lara. I came here to confess something, Mrs. Clarkson. Otherwise I won't be able to live with myself. It was me who pulled up that boundary marker in your field. I tried to, anyway. Let me tell you, when the surveyors plant those things, they want them to stay put." He attempted a chuckle, but it came out like a mangled hiccup.

Disappointment flickered in Aunt Fran's eyes. "Did Theo ask you to do it?"

"He did. I won't tell you why because I'm ashamed to talk about it, but Lara knows a little bit about it. Anyway, I'm willing to pay to have the boundary marker reset."

Lara was beginning to pity the man. He'd actually gone pink with embarrassment.

"I'm not concerned with the boundary marker," Aunt Fran said. She flicked a furtive glance at Lara and her lips formed a mysterious smile. "I understand you'll be taking over as chief editor of the *Whisker Gazette.*"

Chris smiled. "Word gets around fast."

"Good. Lara and I will be working on a project that might require some advertising. I assume you'll offer us reasonable rates?"

Lara felt her heartbeat spike. *Whaaat?*

"More than reasonable," Chris said. "Whatever you need, you got it. Just give me a jingle."

"Um, Aunt Fran, is there something you haven't told me?"

"There is," she said, smiling. "As soon as these gentlemen leave, you and I will have a nice long chat."

The chief rose abruptly, his chair scraping the floor. "We're outta here. Come on, Chris."

Chris followed his lead and the two moved toward the door.

"If I hear anything new, I'll let you both know," Whitley said. "This'll likely drag on for months before a trial date is set." He paused for a long moment, and then quirked a smile at Aunt Fran. "Francine Clarkson, you'll always be the town's cat lady, but you'll never be crazy." He winked at her and followed Chris outside.

Lara blew out an exasperated sigh. "Okay, Aunt Fran, would you please enlighten me? I feel like I stumbled into a parallel time zone. What was all that about advertising? What are we advertising?"

Her aunt smiled, her eyes shining, her face looking as youthful as it had been when Lara was a girl. "If you're still willing, I've decided to take you up on your offer to redecorate the back porch. I'll pay the costs, if you'll do the painting. I've got some furniture in the basement that we might be able to repurpose."

"You mean— You want to start a shelter? For real?" Lara felt her insides tingle with excitement, her mind spinning with ideas.

"For real," her aunt said.

"But...why didn't you tell me sooner?"

"I needed to know for certain before I got your hopes up." She grinned at her niece. "I've been on the phone quite a bit these last few days. Every time you popped down to the coffee shop, I got to work."

"You're a sneaky one," Lara said with a laugh. "I only wish you'd told me so I could have helped." She bit down on her lower lip. "Aunt Fran, are you sure about this? Is this really what you want to do?"

"It is," her aunt assured her. "I know it's not practical for me to have eleven cats, especially with these terrible knees. Before I started taking in strays and rescues, I only had Munster, Dolce, and Twinkles. It's time, now—the others deserve homes where they can be pampered and loved."

Lara swiped at a burgeoning tear.

"I know you'll be in Boston most of the time," Aunt Fran went on, "but I've thought of a way to get some help—financially, at least. I don't know why it took me this long to think of it, but I'm going to refinance my mortgage. Right now I have a small balance. I'll take out enough equity to cover the initial costs as well as a slush fund for the shelter. Oh, and you'll be pleased to know I've already had a chat with your old pal Gideon. He was thrilled that I'd called. Since the shelter will be a qualified nonprofit, he's offered to help with the legal filings, pro bono."

Lara was stunned. "Pro bono. Isn't that like, free? Wait a minute, what am I saying? I told you I wanted to use the money from the artwork I'm doing for Mr. Lefkovitz."

"This way you won't need to." Aunt Fran's face softened, and her eyes grew moist. "Lara, you've done so much already. I'd still be in a horrible mess if you hadn't shown up a week ago."

"I'm happy I came here, too," Lara said. "But you and I have a lot to do now, don't we?" *And a lot to talk about.*

"Oh boy, do we ever," her aunt said, smiling. "Lara, I can't remember the last time I've been this excited about something. I can't wait to hear your ideas for the shelter." Her smile faded. "Was Gabby happy when you told her you were going home tomorrow?"

"She was dancing on air," Lara said softly.

Gabby had been over the moon to hear that Lara was returning to Boston. She'd added, though, that in a week's time, Luca's work ethic had undergone a dramatic change. He was working his *buns* off, to coin a pun, helping her in the bakery.

"Always remember—you have a home here, too. And I got thinking, I don't want you having to rent a car every time you visit. Is there a place to park where you live?"

"In the North End?" Lara laughed. "Not a chance. I'd have to rent a space by the month in one of the big garages. It would cost a queen's ransom."

"That's too bad. I was going to say you could take my old Saturn. It's aging, but it's in good shape. I've been storing it at Jerry's house. He has a three-car garage."

Jerry's house?

Lara couldn't help smiling. "What did you mean by advertising? Are you thinking we'll need some publicity?"

"Yes. Plus, we might want to do some future hiring, if things work out the way we plan."

"You're a surprise a minute today, Aunt Fran. Don't worry about the car rental. I'll try to work out something more economical."

"Speaking of surprises, we're having another visitor today." Her aunt's eyes glittered.

"Who?"

Aunt Fran simply smiled. "You'll see."

* * * *

The visitor turned out to be more than a surprise. Lara was shocked a few hours later when Josette Barnes tapped on the screen door.

"Hey," she said, when Lara opened the door. "May I come in?"

"Of course, Josette. Great to see you." *Even if you did call me nosy.*

Lara ushered the woman inside and offered to take her plain fleece jacket. Josette had abandoned her usual flashy style for a pair of worn jeans and a maroon sweatshirt. Even her perfume had been toned down to a mere floral hint. Lara couldn't help wondering what Josette would think if she knew Lara had overheard her heartfelt confession about her so-called beau.

Aunt Fran materialized from the large parlor. Josette gave her a sincere hug. "I am honestly glad to see you, Fran." She looked at Lara. "And I— I'm glad you're still here, because I want to talk to you both."

They sat in the large parlor, Josette choosing to sit in Lara's favorite chair. Lara and her aunt shared the tufted sofa. Munster eyed the stranger for a moment and then sidled onto her lap, purring and rubbing her arm in a furry welcome.

"Oh, look at you, aren't you a darling," Josette cooed. She ran her hand along Munster's back and then bent and nuzzled his face. He settled in her lap as if he'd known her forever.

"Ladies, I'll get to the point," she said. "I've been thinking about getting a pet for a long time. Everyone keeps telling me I should get myself a little dog, but honestly, I don't think a dog is for me. I'm not too outdoorsy. I wouldn't be good at walking a dog, especially if I had to carry around one of those scooper thingies. That's why I wanted to ask you about, well, maybe adopting one of your cats?"

A zing of alarm went off in Lara. When her aunt didn't respond, she spoke up.

"Josette, I think it's wonderful that you're thinking about having a cat. They make fabulous companions, but it still involves a commitment. And even if you don't have to walk around with a scooper, you still have to maintain a clean litter box. There's some scooping involved there, too, not to mention a bit of scrubbing."

Josette nodded. "I know all that. I've been doing a lot of reading about caring for cats. But I truly feel I'm ready to take the plunge...as long as I can call you whenever I have questions."

"Anytime," Aunt Fran assured her, smiling when Bootsie padded into the room.

The gray cat stared curiously at Josette, and then curled up and rested her furry chin on the woman's worn loafer. "Isn't that sweet," Josette said. She reached down and tickled the cat between her ears.

Lara's gaze drifted to the carpeted cat tree, and her heart bounced in her chest. Perched at the top like a furry lifeguard, Blue sat studying Josette.

She suddenly understood why Mr. Patello saved that stool every day for his friend. Herbie was as real for him as Blue was for Lara.

Lara had read that Ragdoll cats weren't fond of high places, but Blue had obviously made an exception. Her tail twitched once, and then she looked at Lara. She licked her lips as if to say, She's okay.

Josette looked up at the cat tree and grinned. "Oh my, look at those little ones. Are they related?"

"Sisters," Lara said. "Callie and Luna. They're still unsure about humans, but in the week since I've been here I've already seen progress. In a quiet home, I think they'd do nicely, but you'd need to be patient."

"Lara's right," Aunt Fran said. "They're much less skittish than they were. Luna, the one with the pink dot on her nose, sniffed my finger yesterday when I reached up to her."

"Two kittens would be a big commitment," Lara cautioned.

Josette's smile said it all. She tickled Munster under the chin. "I would love to adopt them. I'll do everything in my power to give them a happy home. If you'll give me a list of the supplies and food I'll need, I'll buy everything today. You can release them to me whenever you feel they're ready. And I promise to call if I have any questions. Oh...and let me know which vet you use, Fran. I'll take them for a checkup and shots, and, when it's time, for spaying."

Josette had clearly done her cat homework. Lara had the feeling she was going to be a terrific mom to a pair of lucky kitties. She also sensed that this was the real Josette—the kindhearted woman who'd been hiding beneath a layer of glam.

"Josette, how is Mary doing?" Aunt Fran asked her.

Josette smiled. "Quite well, actually. I'm pleased to report she'll be taking over Theo's business interests. She'll sell much of it, but she's going to keep the downtown block. Instead of razing it, she wants to give it a long overdue face-lift. Something I know a bit about," she whispered theatrically. "But before any of that happens, she and Chris are going to take a vacation. They've always wanted to tour Italy, so they're planning a trip there soon."

"I'm so glad for them," Aunt Fran said.

Lara thought back to Sunday morning, when Chris had first paid her a visit. She'd found it suspect that Munster avoided the man, but her aunt later explained that cats sometimes reacted to scents humans couldn't detect. Chris might have used a soap or aftershave that triggered an unpleasant memory in the cat. Munster had been adopted from a shelter, and his backstory was a mystery.

Lara looked up at the cat tree. Blue was gone, but Callie and Luna had crept to the edge of their perch and were staring at Josette.

It's like they know, Lara thought.

They exchanged pleasantries for a bit longer, and then Josette left. Lara's emotions were bouncing all over the place.

This is it, she thought. *This is the beginning.*

Chapter 31

"There, how does that look?" Lara hopped backward off her step stool. Using fast-drying acrylics, she'd just finished adding the final cat to the border she'd been painting along the walls of the back porch. The whimsical feline faces brightened the room, giving it a cozy, homey feel. More importantly, it spoke volumes: all cats are welcome here!

Aunt Fran smiled up at Lara's hand-painted cats. "You've captured each of our feline residents perfectly, Lara. I love it." She didn't mention Blue, who was among the cats painted on the colorful border.

"Thanks. I have to admit, I'm happy with the way it came out."

"I guess we're about done, then, aren't we?"

"Almost." Lara skimmed her gaze around with a critical eye. She'd painted the walls a light sage, the perfect complement to the speckled, beige tiles they'd chosen for the flooring. The floor would be easy to clean, a necessity with cats and people trekking over it on almost a daily basis. A sturdy square kitchen table, commandeered from Aunt Fran's cellar, had been refinished by Lara in a distressed blue. She'd also found four chairs, in great condition, at a used furniture shop. Painted a shade slightly darker than the table, they boasted cat-themed cushions hand-sewn by Daisy Bowker, complete with washable covers.

"What's left to do?" her aunt asked.

"I have a pine-edged corkboard I want to hang there," Lara said, pointing at the one unadorned wall. "I'm going to stencil the border with tiny cats. We can use it to post photos people send us of their adopted kitties." She grinned. "We already have our first one, remember?"

Josette had sent them an adorable pic of Callie and Luna nestled in their new bed, toys strewn all around. It was obvious the two were loving their new digs.

"That's a great idea," Aunt Fran said, her eyes misting. "I still can't believe how generous everyone's been with their time, and their hard work."

"You have wonderful, devoted friends, Aunt Fran."

"As do you," her aunt reminded her.

A tap at the door to the back porch made them both turn.

"Hey there." Gideon Halley opened the door and popped his head in. "Got time for some good news?"

"Of course we do! Come in," Lara told him.

He looked at Lara for a long moment, a warm smile reflected in his chocolate-brown eyes. Lara felt her insides wiggle a bit.

Gideon kissed both women lightly on the cheek, then opened his canvas briefcase on the table. "It's official. The High Cliff Shelter for Cats is a done deal. Here's your license," he said, pulling out an official-looking document. "And an application to the town to post a sign at the foot of High Cliff Road. It's all completed—you just have to sign it. It'll be on the agenda at the next planning board meeting."

"Oh, Gid, thank you." Lara threw her arms around his neck and then stepped back quickly, feeling her face grow warm. It didn't help that she felt like a grunge in her most ancient of paint-spattered sweatshirts and a pair of jersey leggings.

"I'll take a thank-you like that any day, Ms. Caphart." Wearing a wide grin, Gideon slowly surveyed the room. "Wow. This is unbelievable. You've both done a super job fixing up this porch."

"Lara did the super job," Aunt Fran corrected. "I only stood by and watched." She looked dolefully at her knees.

Recognizing her angst, Gideon quickly said, "Fran, if there's ever anything I can do, please call on me, okay?"

"I will. Thank you, Gideon."

"So, how is this all going to work?" he asked.

Lara aimed her hand at a chair, and they all sat. "Aunt Fran and I have put a lot of thought into this. We're going to start by having the shelter open three days a week, probably Tuesday, Friday, and Saturday. Afternoons only, from one to four, but that could change over time. I've already started a Facebook page for it." She felt a smile split her face. "You can't believe how many people have already liked and shared it. I'll do a Web site, too."

"I'm even getting good at Facebook," Aunt Fran said.

"With each adoption, I'll do a colored pencil sketch of the cat or cats and give it to the owner as a keepsake. Right now, we're working on drafting an application for people looking to adopt. I've checked out the ones used by other shelters, but we're making ours a bit more comprehensive." She didn't add that she was counting on Blue to give prospective adopters a yea or a nay. "I've put out some feelers for volunteers. So far, I've gotten two responses. Aunt Fran will be setting up times to chat with them."

Gideon's brow creased. "So, when do you think you'll open?"

Lara and her aunt exchanged looks, and then Lara replied. "We're hoping by the second of January we'll be up and running. We know we have a lot to learn. We know we'll make mistakes. But we're really excited about doing this."

On impulse, Gideon rose from his chair and hugged Lara. "Right now, I can't think of two women I admire more. And if I didn't have such a busy schedule, I'd think about adopting a cat myself." He smiled at Fran, and then sighed. "Well, duty calls. I've got a closing at one. Will...I see you again soon, Lara?"

"No doubt you will. And Gid, thanks again for everything."

"We'll work on him," Aunt Fran said, after he left. "Busy people still have cats that are healthy and happy."

Lara folded her hands on the table. She glanced through the gleaming porch windows into the yard beyond. Only a month ago she'd stumbled over Barnes's body out there. It triggered a chain of events she couldn't possibly have predicted.

"Brooke would like me to join the classics book club," Aunt Fran said with a smile. "They're down to two, and need new members. It would be wonderful if you could join as well."

Lara said nothing.

"You're quiet, all of sudden. Is everything okay?" Her aunt's face fell. "You're still coming back for Thanksgiving, aren't you? Daisy and Sherry are so looking forward to it."

Slowly, Lara shook her head. "No, Aunt Fran, I'm not coming back for Thanksgiving."

"Oh." Aunt Fran looked away.

Lara couldn't tease her any longer. "I'm not coming back because I'm not leaving. If you're serious about having me, I'd like to move in with you permanently."

"Serious! Oh Lara, this is exactly what I've been praying for."

"Luca is driving up here tomorrow with my things. Except for a few smaller pieces, my furniture belonged to Gabby. The stuff that's mine will fit easily inside Luca's friend's car."

"What about your rental car?"

"Not a problem. Since Luca's friend is going to drive him up here, Luca will take my rental car back to Boston and turn it in." She squeezed her aunt's hand. "And don't worry about Gabby. She's happy that I'm choosing this. She knows it's right."

Tears flowed down Aunt Fran's cheeks. She pulled a tissue from her pocket and blotted them.

"And now you won't have any more excuses about putting off your knee surgery," Lara added.

"But we have to get the shelter up and running!"

"Yes, we do. And we will. But I'll be here for the cats, so you won't have to worry about them while you're recuperating and having physical therapy."

In response, Aunt Fran hauled herself off her chair and squeezed Lara heartily.

"I want the surgery," she said. "But what about your artwork?"

"I can paint from here as well as I can from Boston," Lara said. "I've already found a few galleries in this area that are interested in showing my watercolors."

Aunt Fran's green eyes sparkled. "Sounds as if I'm going to have to share my title. There's a new cat lady in town."

Lara giggled, and then a furry form emerged suddenly from under the table. Blue slipped onto the empty chair vacated by Gideon. Bright turquoise eyes beamed at Aunt Fran, whose expression never changed.

Tail swishing, the Ragdoll cat turned her head, her gaze coming to rest on Lara—the only one who could see her.

Lara felt her heart melting into a puddle. This was Blue, her spirit cat, who'd always been here for her.

Waiting for her to come home.

Lara, Aunt Fran, and their feline friends will return in Linda Reilly's second Cat Lady Mystery, a Lyrical Underground e-book for sale June 2018!

Meet the Author

Photo by Harper Point Photography

Raised in a sleepy town in the Berkshires, **Linda Reilly** has spent the bulk of her career in the field of real estate closings and title examination. It wasn't until 1995 that her first short mystery, "Out of Luck," was accepted for publication by *Woman's World Magazine*. Since then she's had more than forty short stories published, including a sprinkling of romances. She is also the author of *Some Enchanted Murder*, and the Deep Fried Mystery series, featuring fry cook Talia Marby. Linda lives in New Hampshire with her husband, who affectionately calls her "Noseinabook." Visit her on the Web at lindasreilly.com.